To Tiffanys,
Wishing you

HOW TO JUDGE A
BOOK BY ITS
LOVER

& happiness!

Jessica Jiji

STONE
TIGER

First published by Stone Tiger Books in 2020.

The following is a work of fiction. Names, characters, places, events and incidents are either the product of the author's imagination or used in an entirely fictitious manner. Any resemblance to actual persons, living or dead, is entirely coincidental.

Cover and Jacket design by Rob Carter

ISBN: 978-1-7356676-0-7

eISBN: 9781735667614

Stone Tiger Books
225 E. 35th Street, Ground Fl.
New York, NY 10016

For Jeffrey, dreaming my dreams with you...

1

A sweet voice taunted me from over my shoulder. "Still writing about sex but not getting any?"

Mortified, I snapped my laptop closed. What a horrible thing to say! And how depressingly true.

To make matters worse, that barbed observation was made by Portia Thorn, a long-legged, long-haired beauty who was a natural on the downtown scene. She didn't need a tattoo or a scar to convey that she was both glamorous and edgy, half-Hollywood and half-felon. Me, I could put a bone through my nose and still look like the girl next door.

We were at one of the most shabby chic venues in Manhattan—Performance Space 122—where I'd dragged myself to catch the latest lecture in a series on the dialectics of jazz.

Maybe I was single and unpublished, but I kept trying, even just then editing my novel in my seat while waiting to sample another eclectic offering from the culture capital of the world. Until Portia showed up.

"Still getting lots of sex but not writing well?" I countered.

Actually, Portia's prose wasn't all that bad. She was one of the more talented members of our writers group, although that wasn't saying much. I liked a few of them as friends; maybe their lack of success made me feel more at home.

"Don't take offense," Portia said offensively. "I'm sure somewhere out there in suburbia there's a nice, regular guy looking for a sweet, hometown girl like you. Well," she turned on her heel, "see ya Tuesday."

I didn't know which was worse, her smug tone or her stinging insight. There probably *was* a nice, suburban guy out there but I was looking for a cool, urban intellectual. But when you flee the suburbs like I did, you can't help feeling a little too plain for the sophisticated city crowd. Still, I was going to catch up, one history of jazz lecture at a time.

Portia had taken her seat on the other side of the room, but I didn't bother reopening my laptop. The absence of romance in my life had left me struggling to bring any depth or true emotion to the characters I was trying to depict. The Viennese soldier making love to my main character, Marguerite, was much too stiff—and not in the right places. I needed to get to the essence of his motivation in order to add passion to the scene. But who was he? Lacking any crush of my own, I felt completely blocked.

Just then, the lights in the auditorium dimmed and a lanky, dark-haired man in a tailored suit with his shirt untucked approached the podium. After polite applause, he looked up, and his brilliant blue eyes met mine.

Ooh, yes: inspiration at last!

Still lost in that gaze the following day, I headed over to the stately San Remo overlooking Central Park to meet a potential client. The elevator doors opened directly into Suite 15. Stepping into Anderson Gallant's apartment, I took in the breathtaking view and thought of the brick wall that my studio faces. My whole apartment was the size of his front hall. Just another reminder of how far I was from making it big in the big city.

If I had that much space, I might have decorated differently—or at least decorated. Except for a few expensive-looking antiques, the place was bare, with nothing on the walls or floors.

My new client, Cadbury, was maniacally chewing on a couch leg. Anderson should have stopped him, but then again, Anderson was himself maniacally skiing to nowhere on his NordicTrack.

The maid caught his attention by pulling the plug. As he took his headphones off, he caught sight of the pile of toothpicks his muscular boxer was producing.

"Cadbury!" he shouted. "There's only seventeen Biedermeier empire-style loveseats in the world, and you've already eaten four of them." He turned to me and smiled. At more than six feet tall with reddish-brown hair and glasses, Anderson had the smug ease of someone born with a lifetime country club membership who could walk into a boardroom wearing that beat-up SpongeBob T-shirt he had on and still take the chairman's seat.

"Well, they say you're the best. Think you can handle my Caddy?"

"You know that sheepdog named Slobodan who loves Cadbury? She used to eat Coach handbags like they were pastrami sandwiches until I took over."

To prove my point, I put on my best stern look and commanded, "Cadbury, no! Couches are not for eating." Cadbury looked at me defiantly, but his teeth disengaged.

"Cadbury, come!" Shocked, the dog did as he was told. "Cadbury, sit!" I continued in my drill sergeant voice. Secretly delighted, as all dogs are when they perform, he sat.

My tone jumped up three octaves. "Good boy, you good boy!" The pup wagged his tail with delight.

"How'd you do that?" Anderson asked.

"Am I hired?" I asked with false modesty. After all, I had no doubts about my ability to control canines. It was the rest of my life I was worried about.

"Cadbury's worth it," he said, "even though you charge more than my proctologist."

Yeah, but he doesn't scoop your poop, I thought. "So, you want to show me how to work the keys?"

7

"Sure," Anderson said, letting Cadbury sink a set of incisors into the new Air Jordans on his feet. The difficult part of the job is never the dogs; it's always the people. I wondered whether to correct Anderson but decided not to push my luck. "I only use the top lock."

Suddenly, my eye was drawn to a black-and-white photograph on the piano. I could never mistake that thick, gray beard and macho stance. Ernest Hemingway! If I could only write like him I wouldn't be here interviewing for the privilege of cleaning up after Cadbury, who by the looks of what he was putting down his throat would require a thirty-gallon kitchen bag.

"Is that…" I began.

"You guessed it," Anderson said, beaming. "Dear old Dad."

For a split second I tried to recall whether Hemingway ever had a son named Anderson Gallant when it hit me that he was referring to the bespectacled fellow with a walrus mustache standing next to the literary great. "Your father knew Hemingway?"

"Ah, yes. Great writers were as common around our house as I guess suburban ladies were in yours." Looking down at last year's red capri pants, which I knew positively screamed Walt Whitman Mall, I wished I'd worn my usual Manhattan-artist black torn jeans instead.

As much as his comparison hurt, a sudden explosion of hope suppressed my indignation. He was *that* Gallant?! As in the Gallant publishing empire?

It had to be fate. Here I was, a struggling writer looking for a break, and suddenly one of the biggest publishers in New York gives me the keys to his apartment.

As I walked past the San Remo's smartly uniformed doorman and out into the warm spring afternoon, everything looked dazzling. The bumblebee-colored taxis buzzed with the promise of sweet journeys, the streetlights flashed like glimmers of hope, and the handsome guy on the corner just ahead of me looked exactly like my soldier inspiration from the night before.

As I crossed Seventy-Fourth Street, the stranger looked up from his copy of *The World as Will and Representation* and our eyes met. It *was* him! Lucien Brosseau, head critic of *The New York Arts and Entertainment Review* and featured speaker at the Columbus Avenue Arts Center.

Normally I'd have been too self-conscious to say anything to such a brilliant thinker, but it seemed like fate was embracing me. Even my normally unruly hair somehow felt soft and wavy. Plus, I had just sealed my first deal with a publisher—sure it was only to walk his pooch, but still, good sign! And here was my chance to pitch for romance.

"Schopenhauer!" I said, reading from the jacket. "He's one of my faves!" Probably not the most insightful take, but it made Lucien smile, and I felt my heart swell at seeing the soft side of this hardened critic.

"Really? You must be his cutest fan," he said. I blushed as a fire truck careened around the corner behind us.

When the noise of the siren receded, he handed me a flyer. "Maybe you'd like to come," he offered. It was an invitation to a lecture he was giving in a week's time on the influence of nineteenth-century philosophers on contemporary jazz.

"Totally! I'll totally be there!" I replied, as though it were possible to half be there.

"Great," he said, his blue eyes twinkling.

Great? I thought. It was almost too much to hope for, but I decided that no matter the risk to my scared heart, I would dare to admit to myself how happy I felt thinking about seeing Lucien again.

The Hell's Kitchen writers group I'd been in for the past six years met in a basement community room in an anonymous apartment building on Ninth Avenue. As I entered the florescent-lit lobby, the smells of wontons, curry, and *arroz con pollo,* combining like some United Nations of cuisine, engulfed my senses.

There was a bounce in my step on the dirty linoleum floor. After all, I had News. It was the unspoken dream of every member of the group to leave someday, and Anderson Gallant might very well be my ticket out. I couldn't wait to see the look on Portia Thorn's face when she heard. She may have been stunning, but long, sleek hair would only get her so far in life.

My own mousy mop can never decide if it wants to be straight or curly, and with an average bod and no startling eyes or stunning derriere to set me apart, I was a sucker for every product on the market that promised to make me shine.

But I wasn't down on my looks that night, instead relishing the thought that after the session I could dish with my favorite group member, Danny Z., about Lucien. Maybe he'd even know who the hell Schopenhauer was. It all seemed so funny and fun and filled with lucky vibes.

The eight of us scooched our chairs into a circle and started shuffling our marked copies of everyone's work. Margo's *Love Between Consenting Parrots* was at the top of the pile, since we'd left off there last week, and the author herself was perched at the edge of her chair, pen in hand, ready to absorb our insightful comments on her third unpublished novel.

"The improvement in your work since revision nine is really promising," said Seth, a tweed-jacket chemistry professor by day and aspiring science fiction writer by night. "Squeaky's journey from a neurotically self-absorbed boy—I mean bird—to social consciousness when he flies over the slums of São Paulo is evidence of—"

"I'm sorry, Seth, but could I just work in here a moment?" Portia asked.

"Work in" is the expression we use when someone wants to interrupt with a more important observation. Margo braced herself for the usual Portia critique, but none came.

"I'm going to burst if I don't share this with you guys," she continued. I knew how she felt because I was bursting with the news about Anderson Gallant like a girl in the bathroom line at Bloomies during Christmas week. But I didn't mind letting Portia go first, since my news would blow hers away.

"Helen Ellenbogen loved *Wild Asparagus!*" she bubbled. Everyone burst into applause, including me. I think I clapped the loudest because I was pretending Portia's face was between my hands each time they slapped together. Every one of us would have given our hard drives to be represented by Ellenbogen Associates, which last year sold more six-figure titles than any other agent in New York. My news of meeting Anderson Gallant was like a lottery scratch card compared to her paycheck.

We managed to get through the rest of the night, even though I'm sure I wasn't the only one choking on envy. Only Sunny Hellerstein, aspiring author of *Daily Vows for a Happy Future*, really believed that the success of one brings us all one step closer.

I didn't even have the heart to tell Danny Z. about Lucien. After all, it was only a flyer.

Trudging up to my fifth-floor apartment, the coffin-like elevator broken as usual, I was furious that Portia's dumb romance novel had been picked by Helen Ellenbogen Associates when my labor of love, *Napoleon's Hairdresser*, had not, despite possessing all the elements of a great epic: war, lust, and shattered illusions.

There was no justice.

As I turned the key and rammed my shoulder into the door—it only worked with a good push—it was hard not to remember the waves of hope and excitement that had overwhelmed me the first day I'd moved in. Someday my living room-slash-bedroom-slash-study-slash-kitchen would make a touching anecdote on talk shows about humble beginnings and the struggles all great writers endure. Only it wasn't supposed to take eight years.

I slammed the door closed and a chunk of plaster fell and hit my head. Flipping on the lights, I stared at the cracked walls and shabby cabinets. They looked as pathetic as I felt.

There were only two choices: Reach out to a sweet friend, or dive into an even sweeter pint of Ben & Jerry's Chubby Hubby. I dialed Trish.

Her husband answered. I could just picture Tom in their

colonial-style home on Long Island—that suburban sprawl I'd fled so many years before to make it as a writer in the city. "Hello?"

"Hey, Tom. It's me, Laurel."

"What's up?" he said, lowering the volume on their eighty-inch plasma TV.

"You know me, always hopeful," I replied, knowing that he'd want to get back to the Islanders game that was blasting in the background. Just as well. I really needed my friend.

"Cool. Hang on a second; I'll get Trish."

Trish and Tom met at SUNY Stony Brook, shopped at the Walt Whitman Mall, and set up house not five miles away from where each of them grew up. They seemed happy enough, but I wanted to think my future destiny would hold more than manicured lawns and Sunday barbecues.

"Connor, stop hitting the baby!" Trish shouted before getting on the phone.

"Laurel!" she said.

"Trishalicious, how are you?"

"Between smelly diapers and Dora videos, I've never been better. How about you?"

I told her about Portia. Naturally, Trish rushed to my defense. "I'm sure her writing couldn't possibly be as good as yours. I mean, I bet she never won four hundred dollars when her story was published in *Seventeen Magazine*."

She was only trying to help, but the thought that my first short story, "Total Eclipse of the Canoe Trip," might be the highlight of my career made me want to cry. I was twelve when that happened, with no success since. None. I wanted to throw a tantrum about how unfair life was, but I couldn't even dramatically threaten to stick my head in the oven, since it was broken like everything else in this place.

Trish must have sensed my disappointment, because she changed the subject. "Never mind," she said. "I have great news. Remember that cute dentist I told you about?" She paused for effect, and I could imagine the drumroll. "He's single."

I groaned inside. As well as she knew me, Trish never understood that I wanted so much more out of life than another jock turned healthcare professional. "That's so sweet of you, Trish, but I may have a chance at a really amazing guy."

We spent the next half hour analyzing every nuance of the two lines Lucien and I had exchanged on the street corner. By the time we were testing the sound of my first name with his last name, Connor interrupted. "Mom! You promised I could have another Double Stuf Oreo!"

"I did not, Connor Steven! Now brush your teeth and I'll tuck you in."

"You better go," I said, feeling restored to my senses and ready to face the miserable little drip my landlord claims is a shower—until Trish added one final thought.

"Hey," she said, "I saw Jenna at the gas station the other day. She was giving me the third degree about why you never call her."

Jenna. My older sister. She always seems to show up just when I get up from being knocked down.

That pint of Chubby Hubby wasn't going to make it through the night.

2

Luckily, my job offered the perfect chance to walk off the calories. Between the schnoodle on Riverside Drive, the sheepdog at Lincoln Plaza, the Chihuahua on West Seventy-Eighth Street, the Great Dane I collected at an Amsterdam Avenue hair salon, and now Cadbury at what I hoped was my future publisher's home, I was clocking two and a half miles just in the morning run.

"Kingpin!" I shouted, entering the spectacular, modern apartment at the summit of a new glass-tower residence along the river. The little half-schnauzer, half-poodle ran over with a leash in his mouth.

His owner, Maury Blaustein, sat comfortably in the chair that had earned him all these riches.

"Good morning!" I said. It was difficult to ask him what was new, since nothing was ever new with Maury Blaustein, but I tried anyway. "What're you watching?"

"Lifetime television," he replied, pushing a button on the arm of the famous Lounge-Around, the rotating chair that had revolutionized sunbathing. With barely a whisper, it automatically shifted toward me. "Without Lifetime television, I'd have no life," he shrugged.

I had to agree. Since making his millions, Maury Blaustein seemed hard-pressed to figure out how to spend them all. He'd had a top designer import the finest silk fabrics for his matching brocade furniture, all of which went unused, since he practically lived in the Lounge-Around. The kitchen was filled with every culinary gadget in the Williams-Sonoma catalog, but I only ever saw cartons of takeout food in the fridge. A silver-plated coatrack held his smelly old Mets jacket.

I passed it as I led Kingpin out through the hallway, which was decorated with photos of has-been actors sitting in the Lounge-Around. There was Rob Lowe with sunscreen on his nose. The frame next to him depicted Charlie Sheen looking relaxed. At the center, inexplicably, was a picture of the late, great Mother Teresa, looking more beatific than ever on her rotating chaise. She had written "Maury Blaustein should be sainted" across the bottom of the image.

Ten blocks south, the apartment at Lincoln Plaza offered an escape from Lounge-Around Land. There I met Slobodan, my most well-behaved dog, which was no coincidence since her owners were so sweet. The Danilovas were a loving couple living in a comfortable apartment—no ostentatious gadgets, just pictures of their family. Mr. Danilova was a freelance graphic artist, and his wife did PR for the Alvin Ailey Dance Company.

"Hey there, Laurel, you're early today." Mr. Danilova, with his thick glasses and dorky shirts, wasn't going to get any modeling contracts, but he was always ready with a friendly smile.

"You're a woman: Which would you like better, the pink or the striped?" he asked, pointing to a catalog featuring two versions of the same Furla handbag.

"Definitely the pink," I replied. "What's the occasion?"
"Nothing, I just love my wife. Does there have to be an occasion?"

By then, Slobodan was eagerly sniffing Kingpin, so I offered a quick "of course not" and headed off to my next pickup.

Anderson Gallant wasn't home when I finally got to his place with five happy dogs twisting around my legs, and I added

16

Cadbury to the mix without using the speech I'd spent three hours preparing the night before. It went something like this:

It is an honor to look after the dog of a publishing great like yourself, and if my small contribution enables you to concentrate on your important work, that's all the job satisfaction I need. However, I do want to inform you that I am the author of a soon-to-be-completed major novel which I would be honored to have you read.

Perhaps it was just as well Anderson wasn't there; it would give me more time to polish my pitch.

Cad was thrilled to meet his new friends, but as we made our way into Central Park, his enthusiasm started to get on my nerves.

Dogs are pack animals, and they like to walk in a group, but they have to find their position first. I had decided to make Cadbury the left guard on my basketball team, as that would keep him away from Slobodan. Just like in grade school, friends must be separated, or they disrupt everything for the rest of us.

I could feel the stares of people who pitied me walking through Central Park with six dogs and pockets full of baggies, and they weren't above ridiculing snickers when I used those baggies to fulfill my legal obligations and scoop the doggies' poop.

But I got the last laugh, knowing that for a service job, I was making more per hour than any waitress, data entry grunt, or eyebrow waxer in town. Even in torrential rain, I didn't miss my days serving cappuccinos at the Copenhagen Café, where after a shift of aggravating customers, nasty bosses, and lecherous kitchen help, I would be lucky to scrape together fifty dollars in tips.

Besides, what other job would allow me to get great exercise and puzzle out how Napoleon's hairdresser learned the general's deepest secrets?

At the dog run, I unleashed the puppies and pulled out a folder. There was something uplifting about having a project; it seemed to prove that I was more than a dog-walker; I was a creative writer with a manuscript to polish.

The market scene was one of my favorites because it blended

characterization with the promise of destiny fulfilled. At that point in the action, Marguerite was still just a young nobody from the *banlieues,* the suburbs of Paris.

As the wagon—a hand-me-down from her controlling second cousin—bumped along the crowded boulevard toward Le Marche Discounté, Marguerite listened to the church bells with anxiety. "Merde," she cried. "It's nine a.m., and I'm late again because of all the traffic." As usual, there was no place to park her buggy in the crowded lot. Throwing caution to the wind, she took the spot reserved for lepers and smallpox victims, telling herself she had her own disadvantages, chief among them her tragic combination of ordinary background and extraordinary aspirations.

Making her way through the crowded stalls, past the Hoopskirt Emporium and the greasy crepe stand, Marguerite hurried to her chair at La Supercoif.

"Late again!" the muscular proprietress, Madame Le Bouffante, screamed. "I should demote you back to powdering wigs."

```
    Marguerite set to work,
    feeling deep in her heart
    that she possessed a talent
    far beyond the understanding
    of the superficial ladies in
    waiting who—
```

Suddenly, an irritating electronic ringing drew me out of this magical world. I was even more dismayed when I saw who was calling.

Taking a breath, I tapped the phone screen. "Hey, sis," I said, trying to sound happy to speak to her even as I felt the familiar Jenna headache sinking in.

"Well, it's about time you answered your phone! I know you've been avoiding me. It's not like you're busy or anything," she said accusingly.

I wanted to tell her I was in the middle of work, that I never call her at her oh-so-impressive fitness studio, but that would only open a whole conversation about how I didn't have a real career, and I was trying to avoid an even worse headache.

"I told you to get back to me about the family conference that Mom and Dad want to have." Too late. I felt the pounding reach the center of my brain and echo like a bell.

"What's this big conference about?" I asked, imagining my parents finally announcing The Move to Florida.

"You'll find out on Sunday night at seven at Sizzler," she commanded. "And you'd better be on time," she warned. "Mom's therapist said she is not to have any extra stress this month. And you know we can't count on Dad to keep things calm."

I'd rather chew the soggy cardboard I noticed was hanging from Slobodan's mouth than be served up on a platter to my neurotic parents, but I knew I had no choice. "Drop it!" I screamed at the sheepdog.

"One of these days," my sister said, assuming I'd been talking to her, "you are going to have to face reality, and when you do, you'll thank me." She hung up.

Jenna's nasty tone couldn't keep me down as I ascended to the fifteenth floor in the San Remo's gilded elevator. This was exactly the kind of building I'd always pictured myself living in once the world recognized the brilliance of my writing. It had the kind of old-world charm I just knew Lucien would appreciate. The high ceilings, the wood paneling, the tiled fireplaces, and the wraparound balconies would be perfect for our twice-monthly salons with the glitterati of the New York arts scene. "The Booker Prize committee is here to see you, Mrs. Brosseau," I could just hear the doorman announcing over the intercom.

The elevator opened into Anderson's cavernous living room, and I was delighted to see that the man of the house was there, eating a bucket of chicken wings and watching Extreme Candlepin Bowling on some sports channel.

The books lining his shelves everywhere reminded me that I was far from a published writer, just an unrecognized talent unless someone plucked me out of obscurity. Someone like Anderson Gallant.

Cadbury leapt for the greasy fast food, nearly knocking his master to the ground, but Anderson loved the attention. "Caddy! That's your happy face! You like your new walker, don't you?" he said, wiping the boxer's drool off of his Tweety Bird T-shirt.

Encouraged, I leapt in Cadbury's wake. "I'm not just a good canine management professional, you know," I said, studying Anderson's green eyes for a reaction.

"You mean you have another job besides pooper-scooper?"

Undaunted, I drew a deep breath and declared, "I'm a novelist."

I'd said it in front of the mirror hundreds of times during my practice rehearsals for interviews on the "Today Show." In my fantasies, the reply was always, "Who are your greatest influences?" but Anderson Gallant remained silent, and suddenly I realized that he must have heard that hundreds of times from caterers, plumbers, window washers, and other domestic help like me.

"Really?" he asked after what felt like an eternity. "That's interesting."

Interesting as in "Go to hell," I wondered, or interested as in "I'm interested"?

"You should show me some of your stuff someday. I'm in publishing, you know."

At first I felt shocked, and then terrified, and then I thought, *This is it, and I'm ready.*

I sat down at the computer that afternoon with excitement I hadn't felt in years. One hundred and seventeen rejection letters can take the thrill out of revising a masterwork, but with a miraculous chance to bypass all of the agents with their form responses—"Your manuscript does not interest us at this time," "The market for fiction is very tight at this time," "We're not taking on any unpublished writers at this time"—I set a schedule for myself: Polish the first three chapters in the next week. That was how long I figured it would take before he asked for some text.

No sooner had my computer blinked to life than my apartment began to shake as if there was an earthquake. I didn't have to look out the window to know that jackhammers were to blame. The corner underneath my place was apparently among the most blighted in the city—water main breaks, potholes, electrical work—it seemed the sidewalk had to be torn up every other week and repaired on the weeks in between.

After seven years of urban disaster, I had learned how to cope and broke out my handy earplugs. I was calling up the document "Napoleon's Hairdresser Revision Eighteen" when the screen went black.

My vintage computer system was on the brink of death, but I couldn't afford a new model, and I didn't want to ask my parents for the money. After all, they'd already bought me two start-up computers, and each time I'd promised I'd make it before the machines became obsolete.

Repeated failed attempts to reboot didn't dissuade me

from my task. Instead, I took a red pen and the latest printout and began rereading the opening page for what seemed like the millionth time.

```
Long had the world wondered
who was responsible for the
distinctive forward-brush of
the great emperor's coif.
Before the invention of gel,
mousse, and least of all leave-
in conditioner, Napoleon's
hairdresser devised ingenious
ways of keeping out frizz and
keeping in shine.
```

It seemed as irresistible as ever, and I didn't see the point in messing it up, especially with that week's issue of *Celebrity Style* staring at me from the top of the mail pile. Not that I really cared for cheap gossip—it was much more important to read the copy of Schopenhauer I'd copped in preparation for my big date with Lucien—but they wouldn't let me back into Long Island unless I knew something about the latest star to get liposuction.

I laughed out loud reading "Tummy Tuck Tragedies" and then flipped to my favorite segment, "Hollywood Dish," with its inane quotes. That week's issue featured a piece about a starlet who thought Judge Judy was on the Supreme Court. "Luckily, Kimmy isn't on the Senate Confirmation Committee, or 'Do I have "STUPID" written across my forehead?' might be the Court's new motto," the article said.

Who writes this stuff? I wondered, curling up in bed with the trashy magazine. After all, I still had six days left to get my book into shape.

Luckily, I wore all black to the dialectics of jazz seminar Lucien had invited me to, or else I would have stuck out like a girl from Long Island trying to fit in with the intelligentsia. I had spent two and a half aggravating hours trying on everything in my closet before I called my writer friend Danny Z. for advice. "Dollface, there's only one color in this city. Black is the new black, the old black, and all the colors in between. Wear an outfit; don't let the outfit wear you."

"And," he'd added, "you'd better give me details if you get lucky."

I was hoping for just that as I made my way down the crowded aisle at the Columbus Avenue Arts Center, plastic cup of red wine in hand. It turned out that I was seated next to a famous pill-popping socialite and behind someone unrecognizable sporting a fashionable Slavic accent. If only I'd escaped from behind the Iron Curtain instead of just being from the land of superstores, I might have felt worthy of this smart crowd.

Nothing like a little alcohol to loosen inhibitions, I thought, downing my wine in one gulp.

As the lights faded, I felt a strange, buzzing contentment. Of the six panelists, Lucien was by far the most attractive, with his sexy beaded wristband and loafers with no socks. I couldn't resist closing my eyes for a sec to better picture our wedding: A perfect June afternoon . . . the Conservatory Garden in Central Park . . . the scent of fresh flowers floating in the air . . .

Unfortunately, my lids didn't open again until the lights came up and the applause roused me. How mortifying; I had slept through the whole symposium! It must have been the combination of the wine and the muscle relaxant I'd taken earlier that day after Mini nearly pulled my arm out of its socket. I joined the applause, hoping nobody had noticed, and tried to inconspicuously pat down my hair.

Still, I wasn't going to miss my chance to be part of a New York City arts scene power couple. *And every great writer has a bit of dramatic flair,* I thought, bracing myself for a performance.

I nearly forgot all my lines when I caught those sexy blue eyes looking my way, and when Lucien smiled, I practically froze but managed to sputter, "What a fascinating evening! Thank you so much for inviting me."

"So what's your name anyway?" he asked.

"Laurel," I responded, grateful to remember it, given how he turned my brain to mush.

"I'm Lucien," he said.

"I know that, of course," I practically whispered. "You were the best speaker."

"Really? I thought you'd fall asleep," he replied with a casual laugh. "Even I started getting bored when Professor Thackery enlightened us about the theory of phallocentric harmonics."

"I got a little lost there myself," I confessed, thinking about how he is not only smart and cute but also doesn't take himself too seriously! I had to get to date two. "But in general, I find these events really . . . stimulating," I added, feeling a real sensation somewhere well south of my brain.

Lucien absentmindedly stretched, and I could see his skinny, pale stomach through his T-shirt. "Next week's the last event in the series, if you're interested. I'm not on the panel, but I guess I should show up. Maybe I'll see you there?"

Hope was such an unfamiliar feeling, but I was starting to see beyond my self-image as a lonely loser to a future where I could make it as a real artist with an incredible man.

3

Looking forward to my date with Lucien—in my fantasies, it was sure to last until daybreak—kept me happy even as I headed out to the dreaded family meeting on Long Island. As the crowded passenger cars of the LIRR passed the familiar, dreary suburban landscape, I imagined Lucien cupping my face in his hands and giving me that delectable first kiss, but by the time we neared Hicksville station, an odd presence began to disturb my thoughts, and when we hit Plainview, I knew what it was: Jenna.

I think my parents wanted to give Jenna a companion when they conceived me, but all I ended up being was an audience member in the drama that was her life. Sure, Mom and Dad meant to celebrate my kindergarten graduation, but instead they were busy putting out the fire that flared up in our kitchen after Jenna's failed attempt at baked Alaska. Sure, after I won the spelling bee in third grade they said I could have anything I wanted, but when I asked for dance lessons, the money had been spent on Jenna's gymnastics classes. And too bad about that Sweet Sixteen I was supposed to have at Leonard's; Jenna's anorexia was in full swing, and Mom was too preoccupied to organize a party.

Tall, blonde, athletic, and beautiful, you'd think she'd be blessed, but she was just tortured—and tortured everyone else. First it was gymnastics. My parents practically took out a second mortgage just to fund all those private instructors, and then when Jenna came in with the silver medal at the state championships, they spent even more on the psychiatrist to console her crushed ego.

Next came the ulcer—who ever heard of a fifteen-year-old with an ulcer? But Jenna's was peptic and aggravated. And aggravating! Suddenly, every meal had to be planned around her. Only white foods—bread, mushrooms, and mozzarella—and absolutely no spices. My timid request for a pepperoni pizza was met with a horrified rebuke.

Jenna's weird eating ruled the kitchen until she stopped eating altogether, and then it ruled our lives. My parents were in counseling with her at the Stony Brook University Hospital Eating Disorders Center the day I got my first period, and I was forced to go next door and ask Trish's mother what to do. Mom barely noticed that I was walking like a cowboy from putting the tampon in wrong.

By the time Jenna was discharged from the center, our kitchen had been turned into a machine designed to keep her fed. A colored chart tracked her every bite, with gold stars like those a preschooler might receive commending her intake of protein, carbs, and especially fat. I retreated into my writing, consoling myself with the knowledge that all sensitive artists come from bizarre families.

After that history, Jenna went full health, which of course was a relief. Now she picked Sizzler for the family meeting because of its huge salad bar and keto-approved steaks. She'd gone from being a 92-pound scarecrow to a 115-pound fitness fanatic with six-pack abs and buns of steel. I had to give her credit for turning it all around, becoming beautiful, and finding a career in the process, but all I ever felt was that the spotlight never left her, only now she shines so brightly I don't even try to get on stage.

As my taxi pulled up to the restaurant, I imagined the fateful words: "Honey, we finally bought that condo at the Boca Esplanada." Honestly, my parents deserved it. The weather would be warmer, and practically all their friends had moved there already.

Then it hit me—nobody drives around those country club communities; they all have monogrammed golf carts! Excitement swelled in my heart as I imagined my father making the proud announcement: "Laurel, you get the Cadillac."

It would have to go to me, since Jenna already has two cars, not to mention a whole family to drive around in them. Dad would offer kind words, I knew. "Now that you're well on your way in your successful writing career, you'll probably be needing this for your book tours." I decided to be modest and not tell him that television studios would send their own limos to pick me up. And I certainly wouldn't say that I'd be trading in their old-fashioned wheels for a cool little Vespa motorbike. After all, Jenna may have gotten more attention, but my parents never failed to show their love for me, I realized as I entered the noisy restaurant.

With its color-by-numbers, family-oriented atmosphere and waitresses running by with trays of mega bacon burgers, Sizzler was exactly the kind of place that made my skin crawl, but I had to concede that I felt comfortable in the slightly anonymous atmosphere that replaced the ranking, judgmental stares at the East Village poetry houses I hung out in. And if it made my parents comfortable, all the better.

Before they noticed me, I paused for a second to take in the image before my eyes. Sure, Mom, with her chunky costume jewelry, might be a little too shopping mall for a downtown poetry slam, but for a fifty-eight-year-old she looked damn good with her perfectly pressed pants and backless pumps. Dad might not be the towering intellectual he imagined himself to be, but he was so at ease it barely mattered. Finally in his sixties, at the top of his career and with pride in his daughters, he looked ready to conquer the world, or at least the golf course down in Florida.

For some reason, Jenna had left her husband at home. No

doubt Rob preferred to be up in Port Washington polishing his boat. Without her handsome husband standing as living testimony to her ability to find lasting love, Jenna looked almost vulnerable, if you ignored the bulging biceps she showed off with her sleeveless dress. And had she bleached her hair, or was it just the lighting that softened her normally aggressive demeanor?

"Hello, darling," said Mom, leaning in for a lipstick-smeared kiss. Daddy took my hand, and I sat down between them.

While the waitress scribbled our requests, I noticed that Jenna didn't even seem to flinch when I ordered a carb-filled meal including a twice-baked potato and an ear of corn.

After the small talk died down, Jenna gave my parents a meaningful look, and Dad took a deep breath before speaking.

Here comes the car, I thought, preparing to act surprised yet gracious.

"I have a little something for you," he began, reaching into his pocket. Suddenly all those game shows popped into my head—the ones where the host gives an ecstatic contestant keys before pulling back a big curtain to reveal:

"It's an article you might have missed." He unfolded a neat print-out.

I was still hoping the news item had something to do with my windfall, but reality started to sink in when I remembered my parents' annoying habit of giving me book reviews. They were always trying to get me to read the latest mainstream pulp they mistook for good writing.

Sure enough, the clipping was from the arts section, I noticed as my father handed it to me, his fitness tracker peeking out from under his cuff. My ears burned with shame at my stupidity. Obviously, Jenna would be getting the Cadillac and I would be getting a review of the latest mass-market drivel:

Entertainer to the Stars

Which famous rap mogul had to calm their child's tantrum with the promise that Clowny

Zary would entertain their party?

Which British Royal hired Clowny Zary to provide a transatlantic show for her tot?

And which A-list actress refused to conceive with her rock star boyfriend until he booked Clowny Zary for the baptism?

But the real question on everyone's lips is: Who is behind the loud makeup, fright wig, and global phenomenon that is Clowny Zary?

Just when I thought my life couldn't get any more surreal, along came Clowny Zary to prove me wrong. "Why am I reading this?" I asked my family.

"Just keep going," Mom pointed with her chin:

> A year ago, Zarabella Kantwatar was just another wannabe actress pounding the pavement in search of a job. She hadn't passed an audition since, as a teenager, she was cast as an understudy in the ill-fated musical version of "The Plague." The pain of her glaring lack of success, mounting bills, and dilapidated apartment was compounded as she watched her friends fulfill their dreams while she was stuck financing her hopeless quest by teaching driver's ed.
>
> "Finally, it hit me," the twenty-seven-year-old brunette said, reclining on the terrace of her new penthouse duplex. "As an actress, I stink. Time to bow out gracefully."

I hated this woman, and I couldn't understand why—until it

hit me. They think *I* stink, and it's time to bow out gracefully.

Screw you all, I thought, glaring at my family through eyes that were quickly filling with tears of blind rage.

I threw the article on the table.

"I am not dressing up in a rainbow afro and size 16 rubber shoes just so you can have something to tell your friends when they ask what I'm doing with my life," I spat.

"It would be more dignified than dog-walking," Jenna said with a snide little smile.

"This isn't the point at all, Cookie," said Mom, buttering a roll. "We don't expect you to be a clown, just to stop and think about the message here: No matter how long you've been at something, it's never too late to quit."

"If I've learned one lesson from my years in business," Dad put in, holding a breadstick like a cigar, "it's that open-minded people open the way." He took a bite, crunching contentedly.

When the waitress arrived with our dinner, it took every ounce of control I had not to knock over the whole steaming tray and storm out. I cooled off while she distributed the food, and when she walked away, I asked, with suppressed rage, "Is this why you brought me here? To insult me? To humiliate me?"

"Don't be ridiculous, dear," my mother said. "We would never do that to you."

"We love you, Laurel; you know that," said my dad.

Jenna, spearing a cherry tomato with her fork, cut to the chase. "Yes, that's why we brought her here! And you shouldn't deny it. Isn't that what we're all trying to overcome here—denial? I for one am no longer going to pretend that it is okay for my thirty-year-old sister to be picking up doggie doo for a living!"

"Mom, Dad," I stammered in disbelief, "is this true? You all got together in advance to plan this coordinated attack?" They didn't need to answer; the guilt was written all over their faces. "Well, you could have saved yourselves the effort," I declared, deciding to take the high road. "It just so happens I'm on the verge of a major breakthrough." *Please, dear God,* I thought to myself, *let Anderson Gallant be the one.*

"Not another verge," said Jenna, rolling her eyes. "You're the only person I know who's been living on the verge for the last eight years."

"Hold it, Jenna. Remember Dr. Schneider's parameters: no labeling," my mother said sternly, leaving me to wonder just how elaborately they'd been conspiring. "But dear, you must admit . . . No, no, I'm supposed to begin this sentence with 'I' . . . . I feel as if I have heard this before."

Dad nodded, vigorously cutting into his steak. "There was that major breakthrough with your dermatologist's sister who promised to read your stuff but then dropped dead."

Mom bit the head off a shrimp. "And then there was the agency we paid a thousand dollars to read your work, but they still never came through with anything," she recalled, shaking her head sadly and no doubt imagining how many treatments at Elizabeth Arden that money would have bought.

Jenna, brandishing an asparagus spear, had her own memory to share. "What about the time she met that trick-or-treater at Halloween whose daddy was supposedly a big publisher? She threw her novel into the kid's plastic pumpkin."

"It wasn't a pumpkin; it was a goody bag. And the father said my work was Chekhovian," I seethed.

"But he didn't publish it," Dad pointed out. "And neither did any of the dozens of others you said promised a lucky break right around the corner."

I was ready to walk out in fury when my mother reached across the table and put her warm, familiar hand on top of mine. "The point is, we hate to see you suffer," she said. Something in her voice was tender and sincere, and I suddenly felt like a six-year-old girl who just fell off her rollerblades. The pain from all those years of struggle and dashed hopes that had been as backed up as the sink in my apartment came rushing forth. "What am I supposed to do with my life?" I whimpered quietly.

"There, there, let it out," said my sister. "Just go ahead and have a good cry." I felt so vulnerable, even Jenna sounded sweet.

"And when you're done, cheer up!" my father said. "Because I've got a great lead on a real job for you." He handed me a rolled-up magazine while explaining that my uncle Lewis could get me a position there as a staff writer with a starting salary in the low forties.

A magazine, I thought, intrigued. But my glimmer of hope lasted only until I saw the cover. In bland, Helvetica type there was the name of my future: *Girdle and Support Hose Quarterly.*

It took me the better part of the next three days to print out a copy of my novel for Anderson Gallant to read. I'd been using the same printer since the incident with the dermatologist's sister, and it jammed about every other minute, but I finally coaxed out all 732 pages of *Napoleon's Hairdresser,* wrapped it in a crisp folder, and cradled it in my arms as I headed off to pick up Cadbury.

"Well, here it is," I said to my client, who was wearing a Pepe Le Pew T-shirt and reading Snapchat magazines on his phone.

"Oh, you're delivering the dog food now?" he asked. "Just put it over there in the corner."

Not the most auspicious beginning, but I was determined not to let my family crush my dreams. "It's *Napoleon's Hairdresser,*" I explained. When that drew a blank look, I added, "My novel."

Suddenly, Anderson's eyes lit up as if he could picture a future bestseller. "Your novel—of course!" he said expansively. "How exciting! This is the one about the racecar driver who gets cancer, right? I'll read it this weekend."

Not wanting to diminish his enthusiasm, I didn't correct him and instead took Cadbury for the usual walk. I was relieved but worried Anderson would read it too quickly; I wanted to give him a revised version of Chapter 38 based on the comments my writers group was due to give me that week. I planned to slip the new text in on my next visit so that Anderson would have the most polished manuscript possible.

4

I'd never been more eager for feedback than that Tuesday evening when I arrived at the Ninth Avenue community center. I'd taken the advice of José, the only professional editor in our group, if only of children's textbooks, and I was looking forward to his comments, which were dependably supportive.

But when I got there, hoping to see everyone's scribbled-on copies of "Chapter 38: Waterloo 'Do," I was confused to see nothing but pizza and soda all around.

"You look like you could use this," said Margo, handing me a cold 7UP. I'd obviously missed a WhatsApp notification somewhere along the way.

"What's the occasion?" I asked, but before she could answer, Portia walked in and everyone screamed, "Surprise!"

"Congratulations!"

"We knew you could do it!"

"Helen Ellenbogen—she's the best!"

"Don't forget us when you're famous!"

They were all shouting at once. I managed my own tribute: "Your stuff always was the most commercial."

After a round of limp pizza and even more flaccid

compliments, Danny Z. and I escaped, commiserating on the way to the subway. As we walked east toward Broadway amid the theatergoers rushing to make the curtain, he summed up our feelings succinctly: "That bitch Portia couldn't write a customs form. Don't worry, she'll get horrible reviews, her book will bomb, and then we'll have a real party."

It seemed like grim revenge, especially since I couldn't really celebrate anything until my own book was published and my family felt ashamed for ever having doubted me. We'd all be at the Grand Ballroom in the W Hotel, with the chief editor of the *New York Review of Books* congratulating Mom and Dad for raising such a genius. I'd be loving every minute of it, with no stress from Jenna, because her invite would be for two hours later than everyone else's. By the time she'd arrive, there would be nothing but crumbs of stale bread and a stream of well-wishers in line to buy an autographed copy of my book.

Snapping back to reality, I told Danny Z. he'd likely be the next one we'd be celebrating. "I mean, who wouldn't want to buy *What to Wear When You Want More than an Affair*? I know I could use that advice."

"Tell, tell," he said. "I might just oblige."

On Saturday evening, Danny Z. obliged. He and I ripped through my closet in search of the perfect outfit for my date that night.

"Stay away from that skirt; florals indicate neediness," he said disapprovingly. I dutifully hung up the cotton mini.

"What about this?" I asked, pulling out a striped, boatneck crew top.

"Are you crazy?" Danny Z. counseled. "No confusing parallel lines—you want him to think convergence."

He rejected thong underwear—"too suggestive"—open-toed shoes—"too casual"—and a wraparound shawl—"too ugly."

After three hours of debate and a forty-minute lecture on lipstick, it was time to tackle my coif. Unfortunately, Danny Z. was still researching his next book, *What to Do With Your Hair When You Want to be Part of a Pair*, so he couldn't tell me whether leave-in conditioner would make my locks limp or if gel plus volumizer would be a delight or a disaster. We settled on a touch of curl control and hoped for the best.

Glancing at my reflection on the way out, I had to concede that Danny Z. was a genius. Even though I was wearing only jeans and a T-shirt, I had that glow of famous starlets who intentionally dress down, the kind I always envied in my favorite guilty pleasure, *Celebrity Style.* Added to this was the magic fact that every thread in the ensemble was subliminally geared toward getting me hitched.

Even though we hadn't picked a place to meet, I just knew that as soon as I entered the large auditorium, electric attraction would naturally bring Lucien and I together. During the lecture, neither of us would be able to concentrate on the Socio-Economy of Tempos; instead, we'd feel a frisson of excitement each time our knees casually touched. By the time the lights came up he would have taken my hand, and we'd burn to be alone. Back at his place—God knows I couldn't let him see mine—it would be only seconds before we were frantically pulling off each other's clothes. And when the wedding bells finally chimed, Danny Z. would thank me for bringing him fame by proving that it really was much, much more than an affair.

I could feel Lucien's intelligent, masculine presence somewhere amid the black turtlenecks and wire-rimmed glasses, the goatees and ethnic jewelry sported everywhere, and told myself it wouldn't be long before our eyes finally met.

"Hey there," I heard someone call behind me. "I was worried you wouldn't make it." I blushed deeply before I turned around, only to find myself facing a husky-voiced woman calling out to her lover across the room.

Thinking Lucien must be up near the lectern, I made my way toward the stage, where I accidentally became caught up in what in this crowd passes for a barroom brawl.

"Lacan had it completely backwards. The phallocentric simulacrum was never the dominant modality in Irigaray's reaction," a bushy-haired professor-type sputtered.

"Oh, please," replied his bottle-blonde companion. "The feminist critique isn't about reaction; it's about representation," she said. "Every Semiotics 101 student knows that."

"You," she added, planting her Birkenstocks in my path. "Settle this for us. Which post-structuralist paradigm played precisely into the hands of the French *analysand* advocates? I know it's obvious, but humor me."

In all my longing for Lucien I never wanted him more than at that moment, but he didn't magically appear. "Of course it's obvious," I stammered. "Why do you even ask?"

"Because," bottle-blonde said with contempt, "Professor Reactionist-Revisionary over here claims that Lacan's theories are all a result of bad mothering!"

"He said that?" I asked, hoping to change the subject. "How absurd."

"That is not what I said. You completely missed the thrust of my comparative analytical theory…" As their argument resumed, I slipped away.

A second later, the auditorium lights dimmed, and I grabbed the first seat I could find, certain Lucien would be tapping my shoulder at any moment. But just as the speaker approached the microphone, I spotted him sitting on the opposite side of the room. Who could miss that thick hair? Once in a while he would turn, and I'd catch a glimpse of his intense blue eyes. It was all I could do to stay in my seat.

Instead of sleeping through the lecture, I survived it by imagining our conversation at the intimate café he would certainly take me to. "So you say you're a writer?" he would ask, unable to quench his insatiable thirst for information about my fascinating life. But before I could even answer, he'd be leaning across the table to kiss me because my sex appeal was even more magnetic.

When the final applause died down, I rushed over to see him. I imagined the camera pulling back to reveal me pushing my way through the crowd and him doing the same on the other side of the room, both of us desperately searching for each other.

The soundtrack would swell as our eyes met, and the camera would pull in for a tight close-up of our long-awaited embrace.

The movie playing in my mind was interrupted by a sharp elbow jab between my ribs. "Hey!" I said, nearly ready to respond with a punch, when I saw those baby blues gazing at me.

"Sorry," Lucien said. "Laurel, right? Great to see you again."

Perfect! I thought. He'd remembered my name and recited the first line I'd written for him in my head.

"Hey, I wouldn't miss the chance to see you," I said, reciting the second.

"There's someone I want you to meet," he said. *Wait a minute,* I thought. *That's not in the script.* "This is Xhana. She's from Ouagadougou."

Xhana was like a supermodel, with flawless skin, aristocratic cheekbones, and a gentle, friendly smile. I was both instantly in love with her and filled with jealousy.

"Pleasure to meet you," she said in a lilting accent, extending her beautiful hand.

"The pleasure's all mine," I lied through the biggest smile I could muster. When Lucien's arm slipped around her waist, I felt the air rush from my lungs and that special pain that only comes when the heroine loses true love. The musical score rose to a tragic climax. Fade to black.

In the harsh glare of the streetlights, I realized I couldn't even face being among people on a train or bus, so I decided to hoof it the fifty blocks home. The streets were filled with Saturday night couples snuggling over drinks at sidewalk cafés, coming out of theaters holding hands, and otherwise looking blissful. Meanwhile, I got more witchy by the moment, my face frozen in a frown.

For the first ten blocks I was in shock. How could I be so stupid? Why would a babe as accomplished and sophisticated as Lucien ever take notice of me? Of course he'd pick someone from Ouagadougou and not Massapequa. She was probably multilingual and bicontinental; I couldn't even sing *Frères Jacques* and hadn't traveled further than one bad Spring Break spent in Cancún. Her look was haute couture, and I was strictly off the rack. Xhana was the kind of woman who haunted men in their dreams; I was the kind they trusted to walk their dogs.

By the time I hit midtown, I was good and angry. At myself. For being so deluded. I had to admit it wasn't the first time. My mind could no longer run from the litany of disasters. They flittered before my eyes like images from a dating hell scrapbook. There was Giorgio, the foreign exchange student in high school who I was sure would be my prom date but never even knew my name. And those months I wasted when I worked at the Copenhagen Café waiting for that avant-garde filmmaker to ask me out, only to learn that he was married with three kids. I had suppressed the memory of the one right before Lucien: Kenai, the tortured-yet-successful painter whose Irish setter I walked until that awful night I decided to surprise him in lingerie. He arrived home with his real date and screamed in horror.

I felt like screaming in horror myself. *This has to stop. You are ruining your life. Get your head out of the clouds already. Haven't you had enough? When are you going to realize that fantasy is not the same as reality? The longer you spend dreaming, the less you'll have to show for it. Look at your cousin Mindy, who threw away her youth thinking she was the next Lizzo when all she ended up was lonely, unemployed, and living with her parents.*

I recognized my mother's voice in my head but couldn't write it off as undermining criticism. Every word rang true. By Twenty-Third Street, I'd come to an important decision: no more delusions. The time had come for me to make a real life for myself in the real world. The nearer I got to Fourteenth Street, the more I knew I needed a plan, and by the time I had trodden the well-worn steps to my crumbling apartment, I knew what it was.

Once inside, I picked up the phone. Trish answered right away.

"Hey, it's me. Quick question: Your kid's dentist . . . is he still available?"

The next morning, I emerged fresh from the shower and looked in the mirror to see myself with all illusions washed off—no makeup or product, just me: mousy brown hair limp and lifeless, the artificial sheen gone from my cheeks, and chapped, unkissable lips.

Meanwhile, somewhere on the Upper West Side, a sexy art critic was waking up next to his exotic beauty. Lucien would extend a muscled arm across the cream satin sheets and stroke Xhana's lithe shoulder.

For all I knew, they had already been shopping for rings. No doubt he could afford the pink diamond she'd cherish. Even on short notice, Xhana would have connections who could book her the Pierre Grand Ballroom for their reception, and before they departed for their seven-star honeymoon in Dubai, Lucien would remember old reliable Laurel as the perfect person to care for Xhana's three purebred Shih Tzus. She'd get a massage in the Jacuzzi while I'd be left holding the bag of Shih Tzu shit.

In defiance, I decided to throw on the striped boatneck crew top and the cotton mini. To hell with Danny Z.'s precious theories. No amount of wardrobe hocus-pocus would help a plain Jane like me. Lucky I didn't invest in those sapphire earrings from Thailand he insisted would subliminally erase all fear of commitment in a man. What a joke. Even Trish's suburban dentist couldn't be seduced with a trick like that.

For all her mediocre taste, though, I had to admit that Trish made the guy out to seem like he might be my type. "He loves all kinds of music!" she said.

"Don't you mean Muzak? He's a dentist."

"Yeah, and I can't tell you how many single women in this town wish he was drilling them instead of their teeth."

I giggled at the thought of being the envy of all the desperate women on the South Shore. There I'd be at the mall with tacky competitors all around whispering about how the hunky dentist had fallen for the artsy writer from Manhattan: "It's so unfair, I had a nose job, a boob job, and a six-figure real job, and he goes for a girl who looks like an unmade bed? I should have written a novel instead."

If this drill master attracted so many women, he had to have a great bod and super-thick hair, even thicker than Lucien's maybe. And with the new rage in enamel veneers, I knew he made a good enough living to buy me the dream diamond ring. With his bucks and my good taste, our wedding wouldn't be held at Leonard's of Great Neck; it would be at the Conservatory Garden in Central Park.

While walking Xhana's ill-behaved, inbred monsters, Lucien would just happen to be passing at that moment. Looking through the great iron gate, he'd be devastated to realize the radiant bride was me.

Too late, sucker, I thought in my overactive imagination.

Out of the array of bottles, tubes, sprays, jars, and sample packets crowding every available surface in my tiny bathroom, I selected a volumizing mousse and applied it from the roots to the ends.

Determined to tame my mane, I flipped my head upside down and switched on my blow-dryer. Boom! The air conditioner died, the TV shut off, my computer made an awful sound before shutting down, and the lights went dark. I sighed deeply, looked up at the ceiling from between my legs, and faced the hard truth: Too many appliances blow the apartment fuse.

Standing up and staring at my face in the dim mirror, it occurred to me that, by extension, too many dashed dreams can leave a girl really burned out.

As I left the bathroom, I had another profound realization: Any dentist in the market for a blind date has got to be a major loser.

Since my battery-operated phone was the one appliance still working, and my career was the one hope I had left, I dialed José. Portia's little pizza party had robbed me of the chance to hear any feedback on Chapter 38. José's opinion was the only one I really cared about, and I needed it badly to revise my manuscript before Anderson could read it.

Calculating in my head, I counted seven days since I'd dropped it off. Even if Anderson managed to put it down after each chapter, chances were he hadn't gotten to Part II yet. If I rushed, I could replace the old Chapter 38 before Cadbury's morning walk.

I apologized to José for calling at eight in the morning but explained that it was imperative to get his feedback because an industry giant was reading my novel.

"That's great news!" he said. "If you don't mind if I eat cereal while we talk, let's go."

José loved the new chapter title. "'Toupee or not Toupee'— where'd you come up with that?"

"My imagination, I guess," I replied excitedly. There were upsides to my daydreaming. "But what about the crowd scenes? Did they move too quickly?"

"To tell you the truth," he said, crunching his breakfast, "I was a little confused. Is anyone really going to believe that Napoleon, a man who just conquered half of Austria, is constantly thinking about his bald spot?"

"The great general's brilliance at the battle of Austerlitz can be directly attributed to his subconscious drive to overcome a very common case of male pattern balding," I declared. "And it was his hairdresser who gave him the confidence to advance with the famous hundred-gun grand battery!"

There was silence on the other end—even José's chewing had ceased. "But," he began softly, "the fields were carpeted with the dead and dying. I have to say, such vanity tests my threshold of believability. You completely discredit Napoleon's tactical genius, chalking it up to the work of a stylist."

"Exactly! That's my angle," I explained, disappointed by his lack of insight. "Everybody knows he's a brilliant strategist, but nobody knows that his hairdresser was!"

"Well, then you've done an admirable job of rendering the implausible plausible," he conceded.

"Now, José, I need your criticisms as much as your compliments," I chided. "This is my big shot."

"Okay then, here's what I think. You're too obsessed with pre-industrial age homemade hair products. I grant you, it's interesting to learn that ordinary axle grease covers those unsightly grays, but do you really need to elaborate on the chemical properties of lard mixed with charcoal as a precursor to L'Oréal for three full pages?"

My brow was knit. I hated to delete a month's worth of research, but I knew that José's instincts were correct. "It does slow the action," I admitted.

To get the computer—and the rest of my apartment, for that matter—working again, I had to trudge down seven flights to my building's filthy basement and switch on the fuse box. Feeling half-dead when I came back upstairs, at least everything else had come to life, including my desktop, which displayed an iMessage from Mom.

"Hi, Cookie. Here's Uncle Lewis's number at work. He's all excited about hearing from you, and let's face it, you can't be choosy. So give him a call before—"

Before reading the rest of that sentence, I closed the screen and sat down at my desk to pursue my true calling, which was most decidedly not being a junior writer at *Girdle and Support Hose Quarterly*.

5

Half an hour later, with the newly trimmed Chapter 38 safe in my backpack, I set out to do my morning rounds. The moment I opened the door to Anderson's apartment, Cadbury leapt up and started kissing me on the face.

"Cadbury, sit!"

The dog promptly obeyed.

"Well, you certainly have everything under control," Anderson said, emerging from the kitchen.

I thought about asking him if I could replace the old chapter, but after a compliment like that, I didn't want to look flaky. "Thanks," I said. "I try to be creative."

I studied his face to see if it betrayed any sign that he was deeply immersed in my book and amazed to have discovered such a talent, but all he said was, "I won't be here when you get back, but have a nice walk."

"Maybe I'll see you later this week?" I asked, fishing for clues.

"Hope so," he replied.

Now that had to be good news.

The bad news was that my normally enjoyable morning walk

got off to a rocky start. The dogs were all crazy, prompting me to wonder what the lunar phase was, because I've noticed that during a full moon they act up like somebody slipped Red Bull into their water bowls.

Right in the middle of Broadway, Lulu insisted on trying to hump Mini, which was ridiculous because the teacup Chihuahua could only get as far as the Great Dane's knee. I had to stop and lecture them on the center lane island while a bum jeered the oh-so-original observation, "So that's why they call it doggie style!"

We got to Eighty-Second Street without incident, but while I was imagining *Napoleon's Hairdresser* on sale at every airport in the world, Kingpin relieved himself on an old chair that had been tossed out on the sidewalk.

At least, that's what I thought it was until the owner came running over with a furious look on his face. Glancing around, I noticed the area was full of furniture being loaded into a moving van, and I realized that the chair wasn't just old—it was antique.

"You idiot! That's an original Eames chaise lounge! Do you have any idea how much that will cost to clean?"

"No..." I replied sheepishly.

"Well, you're going to, because I'm sending you the bill."

Since I survive on reputation, I had no choice but to hand over my business card and pray that I wouldn't have to pay much more than I did to dry clean a dress.

"I hope you're getting a big tax return," the owner said in a parting shot, "because this is going to cost at least a couple hundred bucks."

My day's pay blown, I tried to cheer up as we approached Riverside Park. After all, the sun was shining, the day was young, and the Chapter 38 in my backpack was sure to blow Anderson away.

At the corner of Riverside Drive, waiting for the light to turn so we could begin our romp in the park, I was approached by a man in blue.

"These your dogs?" asked the policeman.

"No, sir," I answered cheerfully. "Laurel's Pooch Patrol –

The Upper West Side is Our Backyard." I handed him a card. You never know where you're going to get new business.

"Unfortunately, this is not a backyard," the officer said sternly. "And you have to clean up after your dogs."

As a firm supporter of the pooper-scooper law, I was shocked. No one had cleaned up after more dogs in that neighborhood than I had. "I'm aware of that, sir," I replied defensively.

"Then what's this?" he asked, pointing to what looked like an elephant dropping only inches from my feet.

"Ugh!" I replied jumping back. "That's not from these dogs."

"Sure it's not," he said sarcastically, pulling out his pad. That was the moment that Lulu chose to turn her amorous attention toward the cop.

"Hey!" he cried, trying to shake her off his leg. "I was going to give you a warning, but now you're getting a ticket." He began scribbling on the pad.

"Listen," I said, pulling out my stash of baggies, "I'm a professional! I would never leave that on the street. Besides, that must have been there a while."

"I'm sure you know your dog poop, but they didn't waste any time teaching us that at the police academy. If you want to contest the ticket, here's the number to call." He circled a line on the back and left me standing there holding my second bill of the morning, this one for a cool hundred.

By the time I got back to Anderson Gallant's, glad to be dropping off my last charge, I was feeling frazzled but ready to go ahead with my mission. Conveniently, after letting me in, the maid went down to the laundry room, so I had the place to myself.

Now, where would he put my book? Figuring he read it before going to sleep, I tiptoed into the bedroom, where I found a king-sized mattress on the floor, surrounded by various remotes and facing a giant-screen TV. There was a stray tablet nearby but no books in sight.

This publishing empire heir didn't seem to have much taste for literature, I thought, retreating to the study. It was immaculate, lined with bookshelves filled with classics that looked like they had never been touched. The beautiful mahogany desk appeared equally unused, with no papers anywhere, least of all my manuscript.

People do read in the bathroom, I reasoned, entering his, but I didn't find *Napoleon's Hairdresser* there.

I was starting to feel despondent when it hit me—he brought it to work! Of course! I'd just have to hope he liked the old Chapter 38, because I wasn't about to go snooping around Gallant Publishing.

With the place to myself, I figured it wouldn't hurt to go out on the terrace and sneak a peek at the view. After all, with Anderson's help, I'd eventually have to decide which park-front building I'd want to live in.

The fresh air revived me, and my eyes took in the glittering cityscape. Wanting to leave before the maid returned, I pulled open the heavy glass door and began to re-enter the apartment.

That's when it caught my eye: There, supporting a potted ficus tree, was a thick manuscript that looked horrifyingly familiar. I almost couldn't look, but I had to, and that's when I discovered that Anderson Gallant had turned eight years of my love and labor, my creation, my baby, into a plant-stand. It was enough to make me want to throw the whole book off the balcony, except that with my luck, it would probably just get me a ticket for littering. So all I did was turn around and head home.

The rest of the day was a blur, and by evening, I wanted to crawl under the covers and stay there forever, but it was Thursday, my night to visit Mrs. Lilianthaller and her two toy poodles, Bogey and Bacall, and even though I wouldn't get paid, I knew the spiritual reward would be worth it. Poor Mrs. Lilianthaller could barely walk down the block, and a few of us dog-walkers had each signed up for one night a week to give those puppies the exercise they needed. Both the elderly woman and her beloved canines were so grateful, and their smiles more than made up for the work of adding another dog to my long dog-walking day.

"Is that you, deary?" a tiny voice asked through the intercom, nearly drowned out by the happy barking sounds in the background. The door buzzed open, and before I reached the first landing, I could hear the furious scratching of doggie nails on tile as Bogey and Bacall bounded down the stairs, saving me the trip to the third floor.

"My little stars!" I cried, and instantly regretted it as they both leaped from the landing into my arms and proceeded to lick my face until it was soaked. "You guys need to slow down the welcome," I said, putting them down and taking their leashes, "or I'm going to have to enroll you in Over-greeters Anonymous!"

Oblivious to the threat of therapeutic intervention, Bogey and Bacall wagged their tails with delight. As we set off down Fourteenth Street toward Union Square Park, I said, "At least you care about me."

The sky darkened, and I turned up my collar against a sudden cold breeze mixed with exhaust from the avenue. Every time disappointment slapped me in the face, I would recover by imagining myself getting the last laugh when those who refused to recognize my talent saw my name at the top of the bestseller list week after week after week.

But this time, I couldn't muster the energy. The pain of knowing that Anderson Gallant never had and never would help me get published was nothing compared to the harsh truth that this was my pattern. I used to think all the cheerleading in my head would help me get what I wanted, but now I realized it just allowed me to maintain my useless fantasies.

Union Square was bustling with commuters hurrying around with the focused looks of accomplished professionals. Entering the smelly dog run, I unleashed Bogey and Bacall and slumped on a bench, feeling all tied up inside. How many times can you bang your head against the wall thinking you're going to break through, only to be left with a splitting migraine? There does come a moment when you have to cut your losses and move on to Plan B. God, how I've always avoided coming up with a Plan B! I even had a name for it: Plan Bury Me First. Instead, I subscribed to the beliefs of "I am what I imagine!" "I write the script of my own life!" and "What her mind can conceive, a girl can achieve!"

With the dust kicked up by the dogs flying around my face, I realized those were just delusional phrases. I am what I imagine—until I wake up. I write the script of my own life, and somebody tosses it under a plant.

You're a good person, I thought, consoling myself. *Look how happy you made Bogey and Bacall tonight.* The dogs were wrestling with a Shepherd-Collie mix with joyful abandon. To them, this lousy, crowded city dog run was paradise. The pups weren't always looking for greener pastures or reaching for something they could never get.

A ball landed near me, with Bogey making a dive for it. I pet the scruff of his neck. "Maybe you have the right idea," I said. "Just chase what comes to you."

When I got home, I followed my own advice, picked up the phone, and arranged to see my uncle the following Wednesday. For once, I was imagining something I could actually become: a staff reporter at *Girdle and Support Hose Quarterly*.

There was no time to worry about my career when I sat down with Trish the next day, because she was bursting with news about my blind date. "Six-foot-one, one hundred eighty-five pounds of solid muscle, and he knows how to cook," she said, rooting around in her purse. It was our regular girls' luncheon at Sushi and Slushies in the East Fifties.

I slurped on my pistachio-green bubble tea. "But can he kiss? He'd better not be thinking about cavities and molars when I open my mouth."

"Are you ready to die?" she said with characteristic overdramatization, producing a snapshot. "The one in the middle."

It didn't really matter which was my dentist-date because all five guys in the photo looked pretty much alike: backwards baseball caps, baggy shorts, and each holding a can of Bud. Definitely not my scene, but on closer inspection I noticed that the one in the middle, who was obviously laughing, had a casual look of confidence about him. Translation: possibly attractive. "So why's he single?" I asked, narrowing my eyes.

"Because," Trish replied, "he's looking for someone special."

"So why would he want to meet me?" I asked with a snort.

"Oh, come on," said Trish, furiously stirring her frothy pink drink. "You are so much more interesting than the types he attracts. You know, the mall addicts who spend half their life at the gym and the other half trying to find Mr. Right-Income-Bracket."

Trish did have a point. For all my faults, I wasn't your average subdivision single. "Did you tell him about me?"

"Of course. He's totally into the fact that you're a Manhattan artist who reads more than just shopping apps."

By the time we paid the check, I had agreed to at least meet the guy. "I do have to come out to the Island on Wednesday," I said tentatively. "Maybe we could hook up then?"

"Perfect!" replied Trish. "I'll make all the arrangements. You just be there."

"Well, what's the guy's name at least?" I asked.

"It's…" she paused for a second, "Irwin."

Irwin? I thought. A dentist named Irwin? What did I get myself into? And how would I get myself out?

Those were the same questions I pondered later that evening at yet another meeting of the Hell's Kitchen writers group. Sunny couldn't stop talking about how Portia's success showed that we were all going to make it. "I embrace our lucky friend's good fortune and call to the universe to embrace me," said the wannabe published author of *Daily Vows for a Happy Future.*

"I think we should all join hands and say this together," she suggested.

I think we should discuss my book, I thought to myself.

Everyone else loved her idea, though, and before long we were sitting in an awkward prayer circle avowing our universal embrace.

"I just felt the head of Simon & Schuster have a sudden urge to know who did Napoleon's hair," I said.

"Excellent, excellent," Sunny replied, my sarcasm lost on her.

As we held hands and silently put our energies together, I took a hard look at my fellow aspiring artists. What a bunch of losers. Sunny was reciting those vows all the way to the unemployment line. Danny Z.'s theories, as I had already proved, would get you no closer to a man than romance amulets or love potions would. José was the best writer, but really, who would ever buy *Planet Cucumber and the Wriggly Green Virus*? Seth was supposedly "blocked"—his excuse for never showing up with any material. And Margo was just plain ridiculous. *Love Between Consenting Parrots?* What's her sequel, *Rape of the Unwilling Pigeon?*

It was time, I knew, to escape this group of enabling, self-deluding, fantasy-feeding freaks. I couldn't walk out just then, though, because suddenly the affirmations ended, and José pointed out that it was my turn for feedback. "Let's polish this baby and get it ready for the bestseller list!" he said.

If only, if only, if only, I thought.

That night in my mailbox, along with the usual old-school gossip magazine in hard copy, I was surprised to find a yellow package slip from the post office. The next day, it rested in my pocket like a mysterious promise during the morning walk.

I was showing Danny Z. the ropes so he could fill in for me when I went to the Island on Wednesday. "For this kind of money, I'd walk porcupines," he said, obviously impressed by how much more could be made by waiting on animals than on tables. He might actually have the chance to take over, I thought, realizing that if the interview went well, I'd be giving it all up.

"Whatever you do," I cautioned, "don't call the dogs by the

wrong name in front of the owner. That just feeds their fears that to you their precious little darlings are nothing but a paycheck."

"Aye, aye, sir!" said Danny Z., saluting me under the flag in front of the post office. We exchanged kisses, but before parting he asked his favorite question: "So, what are you going to wear?"

I cringed. I'd been avoiding thinking about digging something out of my messy closet that would be suitable for an office. I sure as hell didn't have any girdles. "What should I wear?" I asked.

"No parallel lines."

"Not for the date!" I corrected. "For my job interview."

"Ah, be yourself," he said. "People want to see the real you: creative, inspiring, and pretty when you get your hair under control."

"Thanks a lot," I said, smiling in spite of myself. Danny Z. could always be counted on to tell it like it is.

During the twenty-five minutes I waited in line, I considered all the possibilities of what this mysterious package might be. Probably not a bomb; I'm too unimportant. Possibly a free promotional gift from someone trying to sell me something— that could be good. Or maybe I entered a contest without realizing it and this was my prize! Unlikely, but still…

When the clerk produced a medium-sized package, my hopes lifted—until I saw the return address: 206 Locust Lane, Massapequa, Long Island, home of my obsessively perfect older sister.

I carried it home like it *was* a bomb and stared at it in the middle of my floor, wondering whether I should dunk it in the bathtub to defuse it. Curiosity got the better of me, and using the sharpest kitchen knife I could find, I slashed the package open.

Not an explosive device, I realized, fingering the outer layer of tissue paper that was obviously holding some kind of outfit. Before I could wonder whether Jenna had finally given me my favorite pink dress of hers, I saw the dull navy color underneath.

A suit. A hideous, conservative, I'm-in-the-mainstream-now, double-breasted suit.

Ugh.

But the letter was even worse.

> *Dear Laurel,*
>
> *Congratulations on finally making a sensible move in your life. I know you're new to this, so you can benefit from my knowledge, experience, and even clothes! Enjoy this suit, but make sure you return it dry-cleaned. And don't mess up the look with a pair of suntan stockings or open-toed shoes.*
>
> *I trust you know how to walk dogs, and I hope you take my word for it on how to make it in the real world. You know I only want the best for you because I care and I want to see you become successful.*
>
> *Don't disappoint Mom, Dad, or Uncle Lewis. We're all counting on you to make something of yourself.*
>
> *Sincerely,*
> *Big Sis*

I ripped the letter to shreds and stuffed the suit back into the box, which I kicked under the table, wishing it was Jenna's head.

But that anger was followed by a spasm of guilt. After all, she'd just offered to lend me her clothes. What could be so bad about that? All she wanted me to do was make them proud…

But what about me? She didn't care if I was happy as long as I fit the mold—good family, good career, middle-class aspirations, and a good husband—so that Jenna wouldn't have to be ashamed of her semi-employed, failed artist, crappy-dressing, single younger sister.

Just like at her wedding. She not only told me exactly what to wear but also how to walk, who to talk to, when to shut up, and where to hide when she wanted me to disappear. Her picture-perfect image couldn't be messed up by Laurel's unsightly creativity. I had thought about writing her a special love story for a present but instead just picked something out of the registry. After all, everyone needs a cheese-cutter. Leave it to Jenna to want one made of solid sterling silver.

I set aside the morning of the interview to fully prepare. Remembering Danny Z.'s criticism of my hair, I made sure to get a professional blow-out. It left me looking a little corporate, but I figured that would work. At the nail salon, I selected a conservative pale pink over my usual hot fuchsia, figuring it would go well with the black and white jacket dress I'd chosen as the best compromise outfit to wear for both a job interview and a blind date. All I needed was a fresh copy of my résumé.

For once, my printer cooperated, coughing out the document without much of a fight. I was about to tuck it in my professional-looking fake leather folder when I decided to have a look.

My throat clenched. There in black and white—mostly white—was the pathetic story of my life since graduating college. Or non-story, to be more precise. Exactly two published pieces to my name: the *Seventeen Magazine* story I wrote in high school and a poem in the *Hoboken Herald* four years back.

Sure, I tried to spin my dog-walking gig as entrepreneurial pet-care management, but why would a real job be impressed by that? I could just hear the question: "So, Ms. Linden, I see you walk dogs, but what the hell do you know about copyediting?"

There was my college degree from Vassar, but how relevant was that? A major in Nineteenth-Century European Literature.

With the derisive laughter of experienced journalists ringing in my ears, I reluctantly dragged the box containing Jenna's suit out from under the bed. With those credentials, I was going to need all the help I could get.

Strangely enough, the suit made me stand straighter, as though by dressing respectably I deserved respect. As I headed through Penn Station, instead of attracting smirks and dumb comments—why do people think they're being original when they ask why I bought all those dogs?—I finally blended in with the rest of the working world. And at the ticket booth, for the first time in my life, I was addressed as "Ma'am."

The ride out was comfortable, and I realized that if I got this job I'd probably always get a seat, since most people live on the Island and work in the city, not the opposite. In the future, I definitely wouldn't be wearing my sister's ugly cast-offs; with my new pay raise, I'd be able to afford all kinds of great clothes. I decided I would go for sexy chic—not Donna Karan, just DKNY: sporty minis with matching jackets that would work as well in the office as on Avenue A. *Maybe the dentist drives a little aubergine Porsche, and he'll take me back into the city where we'll dance until dawn,* I thought, adjusting myself to a future full of interesting possibilities.

Assuming I land this job, that is. I'd been so busy fantasizing about my new life that I'd nearly forgotten to prepare for the interview. After some deliberation, I decided to focus on how my years of writing experience would surely enable me to communicate to the *Quarterly's* readers the very essence of the art of underwear.

By the time the train pulled into Massapequa, I was ready to face the chief editor. I imagined him sitting behind a large and imposing desk in a corner office with a beautiful view of a corporate park, but when I got there, I found no park, only a parking lot, and after being buzzed in, I saw that not only was there no corner office, the place had no windows.

I stood in the doorway, taking in the scene: piles of yellowed paper everywhere, two computers that made mine look like the latest model, and icky stockings and girdles draped in odd places, like over the company refrigerator.

A droopy woman beyond the help of even the most optimistic garment came wading through the mess and extended her hand.

"Thank God you're here. Laurel, right? Come on this—" she began, before breaking off into a hacking cough. She waved me past the front room and into a closet-sized cubicle where two overrun desks sat face to face.

"Mr. Burdowski will be back in a sec," she said. "Make yourself comfy." A phone started ringing, and she began lifting stacks of paper and dusty girdles in search of its source. Eventually the noise stopped and she shrugged. "Voicemail will pick up, and the password is somewhere, so I'm sure it will be fine."

"Of course," I affirmed.

"I'm Joan Malone, Office Manager," she said. I had squeezed myself into a rickety metal chair. "And this," she added, gesturing toward the dreary space with its free bank calendar and bronzed girdle on the wall boasting *2017 Industry Best*, "is your new home away from home."

"You mean I've got the job?" I asked, feeling confused. Just then, a slender, elderly gentleman walked in chewing on an unlit cigar.

"Mr. Burdowski, the new girl's here," Joan said.

"You mean you haven't scared her off yet?" he asked. *Well, almost,* I thought. "Don't mind Joan," he added. "She's normally okay, but she hasn't been able to find her little blue happy pills in here for the last two weeks." Joan grimaced.

"I'm going to level with you," he said, lighting the cigar. "We've had three people quit in the past four months, and we're two quarters behind on our quarterly publication. Louie says you're a genius. Frankly, we don't need a genius, but we do need someone who can add up the sales figures and make them sound interesting."

"You'll pick it right up," Joan said.

"Well, enough fun," the boss said, gesturing toward a stack of paper. "Here's the figures dating back over the past six months. Should take you only about a week or two to spot the trends, but you might as well get started."

I was dumbfounded. He meant now.

"I thought this was a job interview…" I stammered.

"It was," he replied.

"You're hired!" Joan said with a smile.

"Well," I began, "I do need to give some notice to my current employer." Say goodbye to all my little mutts? No more

Lulu yapping at my feet? None of Kingpin's sloppy kisses? Never again seeing Cadbury's bright eyes when I walk in the door? I ached at the thought of leaving them.

"This position has been vacant for so long, what's another week?" Joan asked, taking my side.

"Fine, a week," conceded Mr. Burdowski. "But familiarize yourself with some of this," he added, handing me an accordion folder stuffed with paper.

As I moved to leave, Joan grabbed my arm and whispered conspiratorially, "You know, one of our former writers went on to become editor-in-chief at *Lingerie Wear Daily*." When she saw that I wasn't bowled over, she added, "But the best perk here is"—she wiggled her dandruffy eyebrows—"he'll let you take home a support garment if there's one that you like."

It was a nightmare, but if it was anything like the temp jobs I used to do, I knew I could get the work done in an eighth of the time they expected and spend the rest on my own personal projects. In effect, I'd be getting paid to sit at a computer and develop my oeuvre.

I didn't have too much time to consider the particulars, because when I looked at my watch I realized I had only fifteen minutes until my rendezvous with Irwin.

Conveniently, it was right across from the train station, but when I saw the small, fluorescent-lit Spiro's Diner I had to wonder why he'd been so eager to take me there. There was one vehicle in the driveway, and I prayed it wasn't Irwin's because far from being an aubergine Porsche, it was a bland, grandpa-like Chevy Impala.

I closed my eyes and hoped for the best, but when I entered the generic restaurant, which looked twice as large as it really was because of the preponderance of mirrors, I was met by an eager hostess with more frosting in her hair than on the cakes swirling around in their glass stand.

"Party of one?" she asked.

"Actually, I'm here to meet someone," I said, looking around nervously. There were only a few people in the place, and just one anywhere near my age. Although I could only see him from behind, one thing was clear: He was as bald as an eagle.

"Dr. Turnov? He's right over there," said the hostess, pointing to the cue ball.

"Oh, I don't think…" I began.

"Total sweetheart," she winked. "Gave me these caps half off," the hostess added, mouth wide open to show me.

That's when I saw her: my image in the mirror. A corporate clone reproduced from the mold of society's expectations: all unique attributes carefully painted over in the mid-range colors, my naturally wavy hair blown out into a helmet, accordion folder full of meaningless data under my arm, the dull navy suit making me look like every other commuter on the 7:23 train. All in all, Jenna junior—exactly what I'd vowed never to become.

I suddenly felt dizzy. Everything around me seemed to blur into spinning images: that horrible little office entombing me for the next thirty years; every morning being greeted by Joan Malone's hacking cough as she searched for the damned phone; Burdowski handing me piles of papers with that same turdy-looking cigar hanging from his fingertips; the bald dentist husband smelling of antiseptic and driving me from mall to mall in the awful Impala; my hair one huge, frosted cake.

No! I almost shouted out loud.

No, I decided then and there.

"I'm afraid you have the wrong woman," I said, and, pivoting decisively, I walked out the door, dumped the accordion folder in the nearest trashcan, mussed up my hair, and took off running for the next train to Manhattan.

As the city came into view, corny as it sounds, Frank Sinatra was blaring in my head: *If I can make it there, I'll make it anywhere, it's up to you, New York, New York*. It was the same song that had inspired me when I had moved to the city all those years ago, breaking away from the suburban swamp and leaving all the mediocrity behind in my pursuit of artistic excellence.

I nearly kissed the sidewalk as I emerged from Penn Station, and when I got home, even my crumbling apartment felt like a palace of freedom.

I peeled off the odious suit and jumped in the shower, eager to scrub off every last remnant of Plan B, but after dousing my hair in apple-scented shampoo and covering myself in body wash, the water suddenly shut off.

Again.

For the third time that week.

And the eighth time that month.

As far as the year went, I'd long since given up counting.

Shivering, naked and covered with soap, I felt as vulnerable as a newborn and started to cry. There was no use pretending my life was glorious. Sure, it would make a great story on the "Today Show," but the "Today Show" only featured people who succeeded. Their early years of struggle were character-building steps on the path to greatness. But unless you make it, character-building is just a fancy word for hell. It killed me to admit, but my parents were right: I had accomplished virtually nothing in eight years of trying. Without even realizing it, I was headed from wannabe to couldabeen.

I toweled off, still crying, and decided to curl up in bed. I certainly didn't have the stomach for any research on Napoleon and instead opened my hard copy of *Us Magazine*, hoping for a good article on the hidden heartache of a rich, beautiful celebrity to cheer me up.

It was comforting to read about bulimic TV prodigies, botched plastic surgery, and the bitter divorces of famous couples, until I got to page seventy-two. There, in all her splendor, was Xhana, the hot new African opera singer who had been discovered by none other than Lucien Brosseau.

The sobs came in floods. I threw the magazine across the room and screamed "WHY?" Why did I have to see that now, when I was least able to take it? It was as if life had chosen the worst possible moment to kick me where it hurt.

6

The next day, I woke up with red-rimmed eyes and, feeling numb, went about my routine. In the afternoon, I dropped Jenna's suit off at the dry cleaners, knowing that the fourteen dollars to clean it was only the beginning of the price I'd have to pay. "How could you do this to Mom and Dad?" she'd surely ask. "How could you embarrass Uncle Lewis like that? Don't you have any respect?" The only thing that would shut her up would be a publishing contract, and unfortunately the day's mail brought no miracles. There was a copy of *Celebrity Style*, but fearing another Xhana sighting, I dumped it straight in the trash can. Other than that, just two bills and the usual plea for money from my college alumni association. My phone showed three messages, which I ignored, knowing they were from Jenna, Mom, and Trish, who would no doubt all want an explanation.

Seeing the Vassar logo on the envelope reminded me of those carefree years when I truly believed anything was possible. At college, I received the kind of direction, encouragement, and praise that had been absent from my life since graduation. Feeling nostalgic, I opened the envelope. For a change, it wasn't a fundraising solicitation.

Need a new Big Sister? screamed a headline across a bright red flyer.

Did I ever.

I read on:

> **Vassar's Old Girl Network is ready to help. Register now, and we'll match you with a mentor tailor-made to meet your needs. Then join us for crumpets and tea and get started on a new life.**

What the hell, I thought. I filled out the survey and mailed it on the way to my afternoon rounds.

The tea was held a few days later at the University Club on Park Avenue. As I entered through the big oak doors, I felt a familiar hopeful feeling, like I was twenty years old again and earning all A's. At the registration table, a bubbly redhead looked up my name on a list. "Laurel Linden, now you are lucky: Cathy Grayer is your big sis. Nicest, most sensible, intelligent person you'd ever want to meet." She pressed a nametag on my lapel and told me to proceed to table twenty-one.

The room buzzed with excitement as enthusiastic young women paired up with seasoned professionals offering sound advice. Cathy Grayer greeted me with a firm handshake, poured some tea, and started in with the questions.

"You say you've been writing for eight years, but you haven't published anything?" she asked, as if it was impossible for such a fate to befall a Vassar graduate. Reluctantly, I explained my situation, even going so far as to describe my latest attempt to secure a new job. "I just couldn't see myself sitting there day after day writing about girdles," I confessed.

"But how are you ever going to get published unless you accumulate some clips?" she asked, sitting straight up in her houndstooth suit garnished with a bejeweled butterfly broach. "Sure, a little industrial newsletter doesn't seem so glamorous, but next thing you know you'll have a chance to write for a larger circulation commercial journal. That's the only way anyone is ever going to take you seriously: when you have a byline. My advice to you is to show up next Monday at that job like a real Vassar girl would and start yourself on the path to publication."

Feeling hot tears about to burst forth, I thanked Cathy Grayer politely and stumbled off toward the bathroom in search of some privacy. I was full-on sobbing by the time I got there and felt embarrassed to see that I wouldn't be alone. A small, vivacious brunette in a tailored, light green dress was applying clear nail polish to a run in her stocking.

"Swear to God," she said, "I'm going to break my addiction to this college nostalgia bullshit."

Through my tears, I smiled.

The woman turned to face me and realized I'd been crying. "Oh, you look exactly how I feel!" she said. "Utterly depressing, isn't it?"

For the first time in ages, somebody was validating my feelings, and I couldn't hold back the dam that had bottled them up.

"Depressed is better than how I feel now," I said, and before long, I had recounted my conversation with Cathy Grayer. "So do you really think I need to go work for that girdle magazine?" I asked my new friend.

"Absolutely not!" she said, slamming a bangle-laden hand on the marble counter. "That would be the stupidest move possible. Who is ever going to take you seriously as a novelist if all you've ever written about is latex?"

"But nobody takes me seriously now!" I explained. "I'm a dog-walker, not a novelist."

Her large, expressive brown eyes bored into me with a confidence that was almost frightening. "Vanessa Pixley," she announced, grabbing me by the shoulders. "And I'm here to tell you that your great potential can be realized." Letting go, she snapped a business card into my hand. "When you're ready to believe that, you just give me a call."

With that, she left, and I felt like maybe I'd met a real big sister.

I didn't know if it would be too soon to call the next day, but I did anyway. My timid introduction was met with a warm and welcoming invitation to lunch. "How about Aquavit at one-thirty?" she asked.

I knew I couldn't afford one of the best restaurants in New York and hesitated, wondering if I'd reached out of my league.

Sensing my rectitude, she added quickly, "My treat."

"Are you sure?" I asked.

"Of course," she confirmed. "It will be my chance to hear all about your fascinating novel. And together, we're going to figure out how to get you published."

That phone conversation finally gave me the courage to face what I'd been avoiding.

"Hi, Trish," I said, sitting at a Starbucks in between shifts. "It's me."

"Now you decide to call? It's too late. He hates you."

"Big tragedy," I said, taking a sip of my latte and feeling carefree. "Why didn't you tell me he was bald? And his name is Turnoff?"

"It's Turnov. And anyway, look who's talking! You showed up in a double-breasted suit with your hair in a bouffant. I told you he likes artsy types."

"He saw me?"

"You were pretty obvious about walking out on him."

"Well it's not like I'm ever going to hook up with someone named Irwin Turnov. I mean, Trish, give me a little credit."

"Oh right, I forgot you're dating Lucien Brosseau. But how come you weren't mentioned in the article in *Us*?"

Figuring no one could go lower than that, I called Mom. I

was wrong.

"What did Uncle Lewis ever do to you to make you embarrass him like that in front of his closest business associate? Do you realize that man is one of your closest relatives? Okay, so you want to be a failure, but do you have to drag down the rest of us with you? This family hasn't been so humiliated since Jenna gave your cousin a job doing reception at the fitness studio and Mindy spent the whole time eating greasy fast food in front of the students!"

Vanessa wouldn't think that was such a crime, I thought.

There was no one left to call but the calorie policewoman herself.

"I tried, Laurel. You can't say I don't believe in you," Jenna said.

"Believe in me?" I'd finally had enough. "You call trying to make me be something I'm not believing in me? If you believed in me, you might have once come into the city and visited my apartment. Or come to my writing group like I asked you to fifty times. You might have actually read *Napoleon's Hairdresser*. It's not like I didn't give it to you Velo-bound and everything."

For once, Jenna was silent.

"It sounds like an incredible book, and I can't believe you finished it in only eight years. I mean, look at Flaubert—he spent thirty years on *Madame Bovary*, so you're way ahead of the game," Vanessa said at lunch the next day. Seated in such a fancy restaurant, with such an elegant woman taking me seriously, I actually had hope of believing her.

"You think?" I asked, seeking reassurance.

"Honey, in actuality, publishing is all about contacts, not talent. The fact that you have very little to show for your efforts only proves that you've been devoted to your art instead of marketing."

"Maybe I just suck," I said.

"Give me a dollar!" Vanessa commanded. "I'm going to charge you every time you make a self-disparaging remark." I gladly handed over a single, feeling happy that she was really on my side. She tucked it into a small, sleek, black satin pouch produced from her red handbag.

"Laurel, you don't even see how great you are. For eight years everyone has been against you, and you've never once given up on your dream. You've gone out there, you've made your career, you've supported yourself and pursued your craft. It's only a matter of time until someone discovers your creation."

I felt myself glow inside. Seeing my life through Vanessa's eyes, the glass was way more than half full.

"You deserve to be published," she continued.

Full of champagne.

"But let me ask you this: Do you really want to realize your dreams?"

"Who doesn't?" I asked.

"Then say it: Yes, I do!"

"Yes, I do!" I repeated, feeling giddy, as though I'd downed the champagne all in one gulp.

"Congratulations," Vanessa said. "You've just taken the hardest step. Now, here's the next one: When you get home, I want you to throw out everything in your apartment that makes you feel unworthy."

"Are you kidding? There'd be nothing left," I protested.

"Another dollar!" she commanded. "Don't make me rich off of your pessimism. Now try again; can you do it?"

"Definitely," I answered. "I'll have a bonfire."

First off, the *Us* magazine featuring Xhana and Lucien. Added to that were 117 rejection letters from agents, all of Portia's chapters of *Wild Asparagus,* and a folder full of articles my mother had cut out about successful young professionals, with Clowny Zary at the top. Too bad I'd already taken Jenna's suit to the cleaners, but I still had enough hand-me-downs from her to add to the pile, all of them dreadful conservative outfits meant to make me fit in the working world.

I brought this history of loserhood to the alley behind my apartment and set it aflame, watching the papers crinkle and turn black.

"What the fuck is going on?" someone screamed behind me. "You trying to get the fire department on my ass?" It was the super. Funny, he never showed up when my lights went out.

"Relax. Everything's in a metal garbage can."

"What the hell are you doing?"

"Starting a new life," I proclaimed.

To my total shock, when I got upstairs, my father was sitting on the hallway steps outside my apartment.

Not another intervention, I thought.

"Surprised to see your old man?"

"Well, yeah, Dad."

"Happened to be in the neighborhood and I thought, I miss my sweetie. I bet she hasn't been out to a nice restaurant in a long time. How 'bout I take you to Peter Lugar's?"

Shock number two. He could barely remember my birthday, and now he was offering to take me to the best steakhouse in New York for no particular reason?

"Actually, Dad, I had a big lunch. But come inside."

He followed me into the small apartment and made himself cozy on the ratty couch. I handed him a stack of takeout menus, and pretty soon we were chowing down on spring rolls and pad thai.

"So what really brings you here, Dad?" I asked.

"Well, this whole business about your uncle," he began, and I felt my defenses rise. So it *was* another intervention. These people could never think about me just for me, only them.

But my father didn't seem like he was about to launch an attack. Instead, he put his arm around me and said, "Tell you the truth, I never liked the jerk."

I laughed, remembering how Dad always rolled his eyes whenever Uncle Lewis launched into another speech about the garment industry.

"I'll deny this if you tell your mother, but I'm happy you turned down the job," he said.

I hugged him tightly. "Oh, Daddy."

"That kind of work's not for you," he went on. "Smelly little office out on Long Island." He patted my shoulder. "Walk your dogs. Get fresh air and exercise. Write that novel of yours. Who knows? Maybe it's even kind of good."

It was pouring the next morning when I went on my rounds. Normally that was just the type of day to make me bitch about my job, but compared to the office routine hell I'd barely escaped, this was heaven.

When I picked up Mini the Great Dane at Sergio's hair salon, I was, as usual, a total slob compared to all the fashionistas getting their three-hundred-dollar treatments, but for once I didn't feel inferior. Maybe it was because I had made friends with Vanessa—her confidence in my ability was contagious.

Maury Blaustein was as glued to his Lounge-Around as always, but he actually looked up from the Lifetime television movie he was watching and noticed me. "You do something different to your hair?" he asked.

"Well, besides being soaking wet, not really," I answered.

"It's a good look for you," he suggested. I knew I looked like a drowned rat, but Maury was onto something: I felt different that day.

Neither Danilova was home, so I had a good chat with Slobodan when I saw her. "No, I would never leave you!" I said as she wagged her tail and nuzzled me affectionately. "I would never, ever, ever leave you."

Lulu was next, and then Cadbury; mercifully, Anderson wasn't home, and by avoiding his terrace I managed to not think about my book rotting out there.

I let my babies loose in the dog run and sat on a bench in Riverside Park. The rain had eased, and we had the place to ourselves. No longer jealous of the New York professionals and their workaday lives, I stopped to enjoy the tranquility.

But something didn't sit right. It was as though I had left the stove on at home, and after searching my mind, I realized what it was: Trish.

Sure, we'd grown apart, but I only had one friend left from kindergarten. One friend with whom I'd giggled hysterically while making phony phone calls during sleepovers. One friend who always cared about me even when Jenna was the focus of the whole family's attention. One friend who told Jump-Shot Jimmy I had a crush on him and then consoled me for weeks when he broke it off. One friend who made me her maid of honor, even though she had three other girls vying for the position. One friend who, admittedly mistakenly, tried to fix me up with a guy she thought I'd like.

I hit her landline on speed-dial.

"Hi, you've reached Trish, Tom, Connor, and Lily," her voicemail said, as if someone might actually call a toddler or an eight-month-old baby. "Leave a message!"

"Trish, it's me, Laurel. I'm really sorry about the other day with your dentist friend. It's a whole long story I'll tell you when—"

Suddenly, Trish picked up the phone. "Laurel! There is absolutely no excuse in the world for walking out on my cute friend without so much as a goodbye," she said, but I could tell from the tone of her voice she'd forgiven me. "So what's this long story?"

Trish cracked up when I told her about my close encounter with a future in girdle journalism, but she insisted I would have liked Irwin. "He is such a cool guy. You are totally missing out."

Relieved that we'd made up, we confirmed our usual lunch at Sushi and Slushies before getting off the phone. The rain had stopped, the air was fresh, and everything was right with the world, unless you counted the fact that Slobodan had found a piece of trash to chew on.

"Drop it!" I screamed.

7

The Duplex is a legendary club and piano bar on Seventh Avenue South in the Village. I couldn't figure out why it was Step Two on my road to success, but I trusted Vanessa, who had insisted we go there that Thursday night at nine. She'd been delighted to hear about my father's mysterious appearance at the exact moment I'd finished burning my bring-me-down baggage. "Your relationship changed precisely when you effected an inner change," she explained. "That's how it works. And it does work. You'll see."

The club was crowded with aspiring stars: a purple-clad drag queen who thought she was Whitney Houston, stand-up comics mumbling their routines, and musicians frantically studying sheet music. Even the waitresses sang and tap danced when they brought the drinks.

I could relate to them well. Follow your dream to New York City, put it all on the line, and pray for the big break.

Except for her wedding ring, Vanessa looked like the typical single partier. She was dressed all in black with an electric blue scarf thrown over her shoulder. Although she was too short to be a model, she was definitely pretty enough, with that bouncy dark hair framing her petite features. But most stunning of all was her compassion. *Why would a woman like that care about me?* I wondered. Gratefully, I took a seat by her side.

"This place is full of dreamers—can't you feel it?" she asked.

Just then, a trio of men in matching spandex began crooning Barbra Streisand's "Evergreen."

"Love, soft as an easy chair—"

It was a sore subject for me, and I couldn't help but feel a little downcast.

Vanessa must have read my thoughts, because her penetrating brown eyes took me in with profound concern.

"Bad breakup?" she asked.

"Worse. Never even came close."

"Why is that worse? It means you still have a chance."

"Oh, forget that. He would never even look at a girl like me."

"You owe me another dollar." Vanessa held out her hand.

"I refuse to pay. His girlfriend's a famous singer, and I'm a nobody."

"Two dollars." Her hand stayed open. "Every time you think a negative thought you create the condition for it to become a reality."

"Easy for you to say. You're gorgeous and married."

"Laurel, you're beautiful. It's just your thinking that's ugly. Now, answer this: Who do you see yourself with?"

"Probably some bald dentist named Irwin from Long Island. That's who my best friend tried to fix me up with."

"Some friend." Vanessa's garnet-colored lips twisted into a grimace. "Let's put it this way: Who's that guy you *wanted* to be with?"

"His name's Lucien. He's a music critic with the most divine hair and baby blue eyes."

"Oh, the blue eyes. They kill me every time."

"That's just the beginning. He's so skinny and sexy. If I had a guy like that I wouldn't even care about publishing my novel."

"Stick with me, kid, and you'll get both."

On stage now, the drag queen was singing "I Will Always Love You" but hitting only about half of the notes.

"Ow, my ears," I complained.

"Don't criticize too much," Vanessa cautioned. "You're on in three."

"I'm what?"

"Amateur night. I signed you up."

"You didn't!" I was aghast. "But I can't sing to save my life!"

"That's the whole point. You're going to confront your fear of failure."

Suddenly I wanted to kill this mentor lady. How could she trap me like that with no warning? Sensing my anger, she quickly added, "Don't worry, kid, I'm going on first. I'll be an easy act to follow, I promise."

That wasn't entirely true. Vanessa brought down the house with her rendition of a burlesque number from *Gypsy*. She wasn't a great singer, but she held the crowd with her gutsy charisma. When she hit the line, "You've gotta get a gimmick if you want to get ahead," I felt like she was singing directly to me.

Sweaty and proud, she patted my back as they called my name. "Work with the crowd, not against them," she advised.

The only song that came to mind was "Oh My Darling Clementine," which I had performed at a sixth-grade talent show. Lacking my little cowgirl outfit, I felt even less comfortable than I had then, and the audience must have sensed it.

My voice wobbled at the microphone. "This is a number I did back when I was a little girl," I said, on the verge of losing it.

"Shut up!" a drunken heckler screamed. The crowd roared with laughter, and I could feel my face turn beet red. But suddenly, Vanessa's eyes met mine, and her challenging look shot courage right through me.

"You shut up!" I countered. The crowd laughed again, this time on my side. And then, without even realizing it, a new song tripped on my lips.

Pointing right at the drunken heckler, I sang with gusto,

What's a matta you — hey!
Gotta no respect

It was a ridiculous campy Italian spoof by a one-hit wonder named Joe Dolce. I had memorized it unconsciously one summer when a cook at the Copenhagen Café where I used to work insisted on singing it every time a dish was sent back.

Whaddya think ya do – hey
Why ya looka so sad?

I took the mic from its stand, thrust a hand on my hip, and kicked my leg up suggestively.

It's a not so bad – hey!
It's a nice a place…

By this time, the audience was mine, having been won over by my quick comeback. Around the room, happy couples, glittering dancers, brooding musicians, and everyone in between was swaying to the music. Taking a chance, I beckoned them all to join in on the last line, and by magic, they shouted in unison:

AW SHADDUP A YOU FACE!

Everyone applauded enthusiastically, no one more than Vanessa. I hugged her when I triumphantly returned to our table. "But why didn't you warn me I'd be performing?" I asked.

"Because," she said, squeezing my hand. "You would have told me that was impossible. This way I got to prove that the only thing that limits you is you."

I'd heard that a million times before, but this was the first time I actually believed it.

It was another noisy New York morning later that week: sirens blaring, garbage trucks roaring, and the sound of a million people yelling into their cell phones. Mini had just dumped a maxi on the sidewalk, and after I shoveled it up with a baggie I looked up to see none other than Portia Thorn staring at me with pity.

"I see you're still in—what do you call it? Pet care management?" She smirked.

I tossed the baggie in a nearby trashcan and tried to think of a way to get away from Portia before she could start bragging. "It pays the rent," I shrugged.

"I haven't seen you for ages," she said. "I didn't get a chance to tell you there's a bidding war on for my book."

"Really?" I asked, wanting to sic all five of my dogs on her smug little face.

"You wouldn't understand, but it's actually nerve-wracking," she said.

AW SHUDDUP A YOU FACE! I screamed in my mind. The memory of my triumph at the Duplex filled me with an unfamiliar confidence, and I said instead, "Yes, I imagine you're worried that you'll get a huge advance and the sales won't keep up."

"No, Laurel," she replied defensively. "A huge advance means they think you have a lot of potential."

"Right," I countered, "but what if you don't live up to that hype? Then you've actually cost them money, and they'll never publish anything of yours again."

"They're saying *Wild Asparagus* is going to make me this generation's Hemingway," she declared.

Hemingway? She had to be kidding. "Good for you," I said. "Let's hope they're right and you don't end your days as a one-hit blunder."

I had confessed to Vanessa how plain I felt every day picking up Mini at the beauty salon, so I was upset when she told me to meet her at Sergio's one morning after my rounds. "Why here of all places?" I asked her outside the fancy clip joint.

"Why else? You have an appointment."

"Oh no. I'd have to clean up after Mini for a month free if I ever got one of their treatments."

"You're getting three. And don't worry, it's on me."

"That's really nice of you, Vanessa. Except, the truth is, I could afford it myself if I thought it would help. But there's no hope for this mop."

"That's gonna cost you—"

"I'm not kidding, Vanessa. Let me finish. I've had dozens of hundred-dollar haircuts and spent thousands on products, and it always stays the same: kind of frizzy, kind of straight, always mousy. Perms and colors just damage it. The only solution is a good hat."

"Sounds like you've consulted all the experts," she said.

"And then some."

"Except the most important one."

"Sergio?"

"No, Laurel. You! You've lived with that hair for twenty-eight years. Obviously you've bought into the notion that it's ugly, and you've left all the decisions to people who earn their living off of your insecurity. I want you to say something good about your hair. What do you like about it?"

"Well, I guess you could say it's thick," I said.

"And?"

"And when it's not humid out it manages to be wavy."

"And?"

"And it can be worn a lot of different ways with clips and barrettes."

"That's my girl. Now, I want you to march in there and tell them you want a cut that works with the thickness and brings out the beautiful waves, and then I want you to buy their prettiest barrettes. You can pay for those with the money you just saved by seeing what's right with your hair instead of what's wrong."

When I got inside, they were all surprised to see me. "But Mini's already had her walk!" Sergio's assistant commented. This wasn't going to be easy.

"Actually, I'm here for a wash, cut, and cellophane."

"You're *that* Laurel? Well, what do you know," she said, checking my name in the appointment book.

As I stared at myself in the mirror with the plastic apron around my neck, I remembered all the times I'd meekly implored hairdressers to make a miracle with my hideous locks. Inevitably they would suggest something radical, like a tight perm, double-process highlights, or an asymmetrical cut. Hoping for a miracle, I'd thank them profusely and grossly over-tip, but by the time I got home, the disaster would be obvious, and I'd melt into tears.

Not this time, though.

"So what are we doing today?" the stylist asked.

"My hair's really thick and wavy," I said, almost unable to believe those words were coming from my mouth.

"It is!" the stylist affirmed.

"So don't do anything radical," I commanded.

"We'll have to even this out," she cautioned, combing through the strands that had suffered the last asymmetrical disaster.

"Just bring out the natural beauty," I said.

By the time she'd finished, I walked out having to admit I looked pretty good. She'd evened out the cut so that my hair bounced lightly around my face, and I could tell it wouldn't take three hours of effort every morning to make it look this way again. It was me, and I nearly liked it.

Just as I was looking around for Vanessa, my cell phone rang. "So?" she asked. "Am I right? Are you beautiful or what?"

"I look pretty good, it's true," I said with a smile.

"How much longer before you have to go back to work?" I just loved the way she acknowledged my job, which most people treated like a hobby or a joke.

"About two hours," I calculated.

"Great," she said. "I want you to go home, put on your best outfit, and meet me in half an hour at six-eighty-five Broadway on the fourteenth floor."

What did she have in mind this time? I wondered, feeling like I was on a treasure hunt.

Right on time, wearing my favorite jeans skirt, a white lace top with a brown suede jacket, and my Nicole Miller mules, I was shocked when I got out of the elevator in the midtown office tower. Staring me in the face was a sign on the door that read: *The New York Arts and Entertainment Review*.

In other words, I was at Lucien's office.

When I turned to leave, Vanessa came out of the elevator. "Oh, no you don't," she said.

"I can't," I whimpered. "He has a girlfriend who is gorgeous!"

"You're gorgeous," she said. "I adore the natural look." She turned me around. "This haircut is so you."

"What about the clothes?" I asked.

"Great. Just one minor adjustment." She pulled my waistband up and folded it over, making my skirt two inches shorter. "Let him see those sexy legs."

Before I could stop her, Vanessa had pushed me through the door.

"We're here to see Lucien Brosseau," she said.

This time I knew she had gone too far. You can't make a man want you through willpower.

"Is he expecting you?" the receptionist asked.

Just then, he walked by the water cooler. Maybe Vanessa could feel me cringe, or maybe it was the blue eyes, but she instantly knew it was him. "Lucien!" she called. "You remember Laurel?"

"Laurel…" he said, checking me out.

"They're here to see you, but they don't have an appointment," the receptionist announced sourly.

"You look great," he addressed me, ignoring her. "My office is down the hall; come on," he beckoned.

It was just as I'd imagined: books and papers everywhere, with titles like *A Cello in Your Arms* and *La Semoitique du McDonalds*; a heavy old desk with a sleek notebook computer on top; lush plants completed the picture—and not a single copy of *Us Magazine* in sight. *Basically the opposite of a dentist's office,* I thought.

"Sorry for the mess," he said, "but I'm on deadline."

"It's fine," I stammered.

"Have a seat," he offered. "What brings you here?"

I was wondering that myself, feeling a crazy mix of incredible excitement and deep mortification.

"Laurel thinks you're just so sexy," Vanessa said. The mortification deepened. Hadn't she ever heard of playing hard to get?

"Well, I don't know what to say," he replied.

"But I had to come here and find out for myself," she added.

"Because you're her . . . chaperone?" he guessed with amusement.

"No, because she nominated you to be Mr. February in the Thinking Girl's Beefcake Calendar. It's intellectual New York's response to the fire department calendar."

Unbelievable, I thought, but Lucien seemed to believe it. "Really? Me?" he asked. "I haven't been to the gym in a while."

"Oh, you'll have plenty of time before the shoot," Vanessa said. "That is, if you get selected. I hope you don't mind appearing in the buff."

"It's a naked calendar?" he laughed. I was laughing, too. Vanessa really knew how to lay it on.

"Why? Does that disqualify you?" she wondered.

"Laurel," he said, looking into my eyes, "what are you getting me into?"

"Oh, Lucien," I said, working up the courage to flirt. "I'm just sure you have nothing to worry about."

"He might," Vanessa challenged. "How's your girlfriend going to feel about this?"

"What girlfriend?" He looked genuinely surprised.

"Xhana."

"She's not my girlfriend."

"Oh, really? Why?" Vanessa asked. "She's so gorgeous." Ouch.

"I could never go out with a performer," he replied. "They need all the attention. Nothing turns me off more in a woman than an oversized ego."

Wow, I thought. So there really *is* hope for me.

"Excellent," Vanessa said. "Our committee will be in touch."

"So," I urged, not wanting to press my luck, "we'd better get going."

"Wait . . . Laurel. How come I haven't seen you at the lecture series? There's another one this Sunday. Will you be there?"

My heart leaped, but before I had a chance to say "Sure," Vanessa stepped in. "No. She's too busy this week," she said.

I wanted to kill her, but her judgment had brought me this far, so I joined in the lie.

"I'd love to, Lucien, but you're not the only calendar boy we're interviewing."

By the time we got to the street, Vanessa and I were doubled over with laughter.

"Nice work," she said. "He's probably worried you're gonna get it on with Mr. July before he even has a shot!" When we exchanged high-fives, I felt like I was reaching for the stars.

8

I was so busy photographing Mr. February in my dreams that I didn't even mind returning to Long Island later that week to face Uncle Lewis at Mindy's fortieth birthday party. After all, I knew I was just a visitor—not a resident—in that mediocre world.

They lived in yet another colonial house in a neighborhood of nothing but the same. Aunt Helene met me at the door in the uniform of every suburban hostess: palazzo pants, a matching top, and red toenails bunched up in her Candies. "Laurel!" she said, kissing me and then wiping the Revlon ColorStay lipstick off my cheek with her thumb.

"I hope Uncle Lewis isn't still mad at me," I said, entering the foyer with its shag carpeting and flowered wallpaper.

"Of course he is; he's furious, but don't worry. He's been mad at me for the last forty-four years. That's love! He gave me this for our anniversary," she said, dangling a diamond tennis bracelet from her wrist.

Dysfunction junction, I thought.

Mindy was sprawled on the living room loveseat, working her way through a dish of Bugles. "Happy birthday," I said, handing her a gift-wrapped pair of earrings I'd bought on the way over.

"Laurel, you look great!" she said. "Is there a new man in your life?" she guessed.

Was there? I wondered. "I'm hoping," I said.

Right on cue, my mother approached. "What's this I hear?" she asked, kissing my cheek. "Is there someone special I should know about?"

Before I could answer, my Uncle Lewis pulled me aside. "What's the matter, an unemployed writer is too good to work at a trade paper?" he asked.

"I'm sorry about what happened, but it really wasn't for me."

"There's my gorgeous girl!" My father came rushing up to the rescue.

"Your gorgeous girl is on the same sorry path my daughter walked," warned Uncle Lewis, gesturing toward Mindy. My cousin was an amazing singer, but no one ever mentioned that, I guess because, like me, she'd never made it in the industry.

"With a father like you, no wonder she's lonely," Dad said. "My girls know how to get over their problems. Just look at how perfectly Jenna turned out."

My heart sank as I took in the tableau presented by my sister and her picture-perfect family. Jenna was wearing couture sweatpants with a sleeveless top that showed off her toned arms. Her husband Rob was the doting dad, with little Emily on his shoulders and Bobby Jr. walking on his feet. I adored my niece and nephew, but at events like these, they just highlighted how far I had to go to catch up with Jenna.

Soon Aunt Helene emerged with a cake, and everyone started singing. When "Happy Birthday" was over, Mindy blew out the candles and made a little speech.

"You guys, thank you so much for coming. I know you all know my wish—it's the same one I've had since I can remember. Let's hope it comes true, and next year we'll be celebrating at the Grammys…"

It was painful to watch. I knew how she felt, and I loved and hated her all at once.

On the scent of my insecurity, Jenna came sidling over. "I hope by the time you turn forty we don't have to hold another pity party like this," she taunted.

Instead of taking the bait, I turned away from my sister and addressed my mother. "Mom, you know how you are always telling me to keep in touch with my Vassar friends? Well, I finally took your advice, and I'm so glad I did. I met the most incredible woman, and now she's my big sister!" I said the last two words with emphasis for Jenna's benefit.

"Wonderful news, that's wonderful!" my mother replied.

"Oh, Mom, you're going to love her. She's this fun, brilliant, successful woman who really believes in me. What a difference it makes to have someone supportive on my side."

I couldn't be sure, but for the first time in my life, I thought I made Jenna flinch.

Vanessa hadn't returned three of my calls before I finally got through. "Where've you been?" I demanded. "We need to do something about Lucien."

"I've been giving it time," she replied, "because you need to cool off. He wants you now, and we have to let the desire simmer. But don't space out—we're moving on to track two."

"Track what?"

"Your career. Put on your best power outfit and meet me at the corner of Jane and Hudson on Thursday at noon."

Over cucumber rolls and tempura that Wednesday, Trish and I picked apart every millisecond of my encounter with Lucien.

"Of course he likes you!" my best friend was saying. "'Laurel, you look really great'? I mean, he might as well propose marriage right then and there."

"Oh, come on," I said, popping an edamame pod in my mouth. "Really?"

"I swear, those were almost exactly Tom's words when he asked me out. And look where we ended up!" Trish delicately stirred green mustard into her soy sauce.

"Happily ever after," I said, feeling giddy.

"And it turns out Lucien's not even with Xhana! I guess *Us Magazine* is full of lies."

I hated to hear anyone dis one of my favorite reads, but I let it slide. "Can you believe it? He's single!" I effused.

"Not for long, I bet," she answered with a wink. "So Laurel's going to hook up with Mr. February."

I was lost in a daydream about just that when Trish interrupted my thoughts. "But what you said before—that thing about how he doesn't like to go out with someone who needs all the attention—where does that leave you?" she asked.

Trish was a sweetie, but she'd completely missed the point. *I don't need attention,* I thought, *I just need Lucien.*

Having cycled through self-help and fiction, it was Margo's turn again for feedback at that week's writing session. We were analyzing in all seriousness how a parrot would react to repeated rejection from literary agents: fight or flight?

"Remind me again," Danny Z. wondered aloud, "are we talking about the white parrot with the green markings or the green parrot with the white markings?"

Although I couldn't blame him for mixing them up, we *had* been going over this drivel for three years now. "Squeaky's the green one," I clarified.

Margo rewarded me with a grateful smile.

"Squeaky may be despondent," said Sunny Hellerstein, knitting her brow with concern, "but I think it's unrealistic for him to contemplate having an affair with the woodpecker."

"Why?" Margo asked.

"Running away from problems only makes them chase you."

"We're talking about her book, not yours," Danny Z. pointed out. "The parrot doesn't do daily affirmations."

Just when I thought it couldn't get any worse, in through the door walked Jenna. I couldn't believe my eyes. It was Theater of the Absurd: Super Soccer Mom drops in on funky New York writers group.

All eyes turned to her.

"The speed dating club meets Thursday night," José said politely.

"What makes you think I'm single?" Jenna flashed her wedding ring like it was her membership card to the I'm Superior Club. "I'm Laurel's sister. I've heard so much about what an important part of her life this group is, so I thought I'd stop by and see for myself. Mind if I have a seat?" She sat down and looked at me expectantly.

I was too stunned to play the part of the polite little sister.

"Well . . . if Laurel's not going to say anything, I'll introduce myself. My name's Jenna. I live in Massapequa Park. I'm the mother of two adorable kids. I know you're probably all wondering how I keep so fit. Well, it's my job. I'm the owner and manager of Change Your Body Today Fitness Studio. We offer body fat analysis, nutritional counseling, and 28 classes a week. If anyone's interested, I can give you my card."

"Oh, you're *just* like Laurel described you," Danny Z. said.

Count on my friend to be there when I needed him.

"So, what have you written?" Sunny asked.

"Written?" Jenna looked stumped.

"It doesn't have to be a whole novel; even a short story is fine," said Sunny.

"Yeah, Jenna, have you ever written anything besides a shopping list?" I couldn't resist asking.

"I'm just here to observe," she said, looking flustered.

"Well, we're discussing my book, *Love Between Consenting Parrots*," Margo said. "You can feel free to jump in whenever you have something constructive to say."

"That's a beautiful title. I like it a lot," Jenna took up the offer. "My son Bobby Jr. has a book called *Parrot, Parrot, One Two Three*. Much less original."

"This isn't a children's book, Jenna. It's a 750-page attempt at magical realism," I corrected.

"Well, it's a wonderful idea," Jenna said fawningly. "I'm sure it's magical and real," she added. It was neither, and my bullshit tolerance level was reaching the breaking point.

"And very publishable," Sunny added. Another lie.

"You always say that, but do you really think so?" Margo asked. She knew the answer they'd give but wanted to hear it.

"Of course!" Seth said, reinforcing the delusion.

I couldn't take it anymore. This was one crutch that was going to stop propping up Margo's ego. "Actually," I exploded. "*Love Between Consenting Parrots* is a piece of crap."

There was a stunned silence, and Margo began to whimper.

"God, I've been wanting to tell you this for three years now!" I exhaled. "Parrots do not chug beer at the Hofbräuhaus House in Munich. Parrots do not obsess about their figures. And parrots definitely do not have long phone conversations about the hurt they carry inside."

"How dare you?" asked Seth. "That's the whole premise of her book."

"Which doesn't work," I shot back.

Jenna looked dumbfounded.

"I think she has a very moving story," Sunny said, patting Margo on the arm.

"So do I!" I said. "There are some very real emotions here, but they're all lost because she's attributing them to birds instead of people."

Margo let out a loud wail as if I had lanced a boil. "It's true, it's all true," she sobbed.

"Now, Margo, your book isn't that bad," José said.

"No," she shook her head emphatically, wiping away tears, "I mean, this is a true story! It's not about parrots. It's about me and my ex! His name wasn't Squeaky; it was Harold. I only called him Squeaky in bed."

A silence befell the room. It was the most emotional discussion we'd ever had.

"Then why don't you rework it?" I suggested.

"I am," she said. "That's just what I'm going to do. No more hiding behind feathers. I'm going to tell it like it was."

After the meeting, I walked out with Jenna, wishing I could ditch her but knowing that she had finally made the effort to get acquainted with my life, so instead I extended an invitation.

"Why don't you come up to my place and see it for the first time?" I suggested.

I could see Jenna blanch. "Oh, I would love to; I really would. But you know—the kids, and the train, and, well, it's getting so late…"

"I understand," I said, letting her off the hook. The night had been way too long anyway.

Maybe the truth works, I told myself the next day as I rode the gilded elevator up to the fifteenth floor of the San Remo. Maybe if I just say what I really feel, I'll get what I need.

The scene at Anderson's apartment was typical. The maid let me in, I disciplined Cadbury for chewing on the replacement couch, and Anderson waved cheerfully while skiing on his NordicTrack.

Taking a deep breath, I stood in front of him and pushed the stop button.

"Hi!" he said, looking at me with a puzzled expression and then seeming to understand. "You'll find the extra baggies in the kitchen."

"Actually," I cleared my throat, "I was just wondering, have you had a chance to look at my manuscript yet?"
"Oh, yes! *The Fisherman's Guide to Ulster County,*" he said with sudden enthusiasm. "It's right at the top of my desk. I'm dying to get to it." With that, he put the headphones back on, hit the start button, and resumed his run.

I restrained myself from quitting then and there. After all, I obviously still needed my day job.

Truth has nothing to do with it, I realized, hurrying down the block with Cadbury. It's all guile. You get what you want through a judicious combination of flattering people and then holding back just enough to make them want more.

With these thoughts clouding my mind, I walked right past a gorgeous babe smiling at me. I didn't even notice it was Lucien until he called out my name.

"Laurel!" he said. "Finally. I've been waiting all morning for you."

As usual, I immediately lost myself in his deep blue eyes. "You were?" I asked. "Why?"

"I have two tickets to see this new symphony created by MIT students using a four-page mathematical equation. It's this Saturday night—what do you say?"

Lucien Brosseau, critic for *The New York Arts and Entertainment Review*, had actually spent the morning waiting on a street corner just to ask me out? Those blue eyes were looking at me hopefully, eager for an answer. All I had to do was say yes, and my dream would come true.

"No," I said, savoring the expression of disappointment on his face. "I'm so sorry. It's not that I wouldn't love to, it's just that this Saturday's booked." Me, a bag of microwave popcorn, and a good binge watch. That was Lucien's competition, but I sure didn't let him know.

At the appointed hour that Thursday, Vanessa was waiting for me at the corner of Jane and Hudson in a pair of faded jeans. I had to wonder why I'd been instructed to wear my best power outfit. Since I didn't own one, I'd bought a pinstriped suit, crisp white top, and a pair of four-inch heels. Meanwhile, my mentor was wearing sneakers.

"Are you and I going to the same place here today?" I asked.

"I was going to come along with you until you told me how you handled Lucien," she said. "Bravo. You're finally learning that you deserve to get what you want."

"Well, I didn't do so well with Anderson Gallant," I reminded her.

"That's why we're here today." She filled me in on my new assignment. "You're familiar with Yelena Yelenovich?"

"Duh. She won the Pulitzer Prize. I wrote a thirty-page paper on *My Idiot Husband* at Vassar."

"Well, she has a penthouse apartment in this very building, and you have an appointment to meet her"—Vanessa checked her watch—"right about now."

My idol! This was a woman who could write a three-page sentence and have you wish it went on even longer. For once, my assignment sounded pleasurable. "So, what am I doing? Is she interested in my work?" It was too much to hope for, but Vanessa had been teaching me to dare to dream. I pictured the famous Russian émigré and I becoming fast friends. She would write the foreword to *Napoleon's Hairdresser*: "Rarely does an artist come along with the insight of Laurel Linden. A fresh, young voice—"

"Hold on there," Vanessa said, interrupting my thoughts. "Right now you just need her autograph."

That would be easy enough. "Great!" I said. "Did you bring a copy of one of her books?"

"The autograph doesn't go on her book," Vanessa corrected. "It needs to go on a check for two thousand dollars."

"What?"

"Yelena Yelenovich is number one on the list of deadbeats who should have made a contribution by now to the Author's League for Children's Literacy."

"How do you know all that?"

"My husband's a board member. For the past three years, she's been the only Pulitzer Prize winner who won't even return our calls."

"So how did you get an appointment?" I asked, feeling a knot forming in my stomach.

"I didn't. She thinks you're the plumber. Well, hurry along. And don't call me back until you get that check." Vanessa turned to leave.

"Wait a minute!" I protested. "At least tell me what this charity's all about so I can convince her."

"The less you know, the better," she replied. "She's not going to give because she likes the charity."

"So what will make her give?"

"That, Laurel, is for you to figure out."

The doorman regarded me suspiciously when I said I was the plumber, but when I added, "For three hundred dollars an hour, we figure our customers deserve a little leg," he winked lecherously and let me up.

Trying to prepare in the elevator, I imagined Yelena's apartment: ceiling to floor bookcases, no doubt, filled with the greatest works of literature ever written; her own books translated into dozens of languages—*Mon Mari Idiot* and *Mein Idioter Mann*—maybe a silver samovar in the corner, and perhaps a few Fabergé eggs here and there.

My intimidation only grew when I approached her apartment door and heard the obvious sounds of a domestic dispute emanating from within. It was muffled but vehement. That was just like Yelena to have great passion in her life. Tumultuous relationships were her muse.

More intimidated than ever, I pressed the buzzer, trying desperately to come up with a plan of action. I decided I would appeal to her great depth of humanity, well-known love of children, and abiding sense of responsibility for the next generation.

"Come in," she yelled.

I opened the door and stood crestfallen. The apartment was bare, save for a giant portrait of Yelena and a large-screen plasma TV tuned to the Real Housewives of someplace or another.

My literary idol was slouched on a beanbag chair, screaming at the dysfunctional stars of a trashy reality show.

"You slut! I didn't have nine lovers in nine years, and you had them all in one week!" Noticing me, she said, "It's the bathroom sink. It should only take you a minute or two. So don't try charging me an arm and a leg."

Having dismissed me, she turned back to the staged train wreck and continued her rant. "You freaks! In my country, you would get proper psychiatric care."

My head was spinning as I tried to reconcile this crass old loon with the literary genius I had worshipped for so many years. But although my illusions had been shattered, I was no longer paralyzed by a sense of inferiority.

"Your sink is the least of your problems," I began.

She muted the television as a commercial came on. "I know," she said, turning to face me for the first time. "The water pressure is like spit around here."

"No, I was talking about the children of this city. Our future. Are you aware of the latest study showing that forty-nine percent of all high school graduates can only read at a sixth-grade level?"

"What kind of plumber are you?"

"A plumber of souls, so to speak," I answered.

"You've got to be kidding me. Get out or I'll call the police."

"Who was it who said, 'Each child is a star in the sky waiting to light the way for mankind'?" I asked calmly.

"Ah! I see *you* read above a sixth-grade level. That was my character Count Boris. But I never liked him."

"What about the family Krasnipolsky? Their dynasty ended when their neglected children squandered the estate."

"It was fiction," she said. "Brilliant fiction, yes, but still fiction."

"But it's no fiction that right here in New York City, youngsters hungry for knowledge are unable to get the spiritual nourishment they need from books."

"Ach, let 'em watch TV," she said, turning off the mute button.

I grabbed the remote and muted it again. "How can you call yourself a humanitarian and not care about the world's children?" I asked, growing exasperated.

"Just because I call myself a humanitarian doesn't mean I care," she countered. "You called yourself a plumber, but I don't see you fixing my sink."

So the great Yelenovich was just another fraud. It was time to play the game by her rules.

"Well, I suppose you could ignore the world's children, but there's a heavy price to pay," I warned.

"What? Another generation of idiots? Good, more episodes of 'Real Housewives,'" she said.

"I'm talking about a financial cost. To you. I happen to know that *New York Magazine* is working on an exposé of the cheapest humanitarians on the planet."

"No kidding? I bet that miserable Children First goodwill ambassador from Ukraine is number one on the list."

"Quite right," I replied. "It's going to ruin his career when it's published."

"Ha!" she said, letting out a belly laugh.

"Unfortunately," I said gravely, "you're number two."

"Me?" she said, looking shocked. "I grew up in wartime. We could last for a month on what you people waste in an hour."

"But now you're a multimillionaire," I reminded her. "Your past suffering doesn't exonerate you in the eyes of these reporters. They're planning to smear you with a two-page spread." I knew it was blackmail, but I figured only the children would stand to gain.

Yelena was silent.

Feeling guilty, I decided to soft-pedal. "I'm sure they'll change their minds if you give money to a wonderful charity like the Author's League for Children's Literacy."

"Ach, sign me up. I'll brag about my generosity in the press, sell another hundred thousand books, and Las Vegas, here I come."

The whole thing took ten minutes, and I came out waving a check between two fingers. Vanessa was delighted. "I know it may have been a dirty job," she said, "but with this money we can finance tutoring for up to thirty children for a year."

It was some consolation, but it didn't make up for the fact that I'd just lost one of my heroes.

"I thought she was one of the most open-hearted people in the world, and she turned out to be one of the least," I said.

Sensing my confusion, Vanessa drew out the moral of the story. "It just goes to show you, these people who you think have all the power are as weak and human as the rest of us."

I leaned against a mailbox and tried to take it all in. "But that's so depressing," I said.

"Unless you use it to create good," she said. "I look at you, and I see a brilliant author just waiting to be discovered. And then I hear about this Anderson Gallant who intimidates you so much even though he's nothing but a spoiled trust fund brat who doesn't have a fraction of your creativity."

There was no denying the truth of Vanessa's words, and I saw where she was leading. "But it's different when it's my own book," I said.

"Why should you be any less deserving than that illiterate child out there?"

"Anderson has this way of cheerfully ignoring me like I'm nothing but the hired help."

"Well," Vanessa challenged, "Yelena Yelenovich thought you were just a plumber…"

I still felt tainted that evening and decided to visit Mrs. Lilianthaller to cleanse my conscience. "Oh, darling, you're a saint," she said. Her cute puppies Bogey and Bacall licked my face with so much joy that I almost believed her.

At the Union Square dog run, with my charges happily prancing around inside, I lapsed into my usual habit of daydreaming: Lucien kissing my neck over drinks at a jazz club on Bleeker Street . . . Anderson Gallant unable to put down my book . . . my always-riveting appearance on the "Today Show."

While watching Bacall run around, I remembered that time so many weeks ago when I'd decided to give up on my dreams. That was before Vanessa taught me that dreams are great as long as you have the nerve to do what it takes to make them come true.

So I started to plan, step by step. Lucien wouldn't stand a chance, and Anderson Gallant would be putty in my hands.

9

On my way to the San Remo the next morning, I flipped open my cell phone and dialed *The New York Arts and Entertainment Review.*

"Laurel!" Lucien sounded thrilled to hear from me. "What a great surprise."

"How was the concert?"

"Incredible. It was six hours long, including three and a half hours of these amazing monotonal beeps."

I felt a pang of regret that I hadn't been there with him, but I knew I'd made the right decision when he said, "I really missed you."

"So how about giving me another chance?"

"Totally! Tonight this major sculptress from Williamsburg has an opening, and I'm the reviewer. Think you can make it?"

"I'd love to," I said.

"Should I meet you at, say, eight o'clock at our regular spot?" he asked.

How romantic, I thought. We already had our own corner. "Definitely," I replied. "By the way, sorry to disappoint you, but you didn't make the Thinking Girl's Beefcake Calendar. Don't feel too bad, though, because the competition was really, really hot."

"Why, did you meet them all?" He sounded morose.

"Well, I had to," I said, feeling cheery. "But I was only a

consultant. I'm off that gig now."

By the time I reached Anderson's apartment, I was feeling pretty hot myself. As in hot-shot. This time, when I stopped his treadmill, I pulled the plug.

"Hi!" he said, looking at me quizzically.

"Do you even know the name of my book?" He looked abashed. "Do you even realize what a masterpiece you have sitting on your terrace under that ficus tree? How are you going to feel when *Napoleon's Hairdresser* wins the National Book Award and they interview you to find out why you never recognized the talent of your own dog-walker?"

"*Napoleon's Hairdresser*? That sounds like a really interesting idea," he said. "I love historical fiction. You say it's under my ficus tree?" He got off the treadmill and went out to the terrace, returning with my manuscript. "What an outrage!" he said. "That damn maid is always mixing up my papers. But now that I've found it, I'll read it right away."

I'd been there before with Anderson, and I knew his promise wasn't good enough. Only insecurity would motivate him. "You know," my voice lowered to a confidential tone, "some people say you just inherited your position and that you really have no eye for literature."

"They're just jealous," he said defensively.

"Maybe so," I replied, "but if you're the one who discovers *Napoleon's Hairdresser*, you'll shut them up for good."

Anderson didn't answer. He was too busy reading my Chapter 1.

It was the perfect afternoon. Leave it to Jenna to spoil it.

"Hey, sis!" She'd phoned me at home, just as I was about to sit down with the latest copy of *Celebrity Style* and savor my triumph. "Your writers group was really awesome, and I learned something about you. You're not wasting your time; you're cultivating your art! The rest of the family needs to know this, too."

Just as I was cringing at the thought of Mom and Dad

showing up in the Hell's Kitchen basement, Jenna came up with an even worse idea. "I hope you don't mind, but I've invited Mom, Dad, Mindy, Helene, Lewis, and Rob's family to a little reading at my place next Sunday afternoon."

"A reading?"

"*Napoleon's Hairdresser*," she said. "Your best chapter. It's about time they learned what you've been up to."

I was starting to believe I could find love and get published, but it was doubtful I'd be able to survive this one.

As always, Vanessa was completely supportive and explained the whole dynamic in a revelatory light when we next met at Café des Artistes. "You're becoming more confident, and you're changing the whole power balance in your family. Jenna's trying to understand in a context she can control."

I sipped the froth off of my cappuccino. "So what am I supposed to do?" I asked. "My family's never going to get my book."

"Look," she explained, "it's just not possible to make up for all the years that Jenna hogged the spotlight. Accept that, and enjoy your relatives for what they can offer."

"But that's not enough," I said.

"The reality is that you're going to have to find friends outside of your family for the kind of encouragement you really need." Basking in the gaze of Vanessa's warm brown eyes, I knew I'd already found the best one.

I was all decked out in my new off-the-shoulder black sweatshirt and torn jeans outfit, which had set me back three hundred dollars but was worth every penny for my first date with Lucien. Before I left, I just had to call Trish and check in.

"I'm so excited. If he's half as sexy as you described, he's gonna be great in bed."

Trish had read my mind.

"We're going to a gallery opening, not a love motel."

"That's just an excuse," Trish said.

"Only if he likes me."

"Just be yourself, and he'll fall in love. You're the warmest, prettiest, sweetest, sexiest, coolest girl I know."

I was feeling pretty damn good after that, and then Vanessa called to check in. "Well, this is it," I said, reminding her about my big night. "Any last words of advice?"

"Just this: Work with everything you already know about him."

"That he's a sexy, brilliant, single hunk?"

"There was one more important clue he gave us. Remember that day in his office? Think, think. He basically told us what he doesn't like in a woman."

After a pause, we said it at the exact same time: "An oversized ego."

"Precisely," Vanessa said. "Remember: Knowledge is power."

Lucien looked better than ever that night, wearing black jeans, an authentic New York Dolls T-shirt, and, over that, a blue, unbuttoned shirt which brought out the color in his eyes.

He gave me a quick kiss on the lips, and I knew the action was only beginning. "You look beautiful." Hearing it from Lucien sent shivers down my legs. "Glad you still have some time for me after interviewing all those beefcakes."

"You were as good as any of them . . . mostly," I said, trying not to let him hear the pounding of my heart. As if anyone could ever look better than Lucien Brosseau.

He placed his hand at the small of my back, and I felt the shivers reach further.

As we sped downtown in a taxi, we each answered those first-date questions that normally bored me but which were truly fascinating with Lucien. It turned out that he'd grown up on a collective farm in Nicaragua during the revolution after his father left France to support the Sandinistas.

"Wow," I said. "That's incredible."

"The folk art of the indigenous population caught my eye at a young age, and my crude review fell into the hands of a professor from Oxford University. Two scholarships and a trek through North Africa later, I got my first paid job as a critic. But you don't want to hear all of this—tell me all about you."

I wasn't about to confess that the highlight of my youth had been making cheerleading squad at Massapequa High, and remembering Vanessa's advice, I demurred. "When did you start working at *The New York Arts and Entertainment Review?*" I asked.

"Well, that's actually a really funny story." He was halfway through telling me about how a Native American prayer shawl mailed to the wrong address had magically transformed his life when we arrived at the gallery.

The whole time he'd been talking I could barely stop staring at him. Those blue eyes were set against the dark waves of hair framing his face, and his cheeks flushed whenever our eyes met. His hair was so thick I just wanted to run my fingers through it, and his musky aftershave left me misty-eyed.

I'd never been to Lispenard Street before, and I'd certainly never heard of the Mahabharata Gallery. Lucien held my hand, and I glowed with gratitude for bring brought into this exclusive world. Everywhere I looked were fascinating people engaged in deep conversations. I recognized the fashion designer Takako Yamanashi, the famous photographer Marvin Saint-Jup, and Roland Butterfield, the real estate magnate, who had brought his latest trophy boytoy.

Without Lucien, I probably would have mingled only with the caterers, but he knew everybody and introduced me all around. "This is Laurel. She's an up-and-coming writer."

One tweed-jacket type wanted to know all about my novel. "It reviews the Napoleonic wars through the prism of a fictional female character who was closer to the general than his own horse," Lucien said. "In Laurel's imagined world, she's the countervailing weight to his innate aggression."

He hadn't even read the book, and here he was describing it in more articulate terms than I ever could.

"Fascinating!" a woman with huge earrings said, joining our conversation. Pretty soon I found myself at the center of a small crowd of potential readers.

This was heaven—better than heaven—and it proved that my eight years of hard labor had not been wasted. Time and time again, my professors at Vassar had told me, "Write what you know," but I was convinced, even then, that what I knew was boring. Would a crowd of New York's premier intellectuals be standing around me if I'd been introduced as the author of *I Was a Teenage Cheerleader*? My decision to take the hard path of seemingly endless, tedious research and painfully difficult writing had finally paid off. I felt deliciously validated.

As we moved through the exhibit holding hands, Lucien admired the sculptures. To me they just looked like rejects from a Play-Doh factory, but he found great significance in their odd shapes. "These uneven textures reference the eternal conflict between spirit and flesh," he explained. "Here I see a plane of calm next to declivities filled with angst," he added, pointing to what appeared to be a mush on the side of a bump. I was rapt.

He was explaining the modern history of alloy castings when the taxi neared Fourteenth Street. "Well, I guess I have to get out, though I'd love to hear the rest," I said hopefully.

"Hey, come back to my place," he suggested. "I'll show you some examples."

Fantasy, say hello to reality.

It wasn't long before we'd forgotten all about the castings, because exploring the exciting planes and declivities of each other's bodies was suddenly so much more urgent. I took off his New York Dolls shirt while he practically ripped my off-the-shoulder sweatshirt right off my chest. In the dim, candle-lit living room, I could see that his stomach was flat with a light dusting of coarse, black hair. He wasn't quite as muscular as I'd fantasized, but below his belt I could see the growing outline of his interest in me. The more clothes we slipped off, the quicker our breathing got, and as he fumbled with a condom I started moaning with anticipation.

"Ooh, hurry," I purred, not wanting to wait another second to feel his deep thrusting.

"Want to know something funny?" he asked, unrolling the Trojan.

Not really, I thought.

He told me anyway.

"In Japanese, they'd don't say 'I'm coming,' they say 'I'm going! I'm going!' But in Tajikistan—"

For once I didn't want to hear Lucien's lecture. Seeing that the protection was secure, I pulled him close and guided him inside. Whether you want to call it 'coming' or 'going,' I did it. And it was love.

10

Over the next few weeks, Lucien went from crush to boyfriend. As Trish defined it, when you spend every weekend night with someone, leave a toothbrush at their house, and don't make plans without checking with each other, you're an item.

Lucien took me to more openings and concerts than I'd ever been to, and we always ended the night wrapped in each other's arms. Waking up, he'd make Spanish espresso for both of us and kiss me with the taste of coffee on his lips. As often as not, that would get us started, and we'd abandon the hot drinks altogether for even steamier sex. Slick with each other's sweat, we would tumble into his large shower, where he'd shampoo my hair and I'd soap his skinny body from head to toe.

During the workday, he'd reach me on my cell phone, or I'd call him at the office, and it was never an interruption, no matter how busy we were. Once he even put the curator of the Museum of Modern Art on hold just to tell me he missed me.

Remembering his tales of North Africa and how he loved Moroccan food, I learned to make vegetable couscous. It took hours of shopping and chopping, but it was worth it to see the way his eyes squinted with delight when I served it at dinner.

One night, an aspiring actress desperate for some ink in *The New York Arts and Entertainment Review* sent a limo just so Lucien would come see her show, but we got completely distracted making love in the back seat, missed the play, and ended up using the car to travel to a little rustic country inn he knew in Connecticut. We spent the whole weekend eating strawberries and cream off of each other's bodies, and when we got back, Lucien was so happy, he wrote the actress a rave review.

Meanwhile, I kept up the pressure on Anderson.

"Have you made a decision about my novel yet?" I asked him right after he'd started reading it.

"I want to, Laurel, I really do," he said. "But honestly, usually my assistant tells me how to go with these things."

The last thing I wanted was to descend the power rung, so I ramped up the heat. "This is your chance to prove that you're a discerning thinker in your own right," I counseled. "If you show it to your assistant, they'll only undermine your stature by taking credit for discovering me. Go straight to your Dad. He's the only one with your best interests at heart."

Anderson looked perturbed. "Let me ask you something. If your assistant told your father she thought it would be helpful if you finished your bachelor's degree, would you conclude that she's helpful or jealous?"

"Are you kidding?" I asked. "That woman is a barracuda! She obviously wants to rip you to shreds."

He smiled gratefully. "Let me get back to you," he said, and I felt certain that, for once, he meant it.

Jenna lived at the top of a large circular driveway, her beautifully manicured lawn dotted with purple impatiens. After passing through the two-story foyer and down three carpeted steps into the main room, I could see that the family au pair had prepared a table full of calorically correct snacks, and there was enough diet soda to flood the sunken living room.

Jenna had arranged the chairs in a circle, just like at the writers group, and had posted little French flags on top of the pyramid of cheese cubes. There was even a picture of Napoleon pasted on the back of my seat. I was more amused than annoyed at the lengths she had gone to take control of my work and turn it into a theme party.

When Jenna emerged from her powder room and saw that I'd arrived, she clapped her hands officiously. "Okay, everybody, enough socializing!" she commanded, tossing her long, gorgeous hair extensions over her shoulder. "This is a cultural event." With a look, she told the au pair that the children were to be removed, and Emily and Bobby Jr. were quickly whisked into the basement den.

Before I'd even had a chance to greet my parents, Jenna was herding everyone into their seats. "Let's welcome our guest speaker," she said, twisting a finger around her diamond bubble-heart necklace. "I want to hear a big round of applause for Laurel, the author of *Napoleon's Hairdresser,* and my little sister."

As I was about to open my mouth to thank her, Jenna continued. "Ever since we were little kids, Laurel's had her head in the clouds," she said, clasping her hands together with an air of self-importance. "I remember when she came to me crying one day because her little doll had a broken heart. I was so touched by Laurel's imagination that I created a whole set of surgical implements designed to mend that sweet, imaginary heart. Emily still plays with them today—it's so cute. Sometimes I think I should market children's toys."

Uncle Lewis yawned. "You have any breath mints?" he asked.

Jenna ignored him. "Thanks to her older sis, Laurel discovered *Seventeen Magazine* when she was just twelve. It must have been destiny that I was a subscriber and shared my copies with her."

That was a good one, I thought. Jenna would have killed me if she'd caught me reading her magazines. I always had to buy my own.

"That's how she came to have her first published work, when she won a story writing contest about summer camp," she said. "I can't take much credit for that one; all I did was offer some modest suggestions about what I would have done differently."

Which I ignored, I thought.

"Which Laurel followed, and you all know the happy ending: She won the contest."

Unbelievably, Jenna managed to talk for ten more minutes, nine of them about herself, before yielding the floor. By the time she introduced me, Uncle Lewis was snoring, and it took a hard jab from Aunt Helene for him to wake up.

"Well, thanks for coming, everybody," I said, bracing myself. My family watched eagerly as I opened the document on my phone. "Let me set the scene." I felt like a second-grade teacher sitting down to story hour. "At this point, Napoleon has just invited Marguerite—that's his hairdresser—to keep his appearance sharp during his conquest of Europe. Only she knows the secret to thicker-looking hair. In this climactic scene, she confronts her family with the news that she is giving up a steady income at the salon for the promise of glory."

Staring out at their expectant faces, I took a sip of seltzer and began:

Chapter 16

Excited but fearful, Marguerite proceeded down the Rue de Bleu—an ordinary street of thatched-roof houses that all looked so drearily alike. Her parents were hard-working, practical people who would have difficulty understanding the choice she'd made. They would fear for her future and be embarrassed by the scandal of her unconventional career.

The straw carpets inside had been fashionable in the days before the revolution but had long since given way to more

```
popular pinewood planks.
    Marguerite was greeted by
her aunt, who was wearing a
drawstring calico skirt, the
kind favored by the mothers of
the neighborhood who needed to
let out their waistbands a bit.
"Marguerite, my dear! We've all
gathered to hear your news."
```

While reading the text in front of my family, I felt a creeping sense of dread—as though I was about to be caught at something. But what did I have to be guilty about? And then it hit me: I *had* written what I knew, only I hadn't even known it! Everyone in the room was on these pages. How embarrassing! They'd have to hate me if they realized. I prayed they wouldn't and continued.

```
    "Aunt Pascale, I do hope
your husband will understand.
He is given to hot tempers,"
Marguerite said. Her kindly,
homespun aunt, though
unworldly, was reassuring.
"He's been beating me since
we've been married, alas," she
said. "But oftentimes he'll
surprise me with a trinket."
She gestured to the red ribbon
in her hair, and Marguerite
understood that all would be
forgiven.
```

I paused a moment to peer at Aunt Helene, hoping she didn't recognize this funhouse mirror of her life, but she was too busy casting an angry glance at Uncle Lewis, who had started dozing off again.

    The family was gathered on
the sectional wood bench in
front of the hearth, where
Marguerite made her
announcement. As she feared,
her uncle, the family
patriarch, was the first to
react. "So, the banlieue is not
good enough for you?" he asked.
    Her parents were concerned,
too. "For years you've been
speaking of conquering the
world, yet you still sweep hair
for Madame La Bouffante," said
her pious mother.
    "Yes," echoed her kindly
father. "Remember the time you
met Mozart's cousin and
announced that you were off to
Salzburg to do his concert
wigs? But nothing came of it.
You were so heartbroken."
    Marguerite's cheeks flushed
with shame. That had been a
bitter blow.
    "And then there was the
incident with the Czar. Just
because you met the friend of a
friend of his favorite
ballerina, you were packing
your bags for Moscow," said her
controlling sister Louise.
    "I shall get there yet,"
Marguerite cried defiantly.

"Napoleon has promised to take me!"

"Let her go if she thinks she can make it without us," declared Louise, who had a habit of speaking about Marguerite as though she weren't there. "She'll come crawling back on her knees, begging for a chance to live her humble life again."

The only silent one was Marguerite's sweet cousin, Valerie, a talented painter who lived alone. She, too, was a dreamer and could understand Marguerite's quest.

Feeling guiltier than ever, I looked up at Mindy. I never wanted to hurt her, but there she was, unlucky in her career and love.

Marguerite sighed deeply, knowing she would receive no encouragement from these simple people, who could see no further than the limits of the banlieue. Although she knew the days ahead would be fraught with risk and uncertainty, the suffering would be slight in comparison to a lifetime of waking to the rooster, fighting the buggy jams on the way to the Marché, and coming home to another dull evening of

```
listening to her family
complain about their property
taxes. No, she, Marguerite
Frederique Dominique Soufflé,
would be a maker of history,
not merely a witness.
```

By the time I had finished, I was certain that my family recognized themselves. I looked up, expecting to see Jenna's angry glare, my mother's wounded expression, my father's hurt pride, and Mindy in a puddle of tears. Uncle Lewis and Aunt Helene would be mortified, and it would be years before any of them ever trusted me again.

Instead, Jenna coaxed a round of applause and urged me to take a bow.

"That was brilliant," said Mindy, clapping her sticky hands. "I really mean it, Laurel."

"Marvelous," said my mother. "It reminds me of *The King and I.*"

My father patted me on the back. "Looks like you're putting that wild imagination of yours to great use."

"It certainly is imaginative," said Aunt Helene. "Those characters were so unusual. Who would behave that way?"

"Well, she does live in the city," my mother observed. "And you know how crazy people there are. That must be her inspiration."

Their complete denial saved me. I could write a book called *The Lindens of Massapequa,* and they still wouldn't get it.

Bergdorf Goodman on Fifth Avenue was the only department store in New York I was too intimidated to enter alone. Trish and I had made the mistake of wandering in there once and instantly knew we were out of our league, not only because of the sky-high prices but also because the salesladies have a sixth sense that tells them when people just don't belong.

Vanessa had assigned me to meet her there, and I was

thrilled. In all our months of outings she'd never once let me pay, and with her at my side, I'd have not only the finances but also the class needed for Bergdorf's.

"I want you to pick out something for your meeting at Gallant Publishing," she said. Even though none was scheduled, I was delighted at the task, especially when she added, "And don't spare any expense."

I thought about a business suit—maybe one of those chic Yves Saint Laurent numbers—but Vanessa reminded me I was an artist and should look the part, so we rode the narrow escalator up to the designer sportswear boutiques. There we had our choice of all the best labels in the world and solicitous saleswomen eager to indulge our every whim.

I wound up with a silk-lined Agnès B. pink sweater with rhinestone buttons, a classic black raw silk pleated skirt, and a pair of Marc Jacobs high-heeled boots. While wearing the ensemble in the dressing room, I marveled at how far I'd come since I'd become friends with Vanessa. I was the picture of style and confidence, poised to take on the literary world.

As the saleswoman tenderly wrapped each treasure in its own special box, I was overwhelmed by Vanessa's generosity. "Someday, I'll find a way to thank you," I said to her, my eyes welling with tears. "After all you've already done for me, I can't believe you're going to pay for this."

"I'm not," she replied cheerfully. I stared in disbelief. "Not that I don't have the money, and not that I wouldn't love to, but it's time for you to bet on yourself for a change."

I was panicked. I hadn't even looked at the price tags, and I certainly hadn't budgeted for such an extravagance.

"Spending this money will be further motivation for you to get that fat book contract you deserve," she said.

Vanessa had never been wrong before. I handed over my credit card and prayed.

Trish laughed hysterically when I told her about my adventure at Bergdorf's. "So that's the secret," she said. "Pretend someone else is paying, then you have the guts to stand up to those salespeople." We were back at Sushi and Slushies, enjoying our girls' afternoon out.

"So do I hear wedding bells?" she asked.

"He's so incredible," I said dreamily.

"How does he rate compared to Miguel?" she asked, referring to my last true love, an abstract artist who left me for the Marines.

"Oh, God. Miguel was a nice BMW motorbike, but Lucien is a silver Lamborghini," I said.

"Still taking you to all those fancy functions?" she asked.

"Last night we went to the most amazing play," I said. "There was no dialogue, only animal sounds."

Trish looked at me skeptically. "Like 'oink oink' and 'moo moo'?" she asked.

I struggled to explain. "Well, those, but also many others, like 'baa baa' and 'cock-a-doodle-doo.'"

"Sounds like one of my kids' shows," Trish said.

I ignored her. "Did you know that in Greek, roosters say 'kakarisi'? I learn so much from Lucien."

"Best of all, he seems to really, really care about you," Trish said. "I guess it's just as well you ditched Irwin. You'll never guess who got him, though."

"Someone I know?" I asked.

"Implants in her boobs and her butt?" Trish's clue didn't help until she added a nasal imitation, "'As God is my witness, I won't be single when I'm thirty. I don't care how commitment-phobic he is; if I want him, he'll propose.'"

I burst out laughing. "Marisa Monahan? I thought you said he liked artsy types."

"She's a con artist anyway," Trish replied. "And it worked. He's totally smitten."

When the check came, she treated. Vanessa might have been convinced that my book contract was right around the corner, but Trish wasn't taking any chances.

I was struggling to keep up with the Latvian subtitles of a four-and-a-half-hour video documentary on Baltic mythology when I noticed Lucien rubbing his fingers. "Are you okay, honey?" He always had a cute, hurt little boy's look on his face whenever he was in pain.

"This is going to sound crazy," he said, "but I think I'm getting arthritis."

"Maybe you just banged yourself without realizing it," I said, picturing us in our eighties looking back on a happy life as I tenderly massaged Aspercreme into his joints.

"No, no, I just read an article about how a lack of Vitamin E can lead to early onset inflammation in certain—"

Just then my phone rang. I almost didn't pick up, figuring it was probably Maury the Lounge-Around King telling me not to forget the heartworm medicine for his dog, but when I saw who it was, my spirits soared.

"Anderson?" I answered.

"No, I'm Mr. Gallant's assistant, Nona. You'll be hearing from me a lot. He's decided to publish your book. Congratulations!"

Oh God oh God oh God oh thank you God. This was the news I had been waiting for all my life. I could barely concentrate as Nona explained that the particulars of my contract would be discussed at a meeting the next week. I wanted to jump up and down, lean out the window, and shout to the whole city: "I sold my book!"

"So can we expect you on Friday at ten?" she asked.

"Absolutely," I said, knowing just what I'd wear.

I hung up the phone and threw it in the air, screaming, "YES!" Lucien didn't even need to ask. "Oh, Laurel, how wonderful!" he said, hugging me tightly. "Let's celebrate. I think I have some champagne in the fridge."

As he went to get it I made a mental list of all the people to call. Vanessa first and foremost. Then all the members in my writers group, plus my family and Trish.

I was wondering how to get in touch with my old professors from Vassar when Lucien returned carrying on a silver tray the bottle of champagne and two delicate flutes garnished with strawberries. He poured the bubbly, and we toasted. "To my brilliant author girlfriend, Laurel," he said. "I'm sure this will be just one of many great novels in your future."

Our glasses clinked, and I savored the tangy taste of champagne rolling on my tongue. "You know," he said, "Gallant Publishing started as a magazine in 1903. A silly little rag about agriculture that the family built into one of the most powerful media empires in the United States."

"Wow," I said, feeling like I was taking off in a helium balloon. "It will be such an honor to be part of that great history."

"Wait," he said, jumping up. "I think I have a book about this somewhere." Before long, we were studying the list of titles published by Gallant over the decades. Lucien was familiar with most of them and explained a little about each. By the end of the evening, I was an expert on their enterprise, and grateful that a gorgeous personal tutor had prepared me for my meeting.

11

Everyone congratulated me when they heard the news, but no one more effusively than Jenna. "Oh, sis, I always knew you could do it," she said, conveniently ignoring the fact that for years she'd been trying to convince me to give up on writing. Feeling expansive in my good fortune, I chose to ignore it, too.

"Thanks, Jenna."

She insisted on treating me to lunch at the Rainbow Room at the top of Rockefeller Center, and I graciously accepted the invitation. I had to concede she'd been trying hard, and now that she was starting to respect me, maybe we could actually be friends.

We were halfway through our grilled Atlantic salmon and wild rice when Jenna's congratulatory tone turned tender. Placing a gentle palm against my cheek, she looked into my eyes and said, "Sweetie, I'm so happy for you, but the truth is, I'm also a little worried."

Jenna had lived through so many of my near misses, she probably thought this one would fall through too, so I reassured her. "Oh, it's a done deal; I got the word straight from Gallant's assistant."

"I know your book is going to be published," she said, "but that's exactly what concerns me. Your success."

My success was a topic I had always thought I'd enjoy discussing with Jenna, but, leaning back in my chair, I was starting to doubt this would be much fun.

"Victory is a double-edged sword. I know. You probably don't remember this, but it was right after I got the silver medal in the state gymnastics championships that my eating disorder began."

Not remember? I wish. I'd spent half of fifth grade in family therapy listening to Jenna moan about how she wasn't perfect enough.

"Jenna, this is completely different," I said, feeling my teeth clench. "It's not going to be stressful for me to finally be acknowledged and praised after years of lonely struggle. You missed the stressful part. Now you want to have lunch with me, but where were you when I got all those rejection letters?"

"Maybe I could have been more supportive, but I'm trying to help you now. Let me tell you something: When they put that silver medal around my neck, it felt like a noose. Sure, it was an honor, but suddenly everybody was talking about my next meet. On to the nationals. And then the Olympics. I knew I wasn't Olympic material, and all I could see in the future was more pain and disappointment."

"So what are you trying to tell me? That I'm not Olympic material?" I could feel a Jenna headache starting to build.

"Look, I hope you win the Pulitzer. I hope you win the Nobel Prize. But I'm warning you: This is only the beginning of a very long road. Have you given any thought to your next book?"

Leave it to my sister to not even wait for dessert to ruin my congratulatory lunch.

"Laurel," she said, lowering her voice, "I know from experience. The higher you rise, the harder you fall. I just don't want to see you—"

"You just don't want to see me happy, that's all. It kills you that I might get some attention for a change. Instead of admitting that you've been wrong about my writing all these years, you twist my good news into some prophesy of doom just so you can feel superior."

"They're going to ask you at that meeting on Friday what other projects you have, and if you don't have an answer—"

"Thanks, Jenna," I said, cutting her off and throwing my napkin down on the table. "Thanks for being such a sweet, caring, concerned older sister," I spat. "But I think I'd rather handle my life on my own." I grabbed my bag and left.

With tears clouding my eyes, I walked directly to Vanessa's glass high-rise near Columbus Circle. This was an emergency; a phone call just wouldn't do. The doorman recognized me from the many times we'd met in her lobby and rang Vanessa before handing me the phone.

"Do you have some time?" I asked. "I just had the worst fight with Jenna, and—"

"Of course, Laurel. I'll be right down."

As I sat in the luxurious lobby, waiting for my adopted big sister, I marveled at how she was always there for me at the drop of a hat. She never seemed to have any personal concerns that took precedence over our relationship. It was amazing. Sure her husband traveled a lot, but I sensed she still had various responsibilities in relation to the charities she mentioned now and then. But it was almost like Vanessa was a professional friend.

Vanessa took me by the arm and guided me out the door. We crossed the street to the Time Warner Center, where she brought me to a quiet café overlooking Central Park. After I'd cried my way through two packets of her tissues, explaining what had happened, Vanessa rolled her eyes and laughed.

"Your sister is a real piece of work," she said. "Why do you think she's lashing out at you at this particular moment?"

"Because she's a jealous bitch," I said, catching my breath.

"It's deeper than that," she explained in her familiar, soothing voice. "Jenna's not just jealous, she's threatened. Your change in status dethrones her, and she wants to stage a comeback. But first she has to get you out of the way."

"What makes me sick is that she pretends she's doing me a favor."

"Of course she does, because she can't acknowledge to herself her own subconscious inadequacy. It all gets projected onto you."

I sniffled. "So you don't think that after I sign that contract I'm going to stop eating?"

"After you sign that contract, you're going to have the best meal of your life. At the Four Seasons. On me."

With reassurance from Vanessa, my gorgeous clothes from Bergdorf Goodman, and a sexy send-off from Lucien, I was in top form when I entered the venerable Gallant Publishing Headquarters on Broadway. To my surprise and delight, I was ushered into the office of the president himself, and as I took my seat in a maroon leather armchair, I thought of the many brilliant writers who had been there before me.

Nona, a humorless-looking woman with black owl glasses that overwhelmed her face, was poised to take notes. Anderson, wearing a Mr. Bubble T-shirt, was pacing excitedly. His father, Preston Gallant, presided with a stately air from behind his mahogany desk.

"Here she is: my protégé!" Anderson announced.

"This is one long-awaited day," the old man began, stuffing a pipe.

"Yes, sir," I replied. "I began this novel eight years ago, and—"

"Oh, I'm not talking about for you. You may have been writing for eight years, but it's taken me a quarter-century to get my son to do some work. I don't know what it is about *Napoleon's Hairdresser*, but you must have something in this book if Anderson Gallant can get past page three. I don't believe a book has held his attention this long since *Treadmills for Dummies*."

I shifted uncomfortably in my seat.

"Dad, I've been using that NordicTrack every day!"

"Granted you have, son, granted you have, but sports has

never been your weak point," Preston Gallant said. Pointing the pipe stem at me, he added, "We wasted seventy thousand dollars to get this boy into Yale, and all he ever did was ski."

"But I'm really excited about this project, Dad," Anderson said. "We need to mobilize our entire publicity department to start the buzz right away. I want this whole town to know the name Laurel Linden before the first book comes out. Get our biggest authors to write endorsements for the cover. And I want praise. High praise."

"Mr. Gallant, we will need to do some revisions first," Nona interjected.

"Well, you'll take care of that," he said with a dismissive wave.

Anderson was pointing to imaginary headlines in front of him. "'Life-changing!' 'Breathtaking!' 'The literary masterpiece of the century, the millennium, of all time!'"

"You get the idea," Preston said. "We're putting you on the fast track with our A-list authors; you know, the Hollywood madams, ex-wives of sports stars, and political tattletales—all the big sellers."

"You'll be coming out in hardcover with an initial printing of three hundred thousand. I don't need to tell you the advance is six figures," Nona said.

"The best part, kid," Anderson said, "is thanks to my connections, we got a six-book deal—two a year, renewable."

"No, no," I said, blown away beyond my wildest dreams. "This is more than enough. How can I ever thank you?"

"No need, no need. If your book can turn my ski-bum son into a real publisher, it is I who will be grateful to you. Why, you'll be saving the whole future of the Gallant Publishing empire."

I floated out of the office like I was on a magic carpet. Goodbye Fourteenth Street crumbling apartment, hello penthouse suite. Goodbye doors slamming in my face, hello red carpet treatment. Goodbye obscurity, hello fame.

To celebrate, Lucien and I planned a long romantic

weekend in Italy. When I told Trish, she squealed with delight. "Oh, you know he's going to propose now!" she said. "That's it, I'm dyeing my pumps." Count on Trish to know what I was really hoping for.

It had always been my dream to see Florence, and Lucien was my ideal guide. We flew first-class and held hands the whole way over, planning together how to take in as much as possible of this cultural mecca.

We had booked a charming little *pensione* in the heart of the old city. The room had a gorgeous view of the famous old Duomo. I settled back in the king-sized bed, sinking into its cozy depths. Lucien stared out the window, telling me about all the landmark buildings he could see, when they were built, and who their architects were. I gazed at my boyfriend and knew that our relationship was deepening. As soon as Gallant wrote the first check, I'd be leaving my apartment, and although we'd never discussed it, Lucien and I knew this vacation was a sort of rehearsal for moving in together.

"Honey, come here," I cooed. "This bed is so comfortable, but it's lonely without you."

"Why, do you want to take a nap? Are you jetlagged? I brought some melatonin. It's a well-known homeopathic remedy first discovered by a Mexican—"

"I'm not tired," I said, wriggling in the sweet-smelling sheets. "I just want to feel you close to me."

"You're not tired?" he echoed. "Great! Let's get started. I'll hold you close on the way to the Uffizi."

By Saturday night, I knew more about Florence than a PhD candidate in Italian renaissance history. It was a fascinating city; the only problem was that it was a little too damp for Lucien.

"My arthritis is acting up again," he complained. I couldn't see any swelling, but I took his word for it and searched the city for a remedy.

I wanted to have wild sex in our cozy love nest, but Lucien still wasn't feeling well by our last full day in Italy, so I settled for a romantic moonlight boat ride on the Arno river.

"Look at this brochure," I said, showing him a glossy photo of happy lovers cuddling in a lantern-lit boat passing under Ponte Vecchio. "Doesn't it look dreamy?"

"Oh, that's funny, Laurel," he said, "but I'm not in the mood for stupid jokes."

"Who's joking?" I asked, feeling hurt. "It will be beautiful! We'll glide under the old bridges at night bathed in moonlight, sip champagne, and hold each other." When he remained silent, I appealed to his intellectual side. "It will be the perfect chance for you to tell me all about the crimes and passions of the Medici."

"I'm not joining the hordes of polyester-clad Americans on their McTour of Europe," he said with a look of disdain.

Hurt, I turned to the window. Soon Lucien had placed a hand on my shoulder. "I want to tell you all about the Medici, I really do," he said gently, "but in an authentic setting. Why don't we use our last day to visit their palace? It's spectacular— so full of art and history, I could get lost there for a week."

"What about your arthritis?" I asked.

"Oh, I'll live," he said with a wink.

It was during the plane ride back that Lucien surprised me with a gift. "Oh, you," I said, savoring the task of untying the elegant silver ribbon on the large black box. *He must have noticed me admiring the fine leather handbags in the windows of the city's best shops,* I thought.

But when I opened the package and looked inside, I was puzzled to see some sort of carved gargoyle. "What is it?" I asked.

"There's two of them," he said with a smile. "Antique bookends." I removed the dusty wooden planks from their box and set them side by side.

"These are for our living room," he explained, adding shyly, "You know, for when we move in together." We were flying at thirty thousand feet, but that was nothing compared to the heights of happiness I reached.

The following week, my new career began in earnest when I

signed the contract with Gallant Publishing. True to her word, Vanessa took me out to the Four Seasons that afternoon. In the elegant, *moderne* setting, Vanessa laid out her scariest assignment yet.

"Give up my rent-controlled apartment?" Whenever I thought about moving in with Lucien, it was always with the backup of subletting my apartment, just in case.

"As long as you have a Plan B," Vanessa chided, "you're undermining Plan A."

What was I clinging to? Noise, dirt, and less reliable water than the average home in a desert. "Okay, I'll do it!" I said with resolve.

When tea came, I took a delicious sip and marveled at my good fortune. Feeling completely satisfied, I turned my attention to my friend.

"So what's going on with you?" I asked, realizing I'd never posed that question before because she always seemed so selfless.

"I'm just so happy to see that you're so happy," she said, confirming my theory. "There's only one thing left for you to do to get ready for your new life."

"What's that?"

"Well, now that you've got a new job, you won't be needing the old one anymore."

"You mean cut back on the dog walking?"

"I mean cut it out completely."

"But that's where I do my best thinking."

"Laurel . . . give up the starving artist bullshit. Just because you have money doesn't mean you can't be creative. When are you finally going to understand what I've been trying to teach you: With the right attitude, you can have it *all*."

It was finally my turn for a pizza party at the Hell's Kitchen writers group. Thanks to Danny Z., there was even a special guest. "Portia's coming," he informed me with a conspiratorial smirk. "You had to sit through her party, and I wanted to be sure she sits through yours."

When Portia finally walked in, I looked at her long black

hair and naturally cool style without even a hint of the jealousy that used to consume me in her presence. Anyone could get a lucky break, and none of us were really better or worse than any other member of the group. José might yet publish *Planet Cucumber and the Wriggly Green Virus*. Margo was in the process of transforming a disaster into what could well turn out to be a work of solid fiction. And Sunny Hellerstein was right to affirm her publishability every chance she could; self-help books were huge sellers, and hers could be next. Gripped by affection for them all, I made my farewell speech.

"What an incredible six years, guys. I know we've been through some ups and downs, but all in all it's been a hell of a ride. I want you to know that I'll never forget any of you and that you can always come to me if you need advice."

"Here! Here!" José said, raising a plastic cup of 7UP.

"Mazel tov!" proclaimed Danny Z. "Let's eat!"

Seth opened the pizza box.

I didn't want to embarrass Portia with the details of my spectacular contract, so I kept it vague when she asked, but Portia told me all about hers.

"You were so right, Laurel. My advance is really tiny, and I'm only coming out in paperback, but my agent said that for a long-term career it's best not to peak too early." She shrugged and added, "Well, maybe I'll see you at the Frankfurt Book Fair."

Portia gave me a quick hug and left. I wasn't quite sure why, but I suddenly disliked her all over again.

12

Danny Z. leapt at the chance to take over my dog-walking route, and since he'd filled in for me before, my clients were pretty amenable. On my last day at Sergio's, they gave me a free gift certificate for another haircut. "It will be an excuse to see Mini," I said, stroking the beautiful Great Dane.

Maury Blaustein said that if I ever wanted a Lounge-Around, he could get me a deal. "I doubt it," I said, "but promise I can still visit Kingpin." I kissed the friendly schnoodle affectionately.

It was no easier saying goodbye to Lulu, and by the time I got to the Danilovas, I was crying openly. "Oh, Slobodan, I'm sorry for all the times I yelled at you for trying to eat dead pigeons."

Mr. Danilova stroked his dog's ear. "Oh, don't worry about her," he said. "She's going to have the time of her life on our camping trip this summer in the Adirondacks."

"I never realized you were an outdoorsman," I said. With his pale complexion and wire-rimmed glasses, Mr. Danilova looked as though he wouldn't last even a night in the wild.

"Well, it's not really my kind of thing," he confessed. "But my wife loves it, and I love her."

It must have been my emotional state, because in that moment, I thought Mrs. Danilova was the luckiest woman in the world.

Editorial meetings with Nona began later that week. Her office was completely different from Preston's—one-tenth the size but with ten times the amount of books and papers. From behind a desk piled high with folders, she addressed me sternly.

"The Gallants are quite keen on this one, but I keep telling them we have work to do," she said. "I hope you're with me on that."

After eight years of writing *Napoleon's Hairdresser,* I knew better than anyone that there was a sentence or two here and there that could use some polishing, and I was eager to see what this woman's discerning eye had picked up.

"Your manuscript is replete with anachronisms. I've marked them all in red," she said, handing it to me. *She must have spilled cranberry juice on it,* I thought, unwilling to acknowledge that each and every page had been colored by her admonishing pen. "Before we can even begin to talk about plot and character, we've got to make this at least quasi-plausible."

I was shocked. Nona seemed to think I was an idiot. "Quasi-plausible?" I asked. "This is practically a documentary."

"Laurel, Anderson respects your work a great deal, and Preston has high expectations for his son. They're positioning you as the next great writer of historical fiction, and passages like this just won't cut it." She pulled a sheet from the stack and began reading:

```
    The night before the battle
of Austerlitz, Marguerite
prepared herself to face the
Emperor. She had lost many
hours of sleep, and even the
anti-wrinkle cream she had so
vigorously applied had been of
```

little use. *Her legs!* she thought. They should be silky and not coarse to the touch. Using a generous dollop of meringue she'd spirited away from the barrack kitchen, she covered her legs from her knees to her ankles and, with a steady hand, used the fine new feminine-sized razor she'd purchased at Madame Schick's. When her calves were smoother than eggshells, her attention turned to the battle ahead. She must at all costs find a solution to the Emperor's ever-growing bald spot. Searching for inspiration, Marguerite turned to the little self-help book she always carried in her trunk, *The Seven Habits of Highly Successful Monarchs*. But its well-worn passages on the importance of making lists and freeing serfs were of little use. Not since Caesar's time had anyone faced a problem of this magnitude.

Caesar . . . Caesar, she thought. He had also had a terrible bald spot and had worn his hair brushed forward to compensate for the thinness on top. A flush of inspiration coursed through her blood. What if I took the hair and actually covered the bald spot? That's it! Le Comb-over!

Nona removed her glasses and stared at me deadpan. "Le Comb-over?" she asked, dripping with contempt.

"I thought that was original," I said defensively. "This is a work of imagination."

Nona seemed to check her anger. "You are the talent, so I'm going to take your word for it, but I have twenty-eight years' experience in this business, and believe me, I've seen them come and go."

I softened. "Okay, so what would you suggest?"

"It's hard to know where to begin," Nona said with a deep sigh, "but let's start with the leg-shaving. In my understanding, there was no feminine obsession with hairless legs until the mid-twentieth century, and then primarily in the United States. French women certainly didn't shave in Napoleon's day."

"But Marguerite's a trendsetter," I said.

"As a case in point, I happened to check, and the Schick razor was invented in Dayton, Ohio in 1898. You're off by eighty-four years."

"Are you going to pick apart every single instance of poetic license in this book?" I asked.

"If I don't, the reviewers will," she said. "I'm just here to make sure we don't get ripped to shreds by the critics. They can be awfully vicious, you know."

Just then, Anderson walked in, looking merry in his Yosemite Sam T-shirt, and took in the scene. "Don't scare her, Nona," he said. "This girl's my meal ticket."

"No, sir," she replied. "I realize that. I'm only trying to help."

"Well, from the looks of it, she's had enough for one day." He turned to me. "Laurel, take the afternoon off."

"But take this with you," Nona said, handing me back the manuscript. "We've got some serious work ahead of us," she repeated.

By that point, I'd begun packing up my apartment and was

spending every night at Lucien's. When he arrived home looking stressed out, I poured him a glass of his favorite Peruvian brandy, but nothing seemed to mollify him.

"Tough day at the office?" I asked. Too spent to bother cooking, I uncovered the leftovers from last night's Ethiopian takeout and popped them into the microwave.

"Worse. Dreadful experience at the theater. I just came from a preview performance of this hyped-up new playwright who is supposed to be the next Tony Kushner."

I began setting the table. "Was it that awful?"

"Try to imagine a set of characters with absolutely no arc, a clichéd plot ripped off from the very worst television sitcom, scenery that makes your high school production of 'Once Upon a Mattress' look like Broadway, and about as much tension as an afternoon nap."

"My poor sweetie," I said, taking the food from the microwave. "I had a hard day, too."

"But you can't imagine what it's like to have to suffer through this mediocrity! I am going to write the most scathing review imaginable. When it's published, not only will that horrible play close but anyone even remotely connected to it will never work in this town again. I'm going to crucify them all."

Dinner was ready, but I'd lost my appetite.

I left Lucien at home the following weekend when I went to Trish's Fourth of July party. Although she was dying to meet the guy she referred to as my fiancé, this was just the kind of jingoistic American occasion that would set him off, so I made excuses when I arrived on my own.

There were about forty people laughing and milling around the redwood deck and pool area in the backyard. As usual, Trish's husband Tom had taken control of the barbecue. I recognized plenty of other faces; in the past, I would have been mentally tearing them apart for being so mainstream, but given my newfound status as a soon-to-be-published author, I was feeling generous. The girls with their fake nails probably got some satisfaction from their weekly manicures, and as for the guys, if they wanted to drink Bud, more power to 'em. Peruvian brandy isn't for everyone.

But by my fifth conversation about traffic on the LIE, horrible train service on the LIRR, and LILCO's exorbitant prices, I was getting bored. When even three beers didn't make the evening any more interesting, I started planning my exit.

I was looking for Trish to say goodbye when the familiar strains of an old song came on the stereo.

Billy Joel's "Italian Restaurant," one of my parents' favorite songs. Hokey as it might sound, he was a native son from Long Island who perfectly captured the place and its people. I couldn't help but feel swept back in time to the carefree days of school dances when his music would get us all on the floor during oldies sets. Grabbing Trish by the hand, I started to rock as the tune got going.

Suddenly the music stopped. A beefy guy with long hair had yanked the CD off the player, and a round of applause went up. "That is the worst shit ever made," he said drunkenly. "No Billy Joel."

"No Billy Joel! No Billy Joel!" came the echo from all across the backyard. House music soon throbbed from the speakers, and everyone resumed their socializing.

Feeling bad for the guy who had put on the unpopular choice, I went over to him. "I love that song!" I said to the muscular jock wearing a baseball cap.

"I guess you're the only one," he laughed.

"And this music's not really doing it for me," I said.

"Me neither," he replied.

"I was about to leave anyway," I said.

"Well, don't let their bad taste drive you away," he said. "I'll put this on in my car, and we can hang out in the front yard."

Knowing that I had a lifetime of obscure opera and esoteric jazz ahead of me, the thought of one last guilty pleasure was irresistible. "Why not?" I said. "Just that one tune."

We grabbed a six-pack and headed toward his Audi convertible. When the song came back on, we laughed our way through all the verses, which were about a couple called Brenda and Eddie.

As the rest of the album played, we started calling each other by those names. While watching "Eddie's" taut muscles catch the light as we danced in the front yard, I remembered Lucien's arthritis and for a second considered an even more sinful guilty pleasure. It must have been the beer that made me so flirtatious.

"At my high school, if you didn't have this CD memorized, you couldn't graduate," he said.

"At mine, you got expelled," I countered. Neither of us had to ask where the other had grown up; it was obvious we were both hopelessly South Shore.

"I bet you used to go to Field 4 at Jones," he said.

"PAR-TY!" I said, reciting the motto of that famous teen hangout.

Both tipsy, we giddily compared notes about hot times at the far end of the yard when a nasal voice suddenly called out from the front door: "There you are! I've been looking everywhere! You have to see Carmella's engagement ring."

My new friend shrugged apologetically. "I'll be right there, honey," he said before turning to me. "Well, bye, 'Brenda.' Maybe next time I'll learn your real name."

Maybe, but I already knew his. As I watched Marisa lead him off, I realized I'd just been dancing with none other than Dr. Irwin Turnov.

After a few more grueling sessions with Nona and her red pen, I finally got a break at Gallant. They had arranged for me to meet with the top publicists on their roster. I was right under the spotlight as I sat facing three intense professionals, each vying to elicit charming anecdotes from me to use in the press kit. I was loving it.

"What's your favorite color?" asked a dark-skinned beauty with silver bracelets.

"Favorite color?" repeated the husky-voiced girl with a red jacket. "We can't waste our time on that." She turned to me, "I want you to think: any funny stories about writing this book? Where did you find your inspiration?"

"Did you always want to be a writer? Who were your influences?" asked the third, an older man in a business suit.

Unlike my meetings with Nona, I was fully confident at this session. After all, I'd been rehearsing my answers for years.

"Let me think," I began, as though it were all just occurring to me. "Nothing in my ordinary background would explain my desire to write a sweeping historical epic. True, my family watched every episode of 'Dynasty,' but for higher culture I had to follow my calling beyond the Huntington line on the Long Island Railroad."

Silver bracelets interrupted. "I'm getting small-town girl with big-city dreams. Very *Newsweek's* 'People' column."

"Massapequa is hardly a small town," business suit corrected her. "It's a crowded suburb."

"He's right," said the husky voice. "But not exactly an inspiring environment for writing a nineteenth-century romance."

"So you moved to Paris?" her colleague coaxed, scribbling in her notebook.

"No, I moved into the New York Public Library," I said, looking into the distance as though it were a strain to recall those days. "There, for eight years, I labored meticulously to research my great enterprise."

"I'm seeing 'suburban girl escapes from cultural underclass,'" the bracelet-wearer said. "They'll love it on public broadcasting."

I was hoping at least for commercial TV, so I fed them a little more. "As I delved into the period, I found striking parallels to today's strife-torn world," I said.

"So it's allegorical?" asked the man.

"No, not really," I confessed.

"Yes, yes, a haunting allegory about ordinary citizens caught up in a political struggle for world hegemony!" pronounced silver bracelets.

Hegemony—that was a word Lucien loved to use. I made a

mental note to ask him what it meant.

"A gripping tale that could be ripped from this morning's headlines," suggested the other woman.

"A fast-paced account about the lust for power that continues to destabilize our world even today," said the man.

They were talking as though I weren't even in the room, and about somebody else's book—not mine.

"Have any of you read *Napoleon's Hairdresser?*" I asked.

"Not yet," said the husky voice.

"Not exactly," said the woman with the jingling bracelets.

"Why bother?" asked the man cheerfully. "We hear it's going to change completely in the rewrites."

I had three weeks left to get out of my apartment. After eight years of living in the same dump, it seemed impossible to pack up all that I'd accumulated. Fortunately, Lucien said he would help, and we were sorting through my collection of posters.

It was old fashioned to own them, but he understood the nostalgia value—just not the taste.

"Honestly, Laurel, I don't know why you have to move all these to my place," he said, eyeing them with disdain. "This is pure commercialism with no artistic merit."

"You're right," I said, knowing he'd never tolerate my playlists. "I'll just keep some of the old ones." I snuck Billy Joel into the pile of those to be saved.

Lucien began bundling my back issues of *Celebrity Style* to take out to the recycle bin, all the while muttering about how he couldn't believe I read the stuff. To distract him, I started talking about my photo shoot. "They're bringing in a professional hair stylist, a makeup artist, and a team of three wardrobe people," I said. "Can you believe all of that just for a jacket photo?"

"Well, maybe *Celebrity Style* will do a spread on you," he said, heading out to the garbage bin. "You would love that, I suppose," he added, letting the door slam behind him.

His anger felt like a slap in the face, but I reassured myself with the knowledge that when two people deepen their commitment, there's bound to be friction. Still, some irrational impulse made me rescue the discarded posters and hide them in a nearby box.

"To facilitate your research," Nona said when I arrived the following Wednesday morning, "I've begun compiling details that need reworking in the interest of verisimilitude." She handed me a list that looked longer than my book:

– Putting 'le' in front of a word doesn't make it French: le flakes du corn crunchie (note: adjective at end doesn't work either)
– Town criers did NOT give reports on buggy pile-ups
– Cross-Your-Heart bras were not invented until 1956
– Miami Beach was not a resort yet (see Marguerite's fantasy, page 68)
– It's unlikely that M's mother would know about trans-fatty acids
– Napoleonic-era women used ribbons to tie back their hair, not scrunchies.
– Cousin Louise's aquarobics classes in the Seine, simply ridiculous, even if possible . . . where would she find students among the starving masses of Paris?
– Low-carb croissants still don't exist!

"How am I supposed to tackle all of this?" I asked.
"According to your press kit, you used to live at the library," she said. "Why don't you move back in?"

I had no choice but to trudge up the majestic marble steps of the Forty-Second Street Research Library. Once inside the echoing hallways, I found the entrance to the main reading room blocked by a security guard who searched my bag for banned items. They're very strict about not allowing any books in because someone might steal one from the collection, pretending it was their own. When the guard saw all I had was *Celebrity Style*, he waved me along.

Inside the massive hall, hundreds of people worked quietly at long, wooden tables. I pulled up a creaky old chair next to an elderly man poring over a manuscript in some Slavic language or another. Across from me, a prim, pallid-skinned woman around my age was lost in a pile of dusty old tomes. I envied their studiousness. How did they manage to concentrate on all this ancient stuff?

Plotting my own strategy, I realized I would have to wait in line to use the digital catalog. Assuming I found anything relevant, I would have to fill out a request slip, wait for my number to be displayed on the big board, pick up the books, hunt for any pages that might be of use, and then, if I wanted to copy them, begin a whole new process of filling out forms and waiting in lines.

I hadn't lied to the publicists; I really had spent a lot of time here, but I wondered how I made it through. Digging into my bag for a strictly forbidden stick of gum, I remembered: junky magazine breaks.

As I paged through *Celebrity Style*, I felt more restless than ever. *This Salli Simmer columnist had the life,* I thought, stopping to read her latest article. Last week, she profiled the latest ingénue director of the Cannes Film Festival; this week, she was back in Malibu picnicking with an aging rock star at the Hollywood Unites Against the Paparazzi Charity Beach Party.

I reminded myself that in serious circles she'd be laughed at, and she'd never get a boyfriend like Lucien. Refreshed, I joined the line for the digital catalog. Unfortunately, the library closed before my number ever came up on the big board.

13

The tediousness of the research was offset by the excitement of the publicity plans. At my photo shoot I was treated like a model, and since I was all dolled up when it was through, I called Lucien for lunch.

As we sat in the Central Park boathouse looking out on the lake, I pulled out my travel schedule. "Look at all these bookings!" I said with awe. "I'll be doing eighteen major media markets in the U.S. and Canada, and once the book is translated, I'll be traveling all across Europe." I had been elated when they told me they'd already started penciling in dates in anticipation of the major interest that would be generated by the ad campaign.

Looking up, expecting his smile, I was disappointed to see that Lucien was pouting instead, but I felt better when I realized it was only because he would miss me. "Oh, honey, you can visit me any time, you can come on the whole tour. I don't want to be away from you."

"Thanks, but I'll skip the Laurel Linden show," he said bitterly.

"What's that supposed to mean?"

"Look at you. You're becoming just like any pampered little star! Photo shoots, publicity tours. I liked you better when you were a nobody."

"You liked me better when I was struggling and depressed and frustrated and ready to give up?" I asked, feeling the blood rush to my face.

"No, it's not a question of your feelings," he said. Tears began rolling down my cheeks. "It's just that in the old days, you used to look at me with this deep admiration that's gone now. When was the last time you spent hours listening to me explain something you never knew existed? That's when I really connected with you."

When he said it, it dawned on me that I didn't miss those old days. Not because they'd been replaced by photo shoots but because I'd grown tired of his lectures. It had gotten to the point where I thought that if I heard another lengthy exposition on the roots of neo-realist textile patterns I would scream.

"Maybe that's because I want a boyfriend, not a teacher," I said, realizing it for the first time. "Someone who can be happy for me when I'm successful."

"Well, your success comes at my expense," he said.

"What?" I was furious. "Success hasn't stopped me from taking care of you, cooking you dinner, pouring your drinks, running around looking for your stupid arthritis medicine."

"Laurel, I could hire an assistant for all of that. What I need is a girlfriend who shines the spotlight on me, not someone who hogs it."

The food came, and we spent the rest of lunch in silence.

With the clock ticking before I was to move in with Lucien, and our relationship at its lowest point ever, I knew it was time to check in with Vanessa. She insisted on treating me to a spa manicure/pedicure at Ilona of Hungary on Madison Avenue. As we sat side by side sipping iced herbal tea and enjoying foot massages, I relayed the details of my fight with Lucien.

"So why do you think you're sabotaging your relationship now?" she asked.

"Because I'm about to move in with him, and I'm afraid of commitment?" I guessed.

"It's bigger than that," Vanessa said, her hands dipped in

soapy water. "Do you realize that in the six months we've known each other you have achieved each and every one of your biggest dreams? That's remarkable, Laurel. You are one remarkable woman."

I felt my chest swell with pride. Vanessa always managed to lift me above the muck and mire so I could see the panoramic view.

"But six months is a very short time for such a drastic change, and it's no wonder you're so scared with everything going so fast. Unconsciously, you're trying to put the brakes on for fear that you'll lose control and crash."

"Poor Lucien! He's the victim of my insecurity," I said.

"Sweetheart, you have come so far, I'm sure you can think of a way to make up with him."

There was very little left in my apartment that hadn't been boxed, and I was about to unplug the landline and put it away as well when it rang.

"Hey there!"

"Trishalicious!" I was delighted to hear my best friend's voice.

"We're coming into the city on Saturday night—a bunch of us," she explained. "San Gennaro Festival. You and Lucien want to come catch some zeppoles?"

I beat back the image of Lucien gagging on a greasy ball of fried dough. Definitely not his scene, but luckily I had a good excuse to bow out. "I would love to, Trish, but we have tickets that night. I'm treating him."

"Another one of those plays where nobody speaks?" she asked.

"No, it's Niklatumanda Inuit windchimes—a concert in Chinatown."

Trish was silent for a moment. "So meet us afterwards," she suggested.

"Can't. It's a six-hour interpretation of their exodus across the Bering Straits," I said. "Lucien's been going on about it for months."

"Oh, please," Trish exploded. "Laurel, I may not be one of your fuzzy-brained, high-flown intellectual friends, but I do know you. You cannot tell me that a girl who cried through the last episode of 'Gilmore Girls,' who turned her whole room into a shrine for Drake, who used to regularly cut class to stream 'The Bachelor'—with me—cares a shit about some exodus across the Bering Straits."

I would have been mad at Trish, but I was laughing too hard. Just to get her off my back, I asked where they'd be meeting. "We're having dim sum first at Lucky Chen's, so we'll be there from seven to eight," she said. "Stop by when you've had enough of those fascinating windchimes."

Trish was wrong; I was actually looking forward to the concert. It would be a break from the drudgery of the library and a chance to reignite the spark in my relationship. Lucien had been delighted when I surprised him with the tickets and had bought an Inuit–English dictionary for the occasion.

In our seats before the show, after he'd finished translating the names of each song on the program, he asked if his issue of *Granta* had arrived. "Not yet," I said, "but oh, I got the sweetest gift from my writers group! They all chipped in and bought me this goofy, fluorescent pink, personalized stationery with my name and a picture of Snoopy at his typewriter." My heart had been warmed by the gesture, but those blue eyes of Lucien's seemed icier than the Bering Straits.

"I thought we talked about this," he said, looking furious.

"What?" I asked, trying to figure out my crime.

"Snoopy? Personalized pink Laurel Linden stationery? Need I say more?"

Just then, two men in fur walked out on the stage and placed three fans in front of a set of windchimes. The audience applauded, but I was too upset to join in. Lucien's short comment had crystallized the problem exactly: From now on, I was not allowed to mention anything lowbrow or anything Laurel.

There was nothing to do but think with the fans on and the

chimes clinkling. It was like sitting on my parents' back porch, but the scenery was worse. I saw a future with Lucien where my opinions, my tastes, my passions, my interests all but disappeared. Not to mention my sex life. Looking back, I realized that ever since that first time in bed, the lectures had grown longer and the fun shorter.

I kept waiting for the concert to kick into gear, but by the second hour of watching windchimes barely stir, I couldn't take it anymore. If Lucien wanted less Laurel Linden, he could have it. "I need some air," I said, and stepped out.

It was only three blocks to Lucky Chen's, but that was a world away from the frozen Bering Straits I'd left behind. The traditional Italian Festival of San Gennaro was in full swing. A canopy of green and red lights was strung across Mott Street, and it seemed that all of Manhattan and most of Long Island was packed along its few short blocks.

They weren't at the restaurant, but miraculously I caught sight of Tom standing across the street.

"Hey!" he said when I reached him. "You made it!"

"What's up?" I asked. "Where's Trish?"

"I'm meeting her down the block. Come on."

Just then, a familiar face turned from a pitch-ball booth toward Tom. "Hey, buddy! I just won a free game. Wanna play it?"

He tossed the ball to Tom, who tossed it back. "I've got to meet Trish. Catch up with us." Tom headed off.

"Eddie!" I said, surprised to see my fellow Billy Joel fan, the dentist, looking cute in baggy chinos and Adidas sandals.

"Oh, it's you—Brenda," he laughed.

Irwin tossed me the ball. "How's your arm?" he asked.

"I used to be the pitcher for the South Shore Seashells," I boasted.

"Aw, you guys lost every year to North Woodmere," he said. I was amazed he'd heard of my childhood softball team, but then again, something about Irwin seemed so familiar.

I hurled the ball at the target but hit the booth's proprietor instead. "Sorry!" I called out before making my excuses. "Guess I've been living in the city too long."

Irwin bought another try and wound his arm dramatically, as though it were the bottom of the ninth with bases loaded. I couldn't help but notice his six-pack abs as his shirt momentarily rose off of his stomach. He easily won a pink dinosaur, which he presented to me. "Give it to your girlfriend," I said. "Where is she, anyway?"

"Ah, she hates the city," he replied. "And I promise, she doesn't miss me. She's having too much fun rearranging her living room. Again. Take it."

Marisa Monahan hated Manhattan, I remembered. As I accepted the silly gift, which actually did make me smile, I wondered why someone who wanted to hook up with an artsy type, as Trish had said Irwin did, would end up with the girl voted Most Likely to Stay in Massapequa.

We set off to find Trish and Tom, but they were lost in the churning crowds. "Well, I guess I'd better get going," I said, noticing for the first time how sparkling Irwin's dark eyes were. "Oh, come on, Brenda," he said. I was starting to love the sound of that nickname. "At least one whirl on the Ferris wheel? My treat."

We handed in our tickets and boarded the ride. As we lifted up and Little Italy spun before us, I cast a sidelong glance at the tall man at my side, feeling sorry for treating him so badly the first time we'd met. Maybe if I hadn't been in such a horrible mood that day, I would have realized that he was cute. No—more than cute; he was adorable. He had shaved what was left of his hair, which gave him a sort of street-boy look enhanced by his cut-up muscles, but any edge of toughness was offset by his easy laugh, revealing perfect white teeth.

"My turn to treat," I said, not ready to go back and face the windchimes. We made our way toward the Whip.

"Don't be scared," he joked as the bar came down on the quaint old carnival ride, locking the two of us next to each other.

"Are you kidding?" I asked. "I used to ride in the front car of Rolling Thunder at Great Adventure with my hands in the air."

"I love that one! But my real addiction was the Stuntman's Freefall," he said.

"Oh my God, that feeling you get in your stomach when you're looking down the precipice and you know you're going to drop at a million miles an hour?"

"So what other thrills do you love, city girl?" he asked, giving me a look of interest I was shocked to realize I hadn't received in a long time.

Just then, the ride kicked into gear, jerking us back and forth haphazardly before picking up serious speed. We burst out laughing as we were mashed up against each other on one side of our car and then the other. Feeling his body against me, I realized the electricity wasn't only in the ride.

He was holding my arm as I stepped out of the car when I heard my name through the crowd. "Laurel!" said a man's voice. For a second I wondered if Lucien had followed me out of the concert, but when I turned I saw the smiling faces of Trish and Tom.

"Hey, you guys!" I said, as we moved closer to each other.

"So you managed to get away from your boyfriend, Laurel," Trish said.

A look of puzzlement clouded Irwin's features before he said slowly, "Laurel?" Guilty and embarrassed, I realized he now knew I was the girl who had walked out on him at Spiro's Diner so many months before. "So Brenda is actually Laurel," he said.

Confession time. "It was that Impala parked in the driveway. I swear it wasn't you," I said.

"Impala? I went there on my Harley. Anyway, you're looking a hell of a lot better without the helmet hair and ugly suit," he said. "I didn't realize you were so pretty."

His kindness only made me feel worse, and I beat a fast retreat. "I really have to go," I said. It was time to leave the carnival.

Needless to say, Lucien was furious when I showed up at the concert hall holding a two-foot-long pink dinosaur. "*That's* why you had to leave and miss the entire movement on the attack of the giant walrus?" he scolded.

As far as I could see, the fans were still blowing languidly on the same windchimes I had left three hours before. "Oh, woe is me," I said sarcastically.

"Well, I'll try to download the music," he grumbled.

I should have been upset, but for some reason, I was hugging my brontosaurus and smiling from ear to ear.

Later that week, as I finished packing up my apartment, the same silly stuffed animal became a surprising source of angst. It had already bothered Lucien once, and part of me thought it would only be a provocation in our new apartment, but at the same time, for some unexplained reason, I couldn't bear to throw away the bright, cuddly toy.

I sat on a box and stared at the bare walls and found myself feeling utterly, if inexplicably, depressed. Luckily, my torpor was interrupted by a rap on the door.

"It's me, rock star!"

"Vanessa!" It was further evidence of how fine-tuned her nurturing radar was that she'd shown up just in my moment of need.

"I came here to celebrate with you, but my God"—she took in my morose expression—"what's wrong?"

"It's this little animal; I don't know whether to pack it," I began, suddenly starting to cry and continuing incoherently. "The dentist got it for me, and it was kind of sweet, but Lucien hates pink stuffed animals, and now I'm moving in with him, but I don't want to do anything to make him angry, but I want to keep it, and what should I do? I'm so confused..."

With a gentle arm around my shoulder, Vanessa slowed me down until I'd finally explained myself clearly. "Everybody goes through this when they're about to move in with someone," she reassured me. "And if you take a moment to analyze the situation, you'll see that it is not about the dinosaur, it's about your fear of commitment."

"What do you mean?" I sniffed.

"You went out with Lucien, and you had a dull time. And then by chance you met this other person and had some fun.

Now all of a sudden you're having doubts. But wasn't it all fun and games with Lucien in the beginning too? Relationships take work. There are going to be ups and downs, including boring nights now and then. If you're not willing to get through the hard parts, you'll always be thinking that every man who comes around the corner is better than the one you're with."

She was right, I knew. "Yeah, I guess," I said, my choppy breathing returning to normal.

"The real problem, Laurel, is you're afraid you're not sophisticated enough for Lucien, so you're tempted to sabotage this relationship. But I'm here to tell you that even though you come from a mediocre background, you're easily his equal. Okay, honey?"

I was clutching the dinosaur, still feeling uneasy, but I couldn't deny her logic. "So do I throw this away?" I asked.

"No, keep it," she counseled warmly. "Just hide it under the bed."

Jessica Fifi

14

After I'd worked my way through three pages out of Nona's forty-five-page list, I got called in by the legal department at Gallant Publishing to initial two lines I had missed while signing my contract.

I penned "LL" on the two blank spots of the document, which was thicker than a computer user's manual and much more complicated. Only after I'd left the legal department and taken the elevator three floors down did I realize that I hadn't a clue as to what any of it meant. What were the terms of the fabulous advance I was receiving? Before I started spending, I felt I should know.

I raised the subject at my twelve o'clock meeting with the publicists. "Let's say this book doesn't sell," I began. "Do I still get to keep the advance?"

"That's not going to be your problem," one of them laughed. "Look at the venues we've penciled you in for." She proudly handed me a long list.

"Hardball, PBS Newshour, Rachel Maddow, Meet the Press?" Those were all dull news shows. "What happened to Oprah and Today?" I asked.

"Remember, we're positioning *Napoleon's Hairdresser* as an allegory. It's going to sell big, big, big among the news junkies," said the husky-voiced woman.

"All you have to do," added the man, "is go on television and explain how your core thesis illuminates the power politics driving today's clash of civilizations."

Oh, is that all? I thought, mentally canceling the shopping spree I had planned and dying inside at the thought of embarrassing myself on national television.

Thanks to Vanessa's words of wisdom, all the tension between Lucien and I had dissipated, and we focused on the task of moving. The day the truck pulled up to his apartment and I watched my stuff being transferred inside, I felt giddy with the change all around. We were combining all of our worldly possessions. Never again would I be a single girl all alone in the big city.

Lucien seemed happy, too, and ordered us a celebratory takeout meal of Albanian food to go with a bottle of Patagonian chardonnay he'd been saving for a special occasion.

"To us," he said, clinking his glass against mine. "This is only the beginning."

After taking a sip of the dry wine, I encouraged him to say more. "The beginning of what?" I asked, hoping he would say "a long life together."

"Well, you know, someday you'll probably be Mrs. Lucien Brosseau."

It was as near as he'd ever come to a proposal, and I kissed him rapturously. "Laurel Brosseau," I said, trying the sound of it and picturing our wedding invitations. I had long imagined my name in print, but on a book jacket, not on an embossed card. "Except on *Napoleon's Hairdresser* it's going to be Laurel Linden, so I guess I'll keep that as my pen name."

"Laurel Linden? Why would you want to keep that?"

"What's wrong with it?"

"It's so pedestrian."

With its jaunty alliteration and dual syllable groups, I'd always loved my name. "Lots of people like it," I said defensively.

"Yeah, people from Long Island," he answered with

derision. "But trust me, you'll get much farther in life as a Brosseau."

I felt myself stiffen and move away from him. "What makes you think that?" I asked.

"Oh, come on. Admit it, Laurel," he said. "Before you hooked up with me you were a dog-walker who thought you were an intellectual because you read the *New York Review of Books*." Seeing the anger in my eyes, he added gently, "You've come so far since then, but you're not finished yet."

Fuck you, I thought, finally fed up with his condescension. What did he even like about me except the fact that I made him feel superior? I couldn't remember a single time he'd asked me about my life, my family, my novel, or anything that didn't directly relate to him. "Not finished with what?" I seethed through clenched teeth.

"Let's face it, Laurel—you have a long way to go."

I thought about that long way and pictured a lifetime of boring lectures, melody-free concerts, plays with no dialogue, and all other manner of cultural hell. Until the day Lucien let me take him to a Drake show, he'd know more about the music than me. And since that day would never come, the future was clear: I'd always be the subordinate.

This relationship is never going to be equal, I finally admitted to myself. And if I ever did attain Lucien's level of sophistication— as if anyone ever could—he would drop me for the next Eliza Doolittle who would hang onto his every word.

I looked around the apartment, everything blurring through a layer of tears. Boxes full of my clothes and other possessions were piled high in the living room. Even after throwing away half of my stuff at Lucien's insistence, I realized there was no room for what I'd brought. Although there was plenty of physical space, my aesthetically correct boyfriend would never abide a hippo toothbrush holder, my pair of fuzzy beagle slippers, or even old pictures of me as a kid.

Sure, I'd left Long Island and all of its track meets, Dairy Queens, and drinking contests behind, but the images of me growing up in that world had always made my city apartments feel like home. Lucien's walls, with their Norse masks and Quebecois tapestries, looked like they would sooner crumble than have to bear a framed snapshot of me and Trish at graduation.

Glancing down at the meat and potatoes coagulating in their aluminum tray, I knew there was no choice: I had to get out.

"Sorry, Lucien," I said, the words choking in my throat. "I'm leaving."

"You're taking a walk in the middle of dinner?"

"You don't understand," I said, feeling strangely calm. "I'm leaving you. It's over."

The steadiness in my voice seemed to set him off. "What is this, your idea of a joke?" he sneered, starting to rub the supposed arthritis in his fingers.

"I'm totally serious. This is not working for me."

"Fine, go have your fit. I'll be unpacking these boxes, and when the tantrum's over, you can help me clean up."

I seized Lucien's patronizing tone for myself. "I know you like to think that you are so much wiser and more mature than me, but if you were such a sage, you'd realize I'm not being childish, I'm being practical. This relationship sucks. And I don't need you to be a glamorous and sophisticated person. I'm pretty happy on my own. You can keep your fancy French last name. And those hideous gargoyle bookends—they're all yours."

"Isn't that just like you, Laurel, to make a big mess and then walk out."

"It's better than staying in something that's not worth cleaning up."

Down on the street, I stood paralyzed for a moment amid the cacophony of Tribeca's evening rush hour. I was ready to head home when I realized I had no home. Knowing that they'd named the New York Minute after the amount of time it takes to lose a rent-controlled apartment, I desperately pounded my landlord's number into my cell phone. Sure enough, when I finally reached him, my request to renew the lease was met with hearty laughter.

"You've got a good sense of humor, don'tcha. We've already started gutting the place," he said. "After major capital improvements, I'll finally be able to raise the rent and make some money off of it."

That stupid crumbling apartment, with its erratic electricity and weak water pressure, never seemed so dear. But it was gone.

What am I going to do? I wondered desperately. Half of my stuff had been junked, and the other half was in the apartment of someone I never wanted to see again. There was Vanessa, but having never even been invited to her place, how could I ask to stay there? Danny Z. was a sweetheart, but he already had four roommates. The Danilovas were away, maybe I could just go to their place for a little while—no, I'd given back the key when I quit.

Feeling helpless, I slumped against a lamppost and tried to cry, but the end of my big romance with Lucien suddenly seemed so inevitable and so right that the scariest part was that I didn't feel any sadness at all. Just lost and alone.

Well, it's gotten to this point, I thought miserably. *I've ruined my life.* My head was up in the clouds, and, once again, I didn't realize what was happening until it was too late. As usual, I mixed up fantasy and reality. My mother always told me that the longer you spend dreaming, the less you'll have to show for it. I'd thrown away my youth, and now I was ending up just like my cousin Mindy: single and living with my parents.

I grabbed my cell phone once more and hit the first number I'd ever memorized. "Hello, Daddy?"

After the moving van came back and took all of my belongings out to my parents' garage in Massapequa, I wandered in a daze to meet Vanessa at her apartment building. Just hearing her voice when I'd called was like finding a raft to cling to on a stormy sea, and I knew a good cry on her firm shoulder would give me the confidence to go on. *Maybe she'll even invite me to stay with her until I can find a new place,* I thought. We could be roomies like two Vassar girls, sharing conditioner and making coffee for each other. We could stream stupid movies and talk late into the night—something I'd never been able to do with Lucien. As I sat watching the water flow around the marble fountain in her lobby, I realized that the feelings of admiration I had for Vanessa were much more intense than any I'd ever had for the man I'd just escaped a life with.

That afternoon, we never even made it to one of her coffee shops. Vanessa put her arm around me right there in the lobby and sat for as long as it took for me to regain my equilibrium. She explained how sometimes we have to take a step backwards before moving forward, how our inner child acts out from time to time and that's a good thing, and how we can definitely use each of our setbacks as steppingstones. It was advice that I would cling to for dear life in the weeks to come.

The photos I'd rescued from Lucien's apartment had been a security blanket when I lived in the city, but the sight of them in my old room on Long Island was depressing. I couldn't believe I had landed on my ass back in the land of chain stores, strip malls, and parking nightmares. Sitting on my canopy bed, surrounded by dolls that I'd never had the heart to throw out, I was staring dumbly at a framed copy of my *Seventeen Magazine* story when my mother walked in.

"What do you want for dinner: pot roast or Cornish hens?" she asked.

"I don't care," I replied languidly. Seeing I was upset, she sat down next to me.

"Oh, Mom, I'm so sorry I had to barge in on you guys like this," I said. "I guess you were right; my head was in the clouds, and now I'm paying for it."

My mother, who lived on the I-told-you-so, was sweetly comforting. "You're not barging in on us! We're so glad to have our little second daughter back home."

"But you must be more worried about me than ever," I said glumly.

"Laurel, darling, it's just the opposite. You've really proven to us that you are a great writer with a great future. I must admit we had our doubts along the way, but if Gallant Publishing is betting on you, who are we to second-guess? Just don't forget us when you're a world-famous author."

That would have been my chance to say, "I told you so," but somehow, I wasn't in the mood.

Over the next few days, I began feeling like my butt had worn its own special groove in my seat at the library, which I could now only reach by commuter train. For every page of Nona's corrections I managed to complete, I allowed myself one article on a junky style website. My mind would switch from the dreary world of coalitions, naval strategy, and exiles to the much more attractive Hollywood party scene. Out with petticoats and ugly empire-waist dresses, in with rhinestone thongs and couture evening gowns. I was probably the only scholar in that hallowed hall sneaking peeks at the *People* app, but who cared?

By Friday, I had a break. Anderson had invited Nona and I to lunch. The ESPN Zone in Times Square was packed with tourists and filled with monitors broadcasting different sports events, so we could hardly hear each other speak, but we managed to shout our way through a conversation.

"You've gotta try the Zone cheesesteak," Anderson said, reading from the menu. "'Beef sautéed with onions, peppers, and mozzarella on a toasted hoagie roll.' That's what I call class."

I ordered the grilled chicken Caesar, and Nona went for the ESPN burger. She conveyed an air of business with her trademark red pen and pad, but Anderson couldn't stop talking about sports. "Oooh, a line drive into left field, and he's SAFE!" he said, calling the plays. "Amazing."

Nona pushed her owl glasses up the bridge of her nose. "Mr. Gallant," she said gently, "don't forget your 3:30."

"Oh, right, golf lesson," he said with a smile, swinging an imaginary club. To focus his attention, Nona pointed her red pen toward me.

"Career strategy?" she prompted.

"Of course, of course," he said, turning to me. "I didn't just bring you to this fantastic restaurant so you could enjoy the great food and incredible sports action. I want to do some long-term planning."

"Sounds good," I said, grateful that somebody was looking out for my future.

"Have you given any thought to your next book?" he asked. "Because I have. Nona, where's that list I gave you?"

"It was covered with chocolate syrup, sir, so I typed it over. However, I do have some concerns—"

"Oh, Nona, you're always so negative," he said, turning to me. "My nickname for her is No-No Nona. But she did agree that once we carve out a marketing niche for you, there's no end to the bestsellers you can produce. Look at Nigel Fensington— he cornered the market on fictitious alternative gay histories. Twenty-six bestselling novels, from *Mein Queer Kampf* to *Bin Laden's Boy Toy*. You know the series?"

I remembered the big hubbub when *Queen Kong* came out, but considering it was a fictionalized version of a sci-fi movie, I couldn't see the appeal. Who would want to read about a giant gorilla hanging from the Empire State Building while waxing his bikini line?

"Do those books really sell?" I asked.

"Are you kidding? Nona, show her the figures." She handed me a chart depicting how millions of people were fascinated by the new hybrid genre. "Everybody's reading 'em: conspiracy theorists, Washington insiders, rom-com fanatics."

"Remarkable," I said, wondering what all that had to do with me. "So what you're saying is…?"

"You—and I, of course—can have a lifetime of guaranteed success with this series."

"Series?" I asked, starting to feel as scattered as the nacho chips falling on Anderson's lap.

"Laurel Linden: Chronicler of History's Greatest Hired Help," he declared. Nona handed me the list:

Nero's Fiddle Teacher

Gandhi's Seamstress
Nixon's Nanny
Saddam's Personal Shopper

Suddenly, before me flashed a future spent digging through the Watergate tapes and analyzing the Butcher of Baghdad's wardrobe. Ugh! Those titles were a far cry from the second book I'd been planning during my daydreaming sessions at the library. Now that I realized how boring it was being a New York intellectual, thanks in no small part to Lucien, my horizons were broadening.

"I was thinking of something more along the lines of a caper about an A-list movie actress who has multiple homes, multiple personalities, and multiple orgasms," I suggested. "Surely that will sell."

"Sir," Nona said to Anderson, and I thought I detected a glimmer of humanity behind those glasses, "while your ideas are certainly . . . intriguing, I believe Laurel is better suited to illustrating the more superficial aspects of popular culture."

Nona had been looking down at me from her high plane of literary excellence for weeks, but for once her snobbery was welcome. I almost wanted to kiss her, but Anderson was adamant.

"Still trying to replace me, aren't you Nona?" he mumbled under his breath. "Come on," he declared loudly to both of us. "The personal assistant tell-all series is a sure success! Everyone knows how hard it is to get good hired help."

How about *Anderson Gallant's Dog-Walker*, I thought sardonically. The epic tale of a downtrodden young girl who cons a lame-brained publishing scion into buying her book. Only problem was, I didn't know the ending.

15

I'd managed to avoid Jenna for the first two weeks I lived at home, but one Sunday afternoon she showed up with Rob and the kids. The minute she entered the Spanish-tiled foyer with its smoked-glass mirrors, I braced myself. No doubt she'd taken my sudden state of homelessness as proof of her longstanding theories about how Laurel is unable to manage her own life.

We hadn't talked since I'd walked out on her at the Rainbow Room, and sure enough Jenna was scowling when she entered the living room, but I soon realized her anger wasn't directed toward me.

"Ooh, Robert Hailey Junior, if you so much as tap your sister one more time, then you can say goodbye to Spiderman for a week," she screamed, disengaging Bobby Jr.'s little fingers from the toddler's hair.

"Whoa," Jenna's husband complained, "punish him; don't punish me."

"You? You are just going to have to use your imagination and find something else to play with," she huffed. With that, Robert Sr. conveniently disappeared into the den to watch the Yankees game with my father.

I was ready to make an exit too, but as I turned to leave, my mother grabbed my arm. "I made sandwiches, and I cut the crusts off just how you liked when you were kids. Come on out to the patio." It could hardly be worse than spending another afternoon on the canopy bed facing my framed *Seventeen Magazine* story, so I relented.

"Grandma, did you make peanut butter and jelly?" Bobby Jr. asked.

"Actually, today we're having something new," Mom said.

"Yuck," he pronounced.

"Why don't you let Grandma tell you what she made before you decide you don't like it?" Jenna demanded, heaving Emily out of her stroller with an exhausted grunt. Bobby Jr. looked at my mother expectantly.

"Egg salad sandwiches!" she announced.

"I HATE SALAD!" he screamed.

"This kid refuses to eat anything green," Jenna lamented as Emily started crying for no apparent reason. "Bobby, egg salad is just called salad," she said, stuffing a pacifier into her daughter's mouth. "There's no lettuce in it."

"Nooooo, I won't eat it," he declared, stomping his feet.

Mom looked crestfallen. "I have some ice cream in the freezer," she suggested.

"Mom!" Jenna exploded. "He can't have ice cream instead of sandwiches. Don't you even have a clue about nutrition?" My mother looked down sheepishly.

Later out back, Jenna's efforts to relax on a lounge chair proved fruitless. First, Emily kept wanting to go "Up-u." A sandwich triangle kept her busy for a while, but once she'd eaten half and spread the rest all over her hands, she jumped back on Jenna.

"Emily, can't I have one shirt that you don't ruin?" my sister asked, furiously wiping the yellow stains from her midriff-bearing top. Emily started screaming as though she'd been disowned, so Jenna picked her up. "Pumpkin, I'm sorry," she cooed, "but sometimes mommies don't want to wear their little babies' lunches!"

Sensing that his mother's attention had shifted to his little sister, Bobby Jr. jumped on her lap as well. "Oof," she cried. "That's my liver!"

Something was haunting me as I watched the scene, and I realized what it was when Jenna uttered a preemptory "Both of you off, because I can see where this is heading: Somebody's going to get hurt." That was basically her warning to me at lunch, I realized. At the time, I'd dismissed her as bossy and jealous, but in hindsight, I wondered if she hadn't been at least a little right.

Ever since Anderson Gallant had handed me that list of next projects, I'd felt burdened. The struggle to succeed had been replaced by the pressure to maintain success.

Looking at my sister, with her blonde extensions, I remembered when the lightness in her hair was natural and she'd just won that silver medal. I had been astonished that after all the attention she'd received for her gymnastics accomplishments, we had to pay even more attention to console her. *What a phony,* I had thought at the time, *she's lovin' it.* But now, I realized her angst had been genuine.

Having stood up, Jenna was caught with one child hugging each leg. "Am I allowed to pee around here?" When neither of them moved, she turned to me. "How about helping me out?" she asked with exasperation.

I wasn't used to seeing Jenna struggle; usually the au pair was around smoothing out the edges. But with my sister in less-than-perfect mode, I felt sympathetic.

"Hey, you two!" I called to the kids with all the enthusiasm of a carnival barker. "Who wants to come with me to the playground? Last one there is a rotten egg." As I ran out the door with her two children following me, I thought I might have glimpsed a grateful smile on Jenna's lips.

Nona peered at me through her owl glasses as I finished reading the edited version of my first three chapters.

"Better, don't you think?" she asked from behind her messy desk.

I was aghast. Who had written this? All of my imaginative—

if anachronistic—touches had been replaced with historically accurate facts. What had been a colorful fantasy of the past was now a deadweight documentary, part-battle narrative, part-Wikipedia entry, full disaster.

"I'm not sure this is so improved," I said tentatively.

Nona took a deep breath. "It's natural for a first-time author to think that everything they've written is perfect just the way it is, but even the best of them need editing," she said, with a studied patience.

"Yeah, but you're turning *Napoleon's Hairdresser* into a completely different book," I protested.

"Now, now, Ms. Linden," she began in a singsong voice reminiscent of a nursery schoolteacher, "your original manuscript was very, very—how shall I say?—original."

I was glaring at her by that point. She was obviously suppressing her real feelings.

"Rarely in my career have I seen such an original work," she continued. The tone of her voice sounded familiar. "In fact, after twenty-eight years in publishing, I can honestly say you are unique."

Then I recognized it; it was the voice she used when talking to Anderson. The I'm-the-expert-you're-the-boss's-son patronizing lullaby. She thought I was as stupid as Anderson! And why not? I had conned everybody but her.

With a word, I could have Nona fired, I realized. I'm the talent around here, not her, and Anderson, at least, believed in me. But he was an airhead! And she was clearly a seasoned professional with a true eye for literature. Suddenly bashful, I glanced around to make sure no one was in earshot before asking the question that had been brewing in my heart the last few weeks. "Is my book going to bomb?"

"Oh, dear darling, let's not think of these things, let's just take it page by page," she said in her Sesame Street tone.

"Nona," I whispered urgently, "please don't bullshit me. What do you honestly think of *Napoleon's Hairdresser*?" I had grabbed her hand in my desperation.

Pulling it away, she replied simply, "What I think doesn't

matter. Anderson Gallant loves your work, and I'm here to support him."

"Anderson Gallant knows more about SpongeBob than literature," I said, prompting a rare Nona smile. "Give it to me straight," I demanded, locking my gaze with hers.

Suddenly, Nona looked like it was her birthday, Christmas, and the Fourth of July combined. "Well, honestly?" I stared at her by way of affirmation. "Okay, then. Where to begin? Your book lacks any central thesis. Not a single character has an arc—do you know what that is? It means a personal journey, development, a gripping transformation unfolding before the reader. Your characters start at point A and live there. For seven hundred pages. In terms of plot, there is none, only a loosely connected series of anecdotes utterly lacking in plateaus or crescendos. How anyone can write about the great battles of Europe without conflict is beyond me. Massive armies were facing off in wars that would rewrite the map, and the only fear you convey relates to the shortage of styling mousse. But I must say, you are at your worst when you attempt philosophical reflection."

"Should I go on?" she asked cheerfully.

"How much worse could it get?" I said, feeling a strange sense of freedom.

Nona didn't answer. She just pulled out a passage from my book.

```
With Moscow finally
conquered, the Great General
entered on his white horse,
expecting to receive the keys
to the city. Alas, the streets
were empty—all the Russians had
fled. Watching Napoleon's brow
furrow—and making a mental note
to tweeze his eyebrows—
Marguerite reflected on it all.
```

159

"Do you remember your heroine's insight here?" I didn't answer, so she went on:

```
Joining the ranks of the
world's great conquerors is as
difficult as tackling a bad
case of split ends, Marguerite
mused bitterly. And no matter
how much you try to cut or
condition it, victory remains
limp and lifeless without the
final rinse.
```

"Need I read on?" Nona asked.

I shook my head. "So basically, I'm the worst writer you've ever had to work with?"

"Don't flatter yourself," she said, half closing her eyes and squinting at me. "I'm Anderson Gallant's assistant, remember. Besides, your writing does have redeeming qualities, albeit insufficient to meet your ambitions. The character depictions actually have insight and flare, and your sentences are short and pithy. When you are not trying to probe beneath the surface, you can be quite engaging."

I perked up. Coming from someone like Nona, I knew that was a major compliment, but what she said next floored me.

"Unfortunately, you are unable to sustain that quality writing for more than a page or two, and given your other flaws, I'd have to conclude that you have no future as a serious novelist."

"Can you at least rescue *Napoleon's Hairdresser*?" I asked, gripping my chair for support.

"Frankly, no. Let me put it this way: Mr. Gallant won't read the reviews. I suggest you don't either."

After leaving Nona's office, I felt like I was lost on the ocean.

The beautiful ship I'd spent my adult life building was filled with leaks, and I was sinking fast. I had to reach for my lifeline.

"Vanessa?" I texted quickly. "Please call me. Are you home? I really need some advice. Actually, I need a hug. Badly."

I took the elevator down and stumbled out into the crowds on Broadway. The streets were packed with office workers trying to get home and theatergoers trying to find a good restaurant. The giant flashing billboards cast crazy lights on the pavement below, and I wandered aimlessly through the mayhem.

My worst fears had been confirmed: My writing was disastrous, and my book was going to bomb. First, I'd be laughed out of town by the critics, then I'd be skewered on the talk shows. My face would be right up there on the jumbotron, with all of Times Square stopping to laugh at me. Sales would be limited to my family and compassionate friends. Thousands of unsold copies would be remaindered, and I'd have to return the advance. My stunning debut would also be my finale.

I cried all the way to Penn Station, just another ignored lunatic on the street.

But when I got back to Massapequa, I found that the person who mattered most *was* paying attention. "You just missed your friend Vanessa," my mother said.

"She called?" I asked, feeling happy.

"No, she was here."

My sister had emerged from the kitchen and was listening with what I recognized to be malicious curiosity. "Quite a woman," Jenna said.

Although her tone was sarcastic, she had spoken the truth. Vanessa had stopped whatever she was in the middle of to rush to my side. I was yet again overwhelmed with gratitude and admiration for her generous spirit.

"When did she leave?" I asked, regretting that I had spent an hour at the Penn Station café with my favorite sedative, *Celebrity Style*.

"She took a cab about ten minutes ago, but she left a surprise for you upstairs," Mom said.

When I opened the door, I hardly recognized my old bedroom. Vanessa had replaced the teenaged-style trimmings—the heart-shaped mirror, the gunked-up makeup kit, the tacky cheerleading trophies—with cool urban accessories. A jasmine-scented candle was burning calmly next to a new blush palette and lipstick selection from MAC. The old bubblegum pink bedspread had been replaced with an elegant Ralph Lauren comforter. In a final touch, she'd put a framed picture of the two of us at the Four Seasons on the night table.

In my vulnerable state, I felt that the room looked like someone else's, and it did—it belonged to the incredible person Vanessa believed I could become. Part of me hoped she hadn't thrown away the trophies, but the rest knew that it was all for the best.

"Your stuff is in a box in the basement," Jenna said. She'd snuck up behind me.

"Oh, I don't care about that," I replied. My mother had joined my sister at the entrance to my room.

"Can you believe how beautiful it looks?" I asked them.

"I will say, this woman has taste, and she's very nice to have bought this for you," said Mom, "but we liked having your old room; it was a reminder of when you lived with us."

"She's more than nice—she's incredible! Who else would come all the way out here just to show she cares?" I marveled.

"So this is that woman from Vassar you told me about?" Mom asked.

"Right," I replied. "My big sister."

Jenna snorted. "Oh, really? What's in it for her?"

I seethed at the implication that Vanessa was anything but altruistic. "For your information, Jenna, there are people in this world who are genuinely compassionate."

My sister picked up the framed photo of Vanessa and me. "And genuinely into themselves," she goaded.

"Vanessa never asks for anything in return," I said, grabbing the photo and putting it back on the nightstand. "This is a picture of my congratulatory lunch with her," I huffed. "It was a joyful, fun occasion, just like all of my times with her."

"Are you telling me you never once had a fight?"

"Of course not."

"Ha! Then how could she possibly be your big sister?"

16

Back in the New York Public Library, I felt as if I was hard at work building my own execution gallows. Every page I revised was another plank in the edifice I'd hang from. Nona and I were the only ones who knew the terrible truth: My book was going to drop like lead and take me down with it.

Blissfully unaware of the looming disaster, my mother had begun preparations for an elaborate party. "Cookie, remember how you cried when you never had a Sweet Sixteen at Leonard's like all the other girls? Well, now we're making it up to you." Recalling her satisfied grin, I cringed. Leonard's? I pictured half of Massapequa all dolled up in their party outfits, pouring into the banquet hall and taking their seats—for the funeral of my career.

But that wouldn't even be the ugliest part, I realized. Nona had made it clear that I had no future as a writer. No future as a writer—the only profession I'd ever dreamed of. Since I could hold a pencil I'd been keeping journals, scribbling poems, and planning stories in my mind. Now what? Who would I be if I wasn't a writer? No more leisurely musing on my next plot twist. No more dreams of gaining fame and fortune through my craft. No more long dances with a turn of phrase. No more seeing my name in print. No more camaraderie among fellow writers.

Not that they'd always been that friendly, I thought, remembering Portia and the other competitors so eager to cut me down. And I wouldn't miss the harsh red pen of a professional editor, that's for sure. No more tedious research in this stuffy library. Plus, after *Napoleon's Hairdresser* died, it would the end of Laurel Linden: Chronicler of History's Greatest Hired Help.

What a relief.

As miserable as it was going to be to fail, at least I could get out of the rat race and find out what I was really good at.

Back home in the kitchen, my mother emptied a bag of frozen carrots into a pot of boiling water. "I'd loved to, but I can't on Monday afternoon, Jenna," she said into the phone. "I have aromatherapy."

Obviously my sister was trying to worm Mom into taking over some task the au pair had bagged out of.

"I know it's hard to get the kids a dentist appointment," she continued, adding frozen peas to the mix. "Yes, I know Dr. Turnov is the only one who makes them laugh instead of cry." She plopped in a dollop of butter.

Irwin.

I had buried all thoughts of him since that night in Little Italy, but I'd put that pink dinosaur on my dresser, and whenever I looked at it I smiled. "I can take them, Mom," I heard myself saying.

"Oh, honey, you're too busy with your book," she objected.

"I'll make the time."

While driving Jenna's Dodge Caravan to Irwin's office, I developed a splitting headache from being the unwitting judge in the who-can-shout-louder contest between Bobby Jr. and Emily. His voice was deeper and stronger, but wow could that little girl wail, and at an earsplitting pitch.

"Bobby Jr., you are so good at so many things, but your sister is a more annoying screamer," I said, thinking this was a compliment.

"No, I won! I won!" he shouted, straining against the straps in his car seat and bursting into tears. Emily knew enough to join in.

I handed her a headless Barbie that was on the dashboard and him a ball, which kept them quiet until their respective toys fell to the floor, at which point I had to twist around to retrieve them, all the while keeping my eyes on three lanes of traffic. I had always thought the au pair did all the work, but even if she left two percent for Jenna, that little bit could make a person crazy, I realized.

Wedged between a Walgreens and Paco's Tacos, Irwin's office was a sterile-looking storefront with hospital-white venetian blinds, but as I opened the door, I entered a completely unexpected world. A colorful jungle gym took up most of the waiting room, which was decorated with huge blow-up figures of anime characters. One whole wall was covered with a sheet of paper that the kids could draw on using any of the many markers and crayons in jars. Obviously, the paper was changed daily, but that afternoon's scrawlings included a picture of a friendly, if three-armed, doctor surrounded by hearts.

Almost instantly, Jenna's kids went from being sulky brats to playful cherubs. Emily found a blue plastic ball twice the size of her little body that she began to push across the floor. Bobby was having an imaginary conversation with Superman while hanging upside-down from the jungle gym.

After a blissfully calm few minutes, we were ushered into the examination room. Irwin looked far less cool than he had in his baggy jeans and backwards baseball cap. His muscles were hidden under a white dentist's smock, and the antiseptic smell of mint mouthwash hung in the air, but his warm greeting almost made up for the cold equipment and harsh fluorescent light.

"Laurel Linden. Who knew you were connected to Superman's special assistant"—he winked at Bobby Jr.—"and the prettiest princess in town?" He gave Emily a smile.

"Jenna Berliner's my sister," I said. "And these two are . . . quite a handful."

"Oh, we'll manage," he said, but the moment he put Bobby

Jr. in the chair and started rolling on his plastic gloves, the screaming exploded all over again. Emily was reaching for some pretty dangerous-looking tools on the counter, and I was imagining having to explain to my sister that her daughter had poked her own eye out when Bobby Jr. stood up on the chair and said, "It's a bird, it's a plane, it's—" but before he could finish and take a flying leap onto the floor, the room went dark, and we were all stunned into silence.

"Ooooooooohhhhhhh," Irwin said theatrically, "the tooth fairy's coming… She's going to light the room with her special powers…"

Scared and excited, Bobby sat down obediently, and Emma allowed me to strap her into the stroller. I didn't know exactly what Irwin was up to, but whatever it was, it worked. He flipped a switch, and a black light came on. Sure enough, all of the white surfaces glowed magically.

Next, he held a clattering set of glowing teeth and pretended it was talking to the kids. "Hello, children, I'm the tooth fairy's mouth," he said in a high-pitched cartoon voice. We all burst out laughing. "I have something special for the little boy that sits nicely today while Dr. Turnov checks his teeth. And it's not a boring toothbrush," he added.

"It's dental floss!" Bobby Jr. challenged.

"It's not dental floss either," the teeth chattered. "But to find out what it is, everyone has to sit quietly." The two children were perfectly obedient.

Before turning on the light, Irwin started attacking me with the teeth. "I may be at work, but I'd sure like to eat up your auntie," he said in that ridiculous voice, moving the contraption to my neck and making it kiss me all over. It was insane and hilarious and bizarrely cute.

The rest of the appointment went like that—Irwin making jokes, half to the kids and half to me. "Hey, did you swallow a television?" he asked Bobby Jr., prompting uncontrollable laughter. "I'm watching TV in your mouth!"

I was laughing too. "Oh, no! It's another ad for adult diapers! Turn it off!" he screamed in mock horror.

"Diapers," Emily echoed, looking pleased.

When Irwin lifted Bobby Jr. out of the chair and swung him around, I couldn't help but think that this guy would make one incredible father, and it struck me as deeply sexy. At the same time, I flashed on a memory of Lucien and I on our way to see Shakespeare in the Park. When he got struck by a wayward softball, instead of tossing it back to the expectant kid, Lucien ignored it while muttering to me, "There should be a law against people under ten."

"Don't forget your present from the tooth fairy," Irwin said, handing Bobby Jr. a black T-shirt. It featured a big white tooth and the slogan "BITE ME." Irwin turned off the light again, and the T-shirt glowed in the dark. "Wow," my nephew said in awe as the lights came back on. Emily, too, was thrilled with her Day-Glo socks.

As we stepped out into the reception area, Irwin removed his clinical jacket, revealing a sleeveless Knicks T-shirt, and of course his sculpted biceps. A jolt of excitement sent my skin tingling. Was he showing off just for me? As I watched him affectionately give Emily a high-five, it hit me: I was totally turned on by Irwin Turnov.

Knowing that dental appointments are six months apart, my mind raced for a way to see him again, but the opportunity came all on its own—only not in the way I'd hoped.

"It's Marisa; she says it's important." The receptionist handed Irwin the phone.

Oh. Marisa. Shit.

"Hey, there," he said, adding after a pause, "Oh, I don't know, whatever you like." He shot me an apologetic look, but it didn't ease my frustration. I'd blown my chance to go out with this guy months ago, and now he was in the clutches of the Massapequa Marriage Maniac.

"Calla lilies or tiger lilies? Either one is fine with me," he said. Then his tone rose. "Of course I care, but I just don't know that much about flowers; could you please just pick it? I trust your taste completely." After another pause, he added gently, "I'm going to make it the most memorable day of your life, I

169

promise, but I have patients here, and I have to go, OK babe?"

Marisa was his babe. My ears burned with shame for even thinking Irwin would want to go out with me. And he didn't, but he did want a favor. "Sorry about that. My girlfriend's having this huge thirtieth birthday bash, and she's acting a little crazy," he explained. "I want to get her a great present, but I'm afraid she hates my taste."

"Hey, you can never go wrong with the jewelry at Axasonic Fashions in Soho," I said, hating myself for being so nice. I should have suggested a head of lettuce.

"I love Soho! Hey, city girl, how about you come along and help me pick something out? Or would that be too boring for you?"

I almost said, "Wear another sleeveless shirt, and I'll never be bored," but instead I just gave him my cell number so we could make a plan.

It was a bad week. The editing process made my book worse, and my mother's growing invitation list made my party bigger. I tried to talk her out of the whole affair, but she had already told everybody about my great success, and the celebration at Leonard's would be her chance to bask in my glory. If only she knew.

I was contemplating running away to India to become a software engineer when the phone rang. It was Irwin.

Three days later, instead of New Delhi, I found myself in front of a New York deli on the corner of Broome and West Broadway. It was raining, and the streets were slick and shiny. The air was crisp with possibility. Since I didn't have an umbrella, I waited under an awning watching the wet weather send shoppers scurrying even faster than their usual frenetic pace.

Irwin, wearing a beat-up pair of jeans and a vintage gas station attendant jacket, greeted me with a friendly squeeze on the arm, strictly platonic. But when we walked together, huddled under his umbrella, I felt more than friendship. It might have been that gorgeous mouth; not only were the teeth perfect but his lips were smooth and inviting, and even through our jackets, I could feel his hard body. I was melting under his touch.

"I love this weather," he said. "It makes New York look like a movie set."

He was right. Soho was all light and reflection, old cast-iron buildings housing chic new stores, kinetic movement over solid cobblestones.

We ducked into Axasonic Fashions, but although Irwin loved everything there, he was certain Marisa wouldn't.

"Come on, these rose-gold earrings are totally cool," I said, pointing to a pair of delicate strings that would be perfect with an updo.

Irwin pulled my hair back with two fingers and held one up against my ear. "Gorgeous," he said with a sparkle in his eye that made me blush, "but not Marisa."

The scenario was repeated at the next seven stores we visited. A Stella McCartney scarf, a chunky silver necklace, a sexy little anklet—Irwin and I loved them all, but they were vetoed by the spirit of his girlfriend.

I was starting to think that those two were a less-than-perfect couple when Irwin, staring at the endless array of high-end boutiques that run the course of West Broadway, said with a look of utter defeat, "This is impossible."

"Maybe you just need a break," I suggested hopefully, adding in my mind, *from her.*

Irwin hesitated, but when I told him I had the inside track on an exclusive view of the Hudson River nearby, he was sold. Night was falling, and on the way to the stunning Richard Meier glass tower on West Street, I prayed that either Natan or Ricardo would be on shift. They'd remember me from when I used to walk the Maltese of a minor British royal who lived there.

The bad news when we got there was that neither of my doormen friends were on duty. The good news: There was no doorman at all. It could have been a rotation of shifts, a bathroom break, or maybe a celebrity emergency on one of the upper floors, but whatever, we breezed in like we lived there.

I pressed "Roof deck" on the dusted bronze panel of the silent elevator. Irwin and I were giggling like two trespassing teenagers, delighted at the stolen luxury.

The roof deck was ultra-modern, with an illuminated swimming pool surrounded by gorgeous, plush chairs—no Lounge-Arounds in sight. Now that the rain had stopped, the fog was beginning to lift over the harbor. Far in the distance, the Verrazano bridge, studded with white lights, stretched across the sky's velvet background. In the middle of the silvery bay stood the Statue of Liberty, making us feel like we'd just stepped into a postcard.

"Wow," Irwin said. The soft light of a half-moon glowed behind him, and I studied his straight nose, kissable lips, and eyes that shone like onyx. Throwing my shoulders back, I ran my fingers through my hair and hoped the moonlight was being kind to me too. It somehow felt like a momentous occasion. Or at least, the perfect setting for a first kiss.

The reflection from the pool caught my eye, and I turned to face the aquamarine rectangle.

"Should we go for a dip?" he challenged. I blushed again. Why was he always making me blush? Mental note: good sign.

"Don't dare me, or I'll do it," I said, feeling wet already.

"I bet you would," he said, looking sly.

Actually, I wouldn't risk getting caught, so I changed the subject. "The gym is incredible, too," I said, "You would love it." I figured he had to be one of those guys clocking regular hours on the Smith machine, but he didn't seem that impressed.

"Yeah, I guess it's convenient," he replied. "But I'd rather get my workout outside."

"What do you mean?" I asked. "Like an outdoor weight room?"

Irwin laughed. "No, like a messy-as-hell football scrimmage, or a black-diamond slope, or a wild ride down the Colorado rapids."

I pictured him sweaty and pumped from an exhilarating sport. "Whitewater rafting?" I asked. "I've always wanted to try that."

"Oh, you have to come someday! It's what rollercoasters were invented to imitate," he said. "If you like Rolling Thunder, you're going to lose your mind over this rush."

"God, I'm excited already," I said, definitely thinking about riding something other than a river.

He turned to me, sighed sweetly, and put a hand on my shoulder. *Is this the beginning of our wild ride?* I wondered with keyed-up anticipation.

Instead of kissing me, though, he looked out at the cityscape. "So can you see your apartment from here?" he asked.

"Oh, I'm kind of between places," I replied, not wanting to confess the whole living-with-my-parents disaster just yet.

"Why don't you move in here?" he joked.

"Nice view, but it's totally not my style. What do you think?"

"I've always wanted to live in Manhattan but not on the edge of the city."

"I know what you mean. I'd rather be right in the middle of the action any day," I agreed.

"Right," he said, "on one of those eclectic blocks with everything from a raunchy gay bar to a fancy French restaurant."

"And a twenty-four-hour pizza place in case the mood hits at three a.m.," I added. "So why don't you start shopping?"

Irwin looked perplexed, and his hand fell from my shoulder. "I always imagined I'd move to the city first chance I got," he said, looking out at the Statute of Liberty holding her torch aloft. "You know, raise my kids in a place where culture means more than the nearest Gap, where they can be exposed to people from all walks of life, where they can learn everything from community to what a real bagel tastes like."

I was floored. My only hesitation about Irwin had been his settled suburban life, but it wasn't an obstacle at all.

"Anyway," he said, looking down momentarily, "I guess life doesn't always work out the way we plan."

"You never know," I said hopefully. "Sometimes your craziest dreams can come true."

Irwin brightened. Looking into my eyes, he said, "Right, you have a book coming out! Trish told me."

"Well, it's not exactly—"

"I bet your boyfriend is really psyched for you," he said.

I wanted to tell him I didn't have a boyfriend. I wanted to tell him to shut up and kiss me already. I wanted to just kiss him, but at that moment, two security guards entered the private space.

"You guys visiting someone?" one of them asked.

"I came here to see Natan—or do you know Ricardo?" I tried. "They're friends of mine."

The other guard smiled. "You're down with Ricardo and Natan? Okay, cool, but they're not here tonight, so maybe come back another time," he said kindly.

We were still laughing as we burst out into the street and headed for the heart of the West Village. Still high from our stint as pretend bazillionaires, we mused on buying an apartment in each fabulous building we passed. A drizzle started up, and Irwin covered me with his umbrella, and we huddled close, even though there was hardly a need, given the warm, early September weather.

There I was, walking around in my dream neighborhood with a dreamy guy, dreaming about sex, when he suddenly steered me to a shop window. "They're perfect!" he said, pointing to a simple pair of pearl earrings inside. I had completely forgotten why we'd even met that afternoon, and the mention of Marisa's present was a splash of cold water on all my hot fantasies.

"Sure," I said weakly. "Great."

The pearls were ridiculously expensive but totally common. And I was totally smitten but ridiculously deluded.

17

Embracing failure became my new philosophy, though I didn't dare tell Vanessa. She would try to convince me that success was within my power, and I just didn't have the heart to listen to her pep talk. And when it came to the publishing business, No-No Nona was the one in the know. She had made it clear that I was doomed as a writer, so now I could prepare for the worst. Sure, I'd be laughed off all the talk shows, and my name would be synonymous with hackneyed, but hey, at least I'd be alive. And after my fifteen minutes of shame, the public would move on to a new scapegoat, and I could begin anew.

But even as I prepared for failure, the Gallant publishing machine kept planning for my success.

"I'm just so excited the two of you can meet," the chief publicist on my team rasped, introducing me to Nigel Fensington, the alternate gay history wonder boy. "Nigel, you know, will be giving us a quote for your book jacket just as soon as he's read the galleys."

"Why wait?" asked the oily, egg-shaped man. "I'm giving it to you right now."

"Don't you want to read my book first?" I asked.

Instead of answering, Nigel scribbled on the back of a

grease-stained paper bag from which he had removed a grilled Reuben sandwich. "'A stunning tour-de-force, Laurel Linden is surely one of her generation's great new voices.' Will that do?"

"The contract does call for three sentences," the publicist said politely.

"Well, then, make up another two and run them by my assistant, will you?" She nodded obediently and left the room, holding the greasy paper bag gingerly.

"Thank you," I said once we were alone. "I hope it won't reflect badly on you if my book gets panned by the critics."

"Why should I care?" he asked, slurping on his messy sandwich. "The critics have always hated me, but that hasn't stopped me from making a killing in this industry."

What a lucky guy. "How'd you manage that?" I asked. "By carving out your special niche?"

"Ah, that was carved out by advertisers. You think I know anything about gays? I'm not a homosexual. I'm not even a heterosexual. I'm asexual." He took another greedy bite. "Once they set the formula, I was set for life." He finished the soggy bread and started in on some French fries.

"But I guess without critical acclaim, you can't get on any of the talk shows," I said, thinking there might be hope for me yet.

"Oh, our publicists have so much power, they could get a hedgehog on 'World News Tonight.' You'll see, kid."

Trish's invitation for a Labor Day outing at the beach seemed like the perfect opportunity to concentrate on the 411 about Irwin instead of the 911 about my book.

Jones Beach was an expanse of beautiful white sand. We went out to Field 4, where we used to hang as teens. Listening to the ocean's roar, watching the seagulls overhead, and smearing SPF 40 all over, we felt as relaxed as we had back in the day, but I couldn't come out and tell Trish how much I liked Irwin; it would just amount to an admission of how stupid I'd been not to give him a chance all those months back. Everything she had said about him turned out to be true—except the part about him liking me.

After we'd laughed about our families, made fun of ex-lovers, and caught up on old friends, I asked—as if it had just hit me—"Did Marisa Monahan make her goal of getting married before she turned thirty?"

Trish's eyes glinted with delicious malice. "Ooh, I forgot to tell you," she said. "The big three-oh is coming up, and the Marriage Monster is out for blood."

"That same guy?"

"Irwin! Yes! That cutie I tried to fix you up with," she confirmed.

I was burning to tell Trish that I was crazy for him, but since it looked like nothing would come of it anyway, I embraced my failure instead. "So they're happy?" I asked.

"They don't look it—or at least, he doesn't," she said. "I saw her leading him around at Roosevelt Field. He was piled high with her shopping bags and boxes."

Failure wasn't that inviting, and I couldn't resist asking, "So you think they'll break up?"

"No way," Trish predicted. "I hear she's having a huge birthday bash. She's made it known that Irwin's supposed to propose right there in front of everybody. Rumor has it she even ordered the engagement cake."

I felt like choking. It wasn't easy getting used to all this losing. In fact, it was downright miserable. Trish seemed to read my mind and suddenly asked, "Hey, what happened that night at the San Gennaro Festival? You never told me."

"Oh, Trish, we had the most amazing time, but I guess—"

Before I finished, she figured it all out and gasped, "Ooooh . . . You like him! You have a total crush on the bald dentist! I knew you two would be perfect."

"Try telling him that," I said morosely. "All he talks about is Marisa."

"He thinks you're still with Lucien, the big art critic."

"Irwin told you that?"

"He told Tom," she said, shading her eyes to look at me intensely. "We have to let him know that you're available."

I considered throwing myself at Irwin and then realized it

would only be a setup for more rejection. Trish had my best interests at heart, but she hadn't seen that look in his eyes when he found the perfect gift for Marisa. The lower my expectations were, the less likely I'd stumble over them and get hurt.

"Forget it. It's too late," I said with finality, the beauty of the beach blurred by my burning tears.

My resolve nearly cracked when Irwin called me later that night. "Hey, Laurel," he said. "I really wanted to thank you for the best time I have ever had shopping."

Yeah, great, I thought. *I helped you find a present for your girlfriend.* "Oh, my pleasure," I said.

"You really know the city, and it's so much fun to walk around with you."

"Thanks."

"Everything's such an adventure with Laurel Linden, and I managed to learn a thing or two," he continued. That one got to me. It was exactly the kind of phrase that never in a million years would have escaped from Lucien's lips.

"You did? What do you mean?"

"Oh, you know so much about how Jane Jacobs saved the Village from the wrecking ball," he said. Irwin had been listening intently when I told him about my favorite urban hero. "And plus, I love the way you can just march into one of the most expensive buildings in the city and act like you live there. Don't tell me the typical impostor from Massapequa could get away with that."

There I was blushing again. Mental note: I'm in trouble. "Maybe next time we should crash the Dakota," I suggested.

"Isn't that where *Rosemary's Baby* was filmed? I'm there," he said.

Picturing us making love in the elevator at the esteemed apartment building on the Upper West Side, I steeled myself to blurt the whole truth: Lucien and I are over, and I'm living back home with my parents, and I'm available, and I like you, and I'm so sorry I ditched you that day, and—

But before I could speak, a nasal whine in the background

pierced my eardrum. "How's my big chrome dome?" I could hear Marisa ask, all sweet. I almost gagged. Surely he must hate this nag, I thought, until he said to her with the same cloying tone, "How's my little kommandant?" To me, he added quickly, "Well I guess I have to go."

"Sure," I replied, and hung up, grateful, for once, for Marisa; she had saved me from my own foolish hope.

When we finished the fact-checking on my book and Nona said she was ready to start editing in earnest, my anxiety mounted. Luckily, Vanessa had the perfect way to help me relax: Bikram yoga, a special form of the ancient art done in superheated rooms.

"I'm not exaggerating. The writing is disastrous, the hype is enormous, and the critics are going to feast on me," I said on the way to the studio as we walked down the street, carrying our rolled-up yoga mats.

Vanessa frowned. "And who told you this?" she asked.

"Only a twenty-eight-year veteran of the business who basically said I should quit." Shooting me a stern look, her brown eyes narrowed. "Laurel, don't you see what you're doing to yourself? These are natural obstacles on the road to success. If you are going to crumble before each little one, then you'll prove your sister right and grow up to be a loser."

I desperately wanted to believe her, but it was tough. She continued, "It's no wonder that you're receptive to these negative influences, considering who you had as a role model. I met her the other day when I was out at your house, you know. I'm sure Jenna is a lovely person, but, frankly speaking, what a bitch."

We both dissolved into laughter, although I think mine was more nervous than mirthful. "But even if I am a success, I'm not sure I'll be happy spending the rest of my life writing allegorical historical fiction and making an ass of myself on talk shows."

"There you go again," Vanessa chided. "You've got to stop that record every time it plays. I want you to break it. Throw it away!"

We had arrived at the yoga center and entered its quiet front room. "I guess you're right," I sighed.

"Laurel, you are truly one of the most incredible people I've ever met—creative, sophisticated, and beautiful. The only thing that's missing is confidence. I want you to spend the next forty-five minutes while we meditate reaching for your Inner Winner. Okay sweetie?" Her eyes were warm again, as though reflecting a brighter future for me.

"Okay, I'll try," I said. And I did. But the forty-five minutes felt like forty-five hours, and by the end of the relaxation session I still felt like I needed a Valium.

That night, Jenna's whole family was there to witness my tantrum. Maybe it was that stupid sweaty yoga, but I just couldn't stand my mother's boasting.

"Uncle Lewis always said you'd be just like Mindy," she chirped while reviewing the seating charts laid out on the dining room table. "But I said, 'Jenna's not the only one who's going to make something of herself in this family—you watch.'"

The backhanded compliment smacked me in the face, but I found myself defending Mindy. "Would you quit trashing her, Mom? Just because she's not your idea of perfection."

My mother rolled her eyes and went back to reshuffling the seating cards. "I'm putting Irene Hirsch next to Viv Capelle; that should be amusing to watch, since the last time they saw each other was in court."

"Whew, glad I'm on your good side," Jenna's husband Robert said.

"And you'd better stay there," Mom warned, "or I'll put Lenny and Nora at your table. You be the referee."

She proceeded to run down the agenda. "First, there'll be cocktails and hors d'oeuvres, then we'll let everyone get comfortable in their seats. I'll make a little speech, and of course your Dad will want to say something. Mindy's planning to sing a little Mariah Carey, and then da da da da—" she imitated a trumpet—"the main event: Our little Laurel reads from her book."

I dropped my copy of *Celebrity Style*. "Back up, Mom. Laurel does what?"

"Well, of course, dear, you're going to read from your book—that's why everyone's coming! You know they're not there to see each other."

"Mom, it's a party at Leonard's, not the Ninety-Second Street Y," I protested. "Plus, they'll all be drunk by then."

"They will not."

"Maybe she doesn't want to do a reading," Jenna put in.

"What do you mean 'doesn't want to?' Of course she wants to! She's been crying all these years that she never gets any attention around here, and I'm finally shining the spotlight on her, at a nice cost to your father, I might add."

"Oh, Mom," I groaned.

"Don't you 'Oh, Mom' me," she said, removing her reading glasses and pointing them at me. "This is our way of showing how much we care about you, Laurel."

"Right," I spat.

"Your father just wanted to have a little family gathering in the backyard, and I said, 'Are you kidding? This is Laurel's big moment. We're going to Leonard's!' And don't think we couldn't have chosen the cash bar. We said no, for our Laurel, open bar. And we ordered the salmon instead of the Chilean sea bass."

She'd gone from a woman who never even took the time to show me how to use Tampax to campaigning for Mother of the Century. In my frazzled state, it was just too much to stomach.

"I know you went through a lot of trouble, but the truth is I'm not even all that comfortable about this whole thing, and you're wearing my success on your chest like some kind of badge of honor. Meanwhile, the pressure keeps building, and now this is one more event I have to perform at all of a sudden? I wish you'd just cancel the whole damn thing!" I burst into tears and stormed upstairs to my room.

Just like when I was a kid, my mother had no idea I could still hear her loud and clear through the heating vents and went on and on. "How dare she be so ungrateful? I've been killing myself for weeks trying to make this perfect, and she turns into a petulant little child!"

Then came the surprise. "Don't blame her," I heard Jenna say. "Laurel never asked for this party. You're just using her to show off to all of your friends, and you know it. If you're such a loving mother, you should give her what she wants: understanding, patience, love—not Chilean sea bass," she screamed.

"We ordered the salmon," my mother shot back, completely missing the point. "Laurel happens to love salmon."

"From the way she reacted, I don't think she's going to have much of an appetite that night," Jenna said.

"You don't seriously expect me to cancel this?"

"At least don't force her to read."

"Fine," my mother said. "I'll have Uncle Lewis play his accordion instead."

A minute later, Jenna appeared in my room. Although I was grateful, I was too upset to thank her.

"I tried," she shrugged. I nodded listlessly.

"Here," she added, handing me a garment bag. "It's that pink dress you always liked. At least you'll look gorgeous at the big event, even if everyone drives you crazy."

18

The day before the big event, I was almost tempted to wear Jenna's dress to Vanessa's birthday tea at the Palm Court in the Plaza Hotel, but sentiment got the better of me. I decided to go with the pink sweater, black skirt, and high-heeled boots she'd helped me pick out from Bergdorf's. The invitation had been sent by a woman named Felicity Bentencourt and forwarded from my old address to my parents' house just in time for me to RSVP.

As I approached the elegant, sunken dining space surrounded by palm trees in the lobby of New York's grandest hotel, I wondered if I would finally meet the mysterious Mr. Pixley. Vanessa rarely mentioned her husband, but I always had an image of a serious yet adoring forty-something banker type.

Amid the clatter of fine china and the clank of sterling silver, I was disappointed to see that the party was made up of only women. It looked like a Vassar reunion, and when the introductions began, I realized it was.

"You must be Laurel—class of '14, right?" I smiled and nodded. The chipper, aging sorority queen went on. "I'm Felicity Bentencourt, '02, and this is Chloe, Shira, Andra, Janetta, and Karen, '12, '14, '06, '17, and '18. Of course, you know the guest of honor." Before taking a seat, I gave Vanessa a tight hug and handed her the gift-wrapped Oscar de la Renta scarf I'd bought for the occasion. Just then, it occurred to me that I had no idea what year she had graduated or how old she was.

"Honey, I'm so glad you made it," she exclaimed, motioning for me to sit next to her. The white-gloved waiter poured me a tea, and I selected a small strawberry tart from the pastry cart. "You know," Vanessa addressed the group proudly, "Laurel's too modest to say this, but she has a major book coming out next year. She's getting a six-figure advance, which is extraordinary for a first-time author. But then, she's an extraordinary girl." The proper awed gasps were emitted from the well-groomed but unimaginative-looking women around the table.

"It's all because of her," I said truthfully.

"We want the story," Felicity encouraged. Vanessa slapped my arm as if to stop me, but I was grateful for the chance to tell an appreciative audience how much she meant to me.

"When I met Vanessa, I was a miserable dog-walker trying to make it as an author."

"She was single, too. Imagine, a beautiful girl like Laurel unlucky at love! Crazy, right?"

I ignored that comment, since I was single again, and resumed my testimonial. "I had no nerve at all and zero confidence in my abilities. It had been eight years of trying with no success."

"Oh, I know just what you're talking about. That's how I was when—" Andra interrupted enthusiastically.

"Let her finish." Janetta shushed her. "You'll go next."

Somewhat confused, I continued. "Vanessa never told me how to be a successful person. She never gave me lists of instructions or stupid self-help jargon. No. She was just the most amazing and supportive friend anyone could ever hope for. And believe me, I was fed up with speeches and affirmations. But she pierced through my shell by making me laugh, by letting me cry, and by teaching me that it is possible to have ridiculous amounts of fun and still make all my dreams come true."

"Oh, Laurel," Vanessa said. "Stop."

"No, really," I insisted. "She had me doing things and going places that I thought were impossible. And if it wasn't for her, there's just no way I would have gotten my book contract. In fact, I still have my doubts, but she never lets me give in to them."

"With all that she's achieved, Laurel still lacks a little faith in herself." Vanessa's warm brown eyes looked around the table knowingly. "We've all been there," she said, prompting a round of nods. To me, she added pointedly, "I'll never let you give up on that book. It's your ticket to success and happiness, and you have to see it through."

I knew my speech was over, because there was a polite round of soft applause. As promised, everyone then turned to see what Andra had to say. She seemed as eager as I was to rhapsodize on Vanessa's gifts.

"I had so much anger inside me before I met Vanessa. I always felt so deprived—my husband never paid attention to me, my kids were brats, and my boss was a monster. My only outlet was the slot machines, and I ran up huge debts playing New York nickels. You would have thought I was a hopeless case, but Vanessa didn't. Somehow, just being around her made me see myself as she saw me."

Vanessa finished the thought: "A strong, capable, beautiful, intelligent woman."

"See?" Andra said. "That's just who she is. Now my husband is totally attentive, a tiger in bed"—everyone giggled—"my kids are on the honor roll, and I don't hate my boss anymore because it's me! I opened my own company." The applause following her speech was so enthusiastic that a few of the subdued diners nearby shot us dirty looks.

It went on and on like that. Chloe had lost sixty pounds and gained a fiancé, Karen had overcome her fear of flying and got a pilot's license, and Felicity had become the first woman at Dow Chemical to be named Vice President of Development Statistics.

I felt like I was in an echo chamber. Janetta summed it up: "I think we can all agree that we'd be nothing like we are today if we hadn't gone to the annual Vassar Old Girls Network, and that we're forever grateful that Vanessa became our big sister."

I nearly choked on my Linzer torte. Big sister? This was like a 23andMe moment. I had six siblings I'd never even known about.

I felt so uncomfortable that I stopped at Mandee on the way to Penn Station and bought a complete outfit for under twenty bucks. Somehow, I had to get out of those Bergdorf clothes. The TGI Friday's bathroom I ducked into was pretty disgusting, but it was worth it to change out of that constricting costume. *Had I turned into one of those acolytes?* I wondered. A bland, mindless, chipper devotee of the grand Vanessa? Everything I'd said remained true, and I'd always be grateful for the support she gave me, but it felt tainted after seeing how she thrived on all the dependence. I wondered if she had a single friend who was her equal—someone she could cry to instead of comforting. Someone who knew as much about her as she knew about them. Someone who wasn't in her thrall.

As the train rumbled out to the Island, I was grateful my parents were at Leonard's making the final preparations for the party the following night and decided to go straight to bed. Before I did, I removed the tasteful Ralph Lauren sheets and comforter Vanessa had brought me and replaced the old pink cover instead.

I couldn't sleep at all, though, even after I'd folded down the picture of Vanessa and I and packed away the jasmine candle. I turned off the light, but her words were still echoing in my head: "I'll never let you give up on that book. It's your ticket to success and happiness, and you have to see it through."

The air seemed as stifling as a Bikram yoga studio, so I got out of bed and wandered to the living room to distract myself with some television. In between reruns of "I Love Lucy" and a Home Shopping Network sale on power tools, I stumbled across an infomercial for Maury Blaustein's famous creation.

Two frail, old ladies were sitting poolside on regular folding lounge chairs. One got up and tried to move hers. "They can fly to the moon, but they can't come up with a chair that you can turn automatically to follow the sun?" she complained. The camera zoomed in to show that she'd placed the chair far too close to the pool, and as she sat back, both she and the chair toppled into the water.

Then came the jingle: "Lounge-Around, Lounge-Around, the happiest lounge in this whole town."

Next, Blaustein appeared, swinging around in his electronic wonder. "Finally, your dream has been fulfilled. No more scooching across the pool deck in search of a good spot. No more accidental spills and bruises. No more fighting with people blocking your sun. Just a nice, relaxing day at the pool, in the backyard, or even in your living room! Wherever you want to Lounge-Around."

I snapped off the television and leaned back on my parents' sectional couch. Anyone who knew how many thousands of those ridiculous chairs he had sold with that idiotic commercial would think Maury Blaustein was the happiest guy on earth, but as his dog-walker, I knew the truth. The guy had no life. Success had only made him a more comfortable loser. Just like that Nigel Fensington. For a moment I could smell his greasy Reuben sandwich all over again. "Once they set the formula, I was set for life," he'd said. "You'll see, kid."

The longer I sat there, the more the prospect of success seemed even worse than failure. The mold they were casting for me was about to harden, and if I didn't get out soon, I'd spend the rest of my life writing drivel like *Nixon's Nanny* and then parroting prepared answers on "World News Tonight."

Spooked, I went back to my childhood bedroom and crawled under the covers, but try as I might, I couldn't sleep. My head was filled with a ghastly carousel of images: Nona's owl glasses staring with contempt over my bed, Anderson Gallant swinging a golf club at a pile of money, and Maury Blaustein going round and round and round on his chair, unable to stop or get off.

I knew I had to pull the plug. This craziness had to end.

I must have slept well, because it was nine o'clock when I woke up and immediately dialed my publishing house. It was time to go right to the top.

"Preston Gallant, please. It's urgent."

Naturally, his schedule was packed, but when his secretary heard my name she squeezed me in at five o'clock. It would mean fighting the rush hour commute to Long Island to get home to change for my big, doomed party and then dealing with my mother's nervous impatience, but I couldn't turn it down.

Feeling better than I had in weeks, I decided to make myself useful and visit Mrs. Lilianthaller before the meeting.

Through the intercom, she warmly welcomed me back. "So nice to hear from you, dear. The pups haven't been the same since that Holt boy took over Thursday nights."

Bogey and Bacall were even more enthusiastic, drowning me in their usual sloppy kisses. I decided to take a long walk through the park on the Hudson River. The scent of the sea wafted up from the harbor as cyclists, skaters, and joggers breezed by. There was a sense of purposeful optimism in the air. September's rejuvenating energy seemed to animate the city. Or maybe it was just me.

After I passed Charles Street, I crossed over and doubled back, like a criminal returning to the scene of the crime, toward the Meier building. I told myself I wanted to say hi to Natan or Ricardo, but the truth was, I wanted to relive that magical night with Irwin.

As I approached the luxury glass tower, I saw Natan holding open the door of an endless, white stretch Hummer. A small entourage emerged from the building, surrounding a tall, stunning strawberry blonde wearing a fuck-me sequined dress. I didn't have to look twice to know it was Ruxandra del Mar, the hottest actress from New Zealand ever to hit American shores. The scene was straight off a page from *Celebrity Style*—I had seen this group before in shots of them partying in the Hamptons, at the Vanity Fair Oscars bash, and at all other manner of glamorous events. There was Lars of Lars of Beverly Hills, Missouri Culpeper, Personal Trainer to the Stars, and Dr. Aitpat Suwanpradhes, the most sought-after spiritual advisor on the West Coast.

"Bogey and Bacall, sit!" I commanded so I could enjoy the scene. They instantly obeyed, so I slipped them each an Old Mother Hubbard oven-baked dog biscuit.

"And if I see so much as one little camera," the great star was ranting at a harried-looking assistant, "so help me Judith, I'll throw away my lithium, and you can answer the voices in my head."

"Ms. del Mar, I promise: no paparazzi, no reporters, no media, nothing. There's a secret back entrance, and as long as no one notices the Hummer, we're fine."

"Good, because I've had it with the press," the movie starlet said, pushing a perfect golden curl off her forehead indignantly. "Those interviewers are always asking about Roberto and how it feels that he left me for a man twice my age and ugh! I refuse to be humiliated anymore." I suddenly understood why there had only been recycled material from past interviews with her in *Celebrity Style* since her big breakup with the Mexican bullfighter.

"I've got it all taken care of," Judith reassured. "And you'll be happy to hear they're serving deep-fried Twinkies tonight."

"Yum!" Ruxandra said, lighting up like a child on Christmas Eve. Suddenly, the glare returned. "Oh, great," she complained. "I have no power to resist those, my belly's going to blow up like an airbag, and I'm almost out of desiccated hippo liver."

I tried not to laugh out loud. She must have been referring to some fad weight-loss gimmick.

Missouri Culpeper confirmed my hunch. "We'll just have to make up for it on the glute machine," she said. "That stuff is harder to find than a straight single man in his forties."

Ruxandra groaned and turned to her spiritual advisor. "How am I supposed to achieve inner peace when I can't even find competent help?" she asked before stepping in the Hummer and speeding away.

I had a good laugh about it with Natan, and he caught me up on the rest of the building gossip. Pretty soon, though, it was time for me to return Bogey and Bacall and head to my fateful meeting at Gallant.

19

As I approached the venerable president's office, my heart was beating so fast I could hear it in my ears. The danger, the excitement, the stakes—it was much more frightening than the steepest plunge on a rollercoaster, but this time I had no safety bar.

I had hoped to be alone with Preston, but when I entered the room I saw Nona and Anderson, who was wearing a T-shirt that said "I Love Lesbians!"

"I'm a busy man," Preston began, "but I always have time for our new talent."

Anderson tossed me an imaginary football. "The best writer on our roster and the one who's going to make me the prince of publishing."

Nona coughed conspicuously.

"So what brings you here?" Preston leaned back in his big leather chair and smiled as if he could read my mind. "Too many touch-ups on your jacket photo? I know it can be trying for a first-time author, but you've got to trust us. Without good looks, we don't sell books."

"No, sir—" I began, but before I could finish, Anderson interrupted.

"Don't tell me—your cousin's got a manuscript, right? Nona here will look at it." He winked at his assistant, who was struggling to conceal her contempt.

"Actually, it's not that—"

"You're ready to tell us about your next book? Fine thing. We're all ears," the old man said.

All of them looked at me expectantly.

I drew a deep breath.

I considered what I was about to do.

Nobody in their right mind would consider anything like this.

It would change my life forever.

Once I spoke, there'd be no going back.

I realized it was crazy.

But I took the plunge.

"I want to kill *Napoleon's Hairdresser*," I declared.

"Marguerite?" Nona asked. "Your central protagonist?"

"But we need a happy ending!" Anderson protested. "Otherwise, Disney will never buy the film rights."

The absurd spectacle of an animated musical version of the retreat from Moscow flashed through my mind.

Preston studied me closely. "Is this what you're telling us? You want a new ending?"

"No, I want to end it all," I said definitively. "I want out of my contract."

Suddenly, the only noise in the room was the muffled pounding of a jackhammer sixteen flights below.

"Simon & Schuster's up to their old tricks again, aren't they? We'll sue!" Preston said, banging on the desktop.

"I'm not moving to another publisher; I'm leaving the business," I said.

"Hollywood's bought you out, right? Tell them who discovered you. Tell them it was Anderson Gallant." The son banged on the armrest of his chair.

"I'm not writing a screenplay, I'm not writing a book, I'm not writing anything," I insisted. "Because my writing sucks."

The two Gallants in the room looked shocked. Nona just

looked down.

"I know Nona agrees with me, but she's in no position to say so. And Mr. Gallant, I know you'd agree, too, if you'd ever read what I'd written."

"I was trusting my son on this," he confessed. "Anderson, you did read the book, didn't you?"

"Just about . . . most of the first part . . . well, yeah, I might have missed some of it..." he stammered.

"I brought along a sample for your edification," I said, passing out copies of a page from my original manuscript.

Preston sat back in his chair, making a steeple out of his fingers. Anderson wandered to the window and played with the blinds. Nona, for once in her life, put down the red pen and looked at me with an encouraging glint in her eyes.

"Let me set the scene for you," I said. "It's winter, 1812. Napoleon has conquered half of Russia, but the Russians have denied him true victory. Realizing he can no longer stay in the charred remains of Moscow, Napoleon must set out with his glorious legions back across the frozen steppes. And now, as it's rendered in my version."

```
    Despite the ferocious
blizzard raging, Marguerite's
distinctly retro Russian sable
blanket kept her warm in the
sleigh. All around, the
soldiers, so skinny as to
resemble supermodels—were they
not men and actually starving
to death—battled against the
cutting wind. The sight of them
tore at her heart. Under such
dire conditions—the bitter cold
unalleviated by breathable
microfiber lining, the endless
marching with nary a borscht
restaurant in sight, not even
```

an AeroBed to rest their weary bones at night—all of this made the struggle against frizz impossible.

Marguerite took heart in the knowledge that rinsing with cold water leaves hair shinier, but alas, not when it freezes into icicles.

"Are we there yet?" she shouted in despair to the kindly driver struggling to steer through the blinding snow.

"M'lady," he replied, "we've yet to pass the rest stop at Minsk. After that, it should take at least another year."

Thinking of her favorite takeout spot in the Belorussian capital, she longed for a steaming-hot wonton soup.

Just then, to her right, she spotted him: the one soldier in the whole Grand Army who didn't sport the grunge look. Their eyes locked, and she admired his thick, beautifully hydrated hair and wondered if he was using a pro-vitamin formula. He reached his hand out to hers, but before she could take it, he fell face down in the snow, dead. With that, the army had lost its last dashing preppy.

So war-weary was she that Marguerite didn't pause to mourn her fallen hunk. Instead,

her mind turned to more
pressing matters. Ahead of her,
barely visible on his white
horse, Napoleon was leading his
army back from what could
hardly be called a success.
Russia was unconquered, the
army was lost, and the
politicians in Paris would
surely be infuriated. All of
this would only add to
Napoleon's stress and, thus,
his hair loss. The combover
would be of little avail,
Marguerite knew in her heart.
    War, war, war, 'twas a
terrible thing, this war. But
for the violence in the hearts
of men, detangler would be
available to all the world's
children, and humankind could
enjoy a life of fuller, longer-
lasting luster.

When I finished, Anderson was sobbing. "It's beautiful," he said.

Nona had removed her owl glasses, and a small smile danced on her lips. She almost looked pretty.

Preston stood and stared at me, slack-jawed. After a pause, he spoke deliberately. "How much do you want to get out of the contract?"

I was about to say "With my whole heart," when I realized he was talking about money. I hadn't thought I'd be able to keep any. "Ten percent of the advance?" I guessed.

"Deal," he said, clasping my hand gratefully. "You've done the right thing, young lady," he pronounced. "For yourself, for this company, for American letters, and for the reputation of my family, not least that useless son of mine."

"Dad!" Anderson whined. "She was my ticket to respectability."

"Oh, go get a job," he said.

Nona followed me out into the hallway, tears in her eyes. "For twenty-eight years, I've been dealing with shitty authors, dreaming of the day one would do what you just did," she beamed. "For twenty-eight years, I've had no professional recognition. It took Anderson a decade just to stop calling me 'Mona.' The only power I have is to withhold or confer my respect. Laurel Linden, I never thought I'd say this, but I respect you."

It was the highest praise I'd ever get from a literary critic, but in that moment, it was all I needed. I felt luckier than any bestselling author.

That is, until halfway between Hicksville and Plainview, when it hit me: I was headed to a formal affair filled with friends and relatives there to celebrate a book deal I had just walked out on. My hands went clammy, and I started to sweat.

Luckily, my parents had already left by the time I got home and slipped on Jenna's pink dress. Looking at myself in the mirror, I had to concede that whatever other problems I had, this was a perfect fit. It pinched in my waist, pushed up my cleavage, and elongated my legs with a sexy slit. "You can do it," I told myself before heading out to Leonard's.

In the cab on the way over, I decided that the best course of action would be a white lie. If I told everyone Gallant had broken my contract, they'd feel sorry for me instead of duped. I rehearsed my explanation: "The business is just not what it used to be, budgets are being cut, corporations can be so cold, and I've already got a lead on a better deal." *That should mollify them at least until the salmon arrives,* I thought.

When I arrived at Long Island's most famous catering hall, I entered through the courtyard past splashing fountains surrounded by colored lights. In the main lobby, beneath the cherub-gilded ceilings, were dozens of people dressed in evening gowns and tuxedos.

"Lorenzo silver anniversary to your right," directed a young man wearing black pants and a starched white shirt. "Goldenberg Bar-Mitzvah, up the escalator and to your left. Linden book party, garden terrace in the back." I left before hearing the rest of the evening specials.

My stomach lurched. I'd have to use whatever money was left from my advance to pay my parents back for this. As I entered the banquet hall, festooned with white candles sparkling under crystal chandeliers, my anxiety grew.

"Where the hell have you been?" my father asked, gesturing wildly to my mother across the crowded hall. When she saw I was there, she ran to the dais. "The guest of honor has finally arrived," she said into the microphone.

Applause went up around the room, and I walked toward the head table past a panorama of faces from different parts of my life, all there, unknowingly, to witness my humiliation. There was the table with Trish's family plus three of our best friends from high school. There was Danny Z. holding court over the rest of the writers group: Margo in a peach chiffon dress, Seth, who had brushed his hair for the occasion, José in a tweed jacket, and Sunny Hellerstein giving me the thumbs-up. Aside from Aunt Helene, Uncle Lewis, and the rest of my immediate family, there were relatives I hadn't seen since the last funeral. Even my former dog-walking clients had been contacted by my overzealous mother: the Danilovas holding hands, Sergio and his crew from the beauty salon, and Maury Blaustein trying to make the best of a straight-backed chair.

But the most unnerving sight was Vanessa. She was the only one who hadn't stopped clapping when the applause died down and looked almost maniacally proud. I averted my gaze and took my seat.

My mother tapped the microphone again. "Hello? Hello? Can you all hear me?" she asked. "I'd like to thank you all for coming, some of you from as far away as Jersey and Staten Island. You know the good news already: a six-figure book deal from one of the best publishers in the country. Little Laurel got this all on her own, through determination and guts. Ever since she was a little girl, she wanted to be a writer, and we did everything we could to support her dream: creative writing classes after school, a major in English Literature at Vassar, and then years and years of working on her novel. Writing is Laurel's destiny, and now she's arrived. So without further ado, here she is: my daughter and future bestselling author, Laurel Aimee Linden."

As I stood at the microphone, my vision blurred from the dazzling lights of the crystal chandeliers, and my prepared speech evaporated before my tear-filled eyes. For a minute, I thought I had no power to speak at all, but I told myself the deed was done and now all I had to do was deliver the bad news.

"I want to thank you—really very much." I sucked in a deep breath, savoring the pause. "Your love and support means the world to me. And I hope I have your understanding, too. Because the thing is, today I broke my book contract."

A hushed murmur traveled the room. Even the waiters stopped serving and turned to stare at me. Taking an even deeper breath, I continued. "It was the most difficult thing I've ever done in my life, but see, I'm not really a novelist. I wanted to be an author, maybe because it was glamorous, or fun, or to be famous, but when I finally got the chance, I had to face the hard reality: It's really not for me. Yes, I had a six-figure contract. I had publicists telling me how to behave. I had editors trying to get my book into shape. I even had a headshot that made me look like a fascinating intellectual. You might be thinking I'm behaving like a total brat, that I should just do the work, collect the paycheck, and shut up about it. But that would be wrong. I don't want to take advantage of people, take their money, string them along for something I honestly don't believe in. Even though I won't be publishing a book, I gained something that no amount of fame or publicity can equal. I made peace with a demon that had been tormenting me for years. I let go of my contract, and when I did, I also let go of the notion that I had to prove I'm special in order to be special. No,

I'm not going to be a published author. I'm just going to be plain old Laurel Aimee Linden. But that's cool."

Jenna started clapping, and everyone else joined in. Seeing my sister's grin gave me the last drop of courage I needed before fleeing. "At least you didn't come here for nothing," I said. "Not only is there plenty of food and drink, but you're about to get a very special treat. Mindy?" My cousin looked reluctant, but I beckoned her, and, waving to the crowd, she approached the stage and signaled the band. I was halfway to the door before she hit the first stanza of "Hero" in true Mariah Carey style.

Jenna caught up with me and squeezed my arm. "Go, go," she urged, as if this was a relay race. "I'll instigate a fight between Irene Hirsch and Viv Capelle, and pretty soon everyone will forget what you just did."

We both giggled, and I gave her a tight hug. "Oh no, I'll wrinkle your dress," I said, stepping back.

"It's yours," she said. "Looks prettier on you than me." She gave me gentle push forward, and I continued my escape.

As I hurried down the hall, I could still hear Mindy singing. Damn, that girl had a great voice.

Just when I thought I was free, I heard a stern voice behind me. "Stop!"

I turned to face Vanessa. Her normally warm eyes exuded frigid anger. "What do you think you're doing?" she demanded. "I've been trying to hold this in for a long time, but you've finally crossed the line, Miss Thing. First it was Lucien. How a girl like you could give up a guy like that is beyond me. And to do it the night you move into his house—how much more irrational can you get? Oh, but I guess you can get more irrational—witness this little psychodrama. I've never seen such acting out, and believe me, I deal with a lot of basket cases."

"That's your specialty, isn't it?" I asked, feeling strangely calm. Her anger only rose.

"Your hostility is so outrageous, Laurel," she said. "I'm sorry if I've offended you in some way." Although her tone was sarcastic, I took her at her word.

"No, Vanessa, you've been a really good friend. The thing

is—"

"The thing is this: You think the choices you're making are correct, but you obviously still have a lot to learn."

"Yeah, I know I have a lot to learn," I said. "We all do. Don't you?"

"That's beside the point," she huffed.

"I don't think it is, Vanessa," I said with studied patience. "It's exactly the point. You're only comfortable giving instructions to poor little weak girls like me. And, frankly speaking, I'm tired of playing that role. It was great hanging out with you; I learned a lot, I really did. But I never learned anything about you. That's not a friendship. If all you want is another patient for your clinic, you're going to have to look somewhere else."

Feeling a huge rush of liberation, I turned and left.

20

Taking the nearest exit, I found myself in a moonlit garden full of roses and gurgling fountains. In a strange mixture of euphoria and terror, I sat on a bench under a trellis. I didn't have a book contract, I didn't have an apartment, I wasn't a dog-walker anymore, and I wasn't an aspiring author. Who was I? And who would help me? The boyfriend I'd had weeks before was gone, and I'd just chucked my Big Sister. My real family, never too helpful to begin with, was probably filing legal papers to disown me. I thought I had met a nice guy, but he was attached to someone else, and pretty soon, they'd be permanently attached.

Tossing my arm over the back of the cast-iron bench and looking up at the stars, I realized that although I had nothing, I had nothing left to lose. Six-hour concerts of random sounds were a thing of the past. I'd never have to worry about discussing hegemonic imperialism on a news show. I no longer owed Vanessa a mountain of eternal gratitude.

I felt so light and free, like a balloon untethered, I almost floated off the bench. Anything could happen, I realized, anything! I could join the Peace Corps. I could become a sushi chef. I could work on a cruise ship. Even that cute guy in the distance I could just make out might possibly be coming right toward me.

He was!

A second later, I realized that not only was he cute, he was Irwin.

Had my mother invited him to the party? Impossible. Why else would he be here? And then it hit me: In a sick twist of fate, Marisa's birthday party was tonight at where else but Leonard's.

His eyes were glowing, and he looked just as surprised to see me as I'd been to find him in this secluded spot.

Why did he have to look so damn good? Irwin was as tall, athletic, and graceful as ever, but this was my first look at him in a suit, and it was a painful thrill. I'd already seen him looking sexy in a sleeveless shirt. Even in that cold dentist's smock, he was amazing husband material, and now he stood in front of me, sharp and classy, looking like he had just stepped out of the pages of Italian *Vogue*.

"Laurel," he said, smiling at the miraculous coincidence. "What are you doing here?"

"Oh, it's a long story," I said, "and not a very pretty one."

"What do you mean?"

"I just went and changed my whole life forever," I sighed.

"Oh, I know the feeling," he said, sitting down next to me. "Believe it or not, I just did, too."

The pain was sudden and severe. Of course—he had just proposed. Marisa always said she wouldn't turn thirty without a rock, and pretty soon she'd be serving that engagement cake.

"Aren't they going to miss you at your party?" I tried not to let Irwin see my tears, but he immediately noticed something was wrong.

"Hey, city girl, don't cry. What's the matter?" he asked gently.

"First of all, I'm not city girl anymore," I confessed, deciding that since Irwin was already attached, I might as well let him see how pathetic I really was. The whole story came tumbling out in sobs. "So that's pretty much it," I concluded. "I just turned my back on everything I spent my whole life trying to get."

"Sounds to me like the boyfriend was no loss, the Big Sister was a Big Control Freak, and you acted with a lot of integrity when it came to your book," he said, unbuttoning his collar and loosening his silk tie. *Stop being so sexy!* I wanted to scream.

It was time to end this misery. I knew that if I brought up his fiancée, that would get rid of him. "So how'd you end up with Marisa?" I asked. "You never told me." People get all romantic when they recount the whole how-we-met tale, and I braced myself for the worst.

"Funny you should ask," he said. "It was all your fault."

My fault?

"I'm stupidly romantic, always have been," he continued, "and I really wanted to find someone special. Trish had told me all about her gorgeous, cool, artistic friend. After weeks and weeks, she finally managed to set me up with her, and, well—"

"I'm sorry about that, Irwin."

"No, you shouldn't be sorry, let me finish. So I'm sitting in Spiro's Diner, thinking here I am about to meet the perfect girl—she's from my hometown, but she's gone out in the world. We'll have everything in common, and we'll still have so much to learn from each other. My crazy romantic side took over. Until she showed up wearing a dreary, double-breasted navy suit, her hair plastered into the same shape as every other woman on the 7:23, with an accordion file under her arm like some kind of office drone."

In spite of myself, I laughed. "I had a job interview that day," I explained.

Irwin, looking into the distance, continued as though he hadn't heard me. "So I think to myself, 'She's hideous. Definitely not the one I've been dreaming of. But Trish's husband is a good friend, so I'll make nice, buy her lunch, and then get rid of her as politely as possible.' But no! She catches a glimpse of me from behind and ditches me! How much worse can it get?"

"What does that have to do with Marisa?" I asked.

"All this time, Marisa was calling me, coming by, taking all her friends' kids to my office. I'd never liked her much; she was exactly the kind of girl I'd been trying to avoid in favor of my romantic fantasy—the artsy city girl—but I always struck out with those types, and that afternoon, when an ugly version of one turned me down, I knew it was time to let go of the dream. Marisa was waiting for me at the office, I asked her out, and that was how it all began."

"I hope you don't still think I'm a hideous office drone," I said, running my fingers through my hair in an attempt to muss it up.

"That's the worst part," he said. "I didn't like you much when I first met you, but after that, I fell really hard. You were everything I ever dreamed of: fun, funky, gorgeous, and cool." As Irwin spoke about how much he liked me, I felt myself go liquid.

"Why is that so bad?" I asked.

"Because I knew you existed, but you were totally out of my league. Your boyfriend was some French art critic who grew up in Nicaragua, and me? I'm just a dentist from Long Island."

"Oh, Irwin, you're so much more than that," I said, wishing I'd realized it the first time we'd met and that I could trade lives with Marisa.

"Come on. You probably bolted as soon as you heard my name. Don't tell me you didn't think of it: Turnov, as in he's a big turn-off? It's a good thing my middle name isn't Michael Andrew, or I'd be I. M. A. Turnov. I could never join the army because I might someday become a Major Turnov. And if I married someone named Delight, my kid would be Baby Turnov Delight."

I'd been laughing, but at the mention of marriage, I remembered Marisa. With all my heart I wanted to jump into Irwin's arms, but my mind knew he'd just gotten engaged. "Don't you think it's time for you to get back to your party now?"

"I guess," he said. "But it's not going to be easy. She didn't exactly like the gift we picked out."

"That's too bad," I said, thinking, *Hmm . . . that's good.* "What happened?"

"I gave her the pearls in the limo on the way over, but she threw them right back in my face." I felt hopeful, and hot, and I hung onto his every word. "She said she wanted a diamond. As in an engagement ring. Gave me an ultimatum: Either I propose tonight, or it's over."

I could barely take the suspense. "So what happened?"

"What can I say? I'm a gentleman. Of course I'm going to do the right thing."

He proposed!

"I broke it off. Marisa was my rebound girl, a good salve for my ego after you ditched me. But that lasted about a week. After that, we fought constantly. All she wanted to do was go from mall to mall looking at engagement rings. She liked to talk about our kids, but only in a superficial way, like whether I liked the name Tyler. She never wanted to address the hard questions involved in raising children—how to educate them, discipline them, turn them into people who will make a contribution to this world. Instead, she just wanted to know if I would get someone named Clowny Zary to perform at their birthdays. It was surreal."

As he spoke, we had inched closer to each other, and he lifted his strong hands to cup my face. "That was cause enough to end it, but it wasn't the main reason."

"What was?" I whispered breathlessly.

"It all goes back to Laurel Linden," he said, tucking a lock of my hair behind my ear and looking at me like I was Miss Universe. "I couldn't propose to someone else, because that would close off any chance I might ever have with you." He locked eyes with mine. "So do I have a chance?" he whispered.

I didn't have to answer. We just melted into the most delicious, passionate, all-encompassing kiss of my life.

After a few minutes that felt like an eternity, he pulled back. "God, I want to stay here with you all night, I really do. You're so fucking gorgeous to me." From the king-sized bulge in his pants, I knew he wasn't lying. "But I can't just vanish. I really have to go back."

Although I wanted to rip off his shirt and touch those cut-up pecs, I realized that what he'd said was true for me, too. "I guess I should show up at my party also."

We kissed more, and when he licked my neck I thought I'd lose all control. "We really should go."

"Yeah," he said, running his hands up the sides of my dress. "Yeah."

I almost started screaming "yes, yes, yes," but Irwin spoke instead, pulling back with finality. "Let me go make a clean ending so you and I can have a perfect beginning." He splashed his face in a nearby fountain. "I could sure use a cold shower first, though."

He was so sexy I could hardly stand the wait, but I knew I had to.

Stirring under my pink blanket the next morning, I awoke before opening my eyes and saw a parade of images from the night before. Did Uncle Lewis really play the Macarena on the accordion, causing Aunt Helene to throw out her hip? Did the members of my writers group stage readings of their work, with Margo bringing down the house? Did Viv Capelle and Irene Hirsch really come to blows at the Viennese table?

And did I really have the most mind-blowing kiss of my life from Dr. Irwin Turnov?

I opened my eyes and looked around.

And will he call?

Getting up, I saw the bruise on my wrist from when I tried to stop Irene from pressing Viv's face into a seven-layer cake. On my night table I found the wine-smeared chapter of Margo's book, which had become really touching now that she'd changed the main characters into humans. And I knew I couldn't have dreamed up the image of Aunt Helene trying to continue dancing as she was wheeled off by emergency medical technicians.

As for Irwin, I could smell his delicious scent on my skin, and if I really tried, I could almost recapture the ecstasy of his lips against mine.

So when will he call?

I brought my cell phone into the bathroom while I showered and then down to breakfast, where I found my parents in their usual Saturday morning routine. My mother was microwaving waffles, and my father was deeply engrossed in the sports pages. I gathered my courage and entered the room.

"We have waffles, muffins—or cantaloupe if you're feeling a little bloated from last night," Mom offered.

"Listen, guys," I said, trying to make eye contact. "Dad?" My father looked up. "I'm so sorry about all the trouble I caused. I know you worked really hard to host an elaborate party, and I ruined it."

"Ruined?" my father asked.

"You didn't cause any trouble, honey," my mother said. "It was your sister who had to go and bring up the subject of the Hirsch–Capelle lawsuit."

I silently thanked Jenna but pressed my parents. "Seriously, didn't my decision put a damper on things?"

"Aw, who noticed?" Mom asked.

"By the time the ambulance came, everyone had forgotten all about you," my father said. "Anyway, it was worth it to see Viv up to her neck in buttercream."

Leave it to my parents to not even notice when I back out of an eight-year career pursuit. "Well, I was going to offer to pay for the party," I said, "since it was to celebrate a book that I'm not publishing."

Mom squeezed my cheek. "Cookie, we're actually relieved there'll be no book. As far as we're concerned, that's worth celebrating."

"You finally learned to get your head out of the clouds," my father put in, resuming his backwards leafing through the paper.

"Keep your money—you'll need it," my mother said. "Just next time, pick a career that won't give me acid reflux disease."

When the phone still hadn't rung half an hour later, I checked my messages, and my heart leapt when the electronic voice announced that I had one, but I was disappointed to hear it was only a lawyer from Gallant saying the papers breaking my contract were ready and I should stop by on Monday morning to sign them.

That made it all the more real. In two days, I'd be out of a job. I took my trusty cell phone to the computer in the den and started frantically surfing career help websites. Within minutes, I'd learned that with my qualifications, I could make half as much money as I did walking dogs by working twice the hours doing data entry, cleaning hotel rooms, or wearing a sandwich board advertising sample sales. *Girdle and Support Hose Quarterly* was starting to look good, only they'd never have me.

I was hysterically trying to plump up my résumé when the doorbell rang. Figuring it was Viv or Irene about to serve papers on my parents, I ignored it, but a second later he appeared in the room: Irwin, wearing a faded green T-shirt that brought out the olive tones in his skin and a beat-up pair of jeans faded in all the right places.

"I found you," he said, coming over and giving me the lightest, but sexiest, kiss on the lips. "Ready?" he asked.

"For what?"

"Our great new beginning." He pulled me to my feet, put those strong hands at the base of my back, and kissed me again, this time excruciatingly slowly. I felt so wet I almost forgot about my career problem. Almost.

"I want to, I really do, but I'm in serious trouble here. I've got to figure out what to do for the rest of my life."

"How about spend it with me?"

It was so forward, I blushed deeply. "No, I mean my job. I have no marketable skills, unless you count poop-scooping."

"You think it's time to bag that?" he joked.

"Seriously, I have a college degree in English Literature, but these days that's not even as good as a beauty school diploma, and I don't know Adobe or Spanish or any other special skill, and I'm twenty-eight years old, and—"

I could have gone on and on, but Irwin started unbuttoning my shirt. I squealed, but I was too into it to stop him and started tearing at his clothes, too. He was unclasping my bra, and I was gasping for breath when it hit me: My parents were one flight up!

"No, no, stop," I said with difficulty.

Irwin pushed me back against the couch, and, forgetting myself, I started grinding my hips against his oh-so-hard on. But when I began to moan, I imagined my parents bursting in on us, and the ridiculous high school scenario was just too much. "Stop," I said, pushing him away but smiling. "This would be a bad way for you to meet Mom and Dad."

Irwin kept tracing his fingers around my breasts, shoulders, neck, and back. "Come to my place then," he said urgently.

We just barely made it over there before making crazy love all over his living room. I hung onto the staircase railing as he stripped me bare and caressed my entire body with his gorgeous hands. We fell together onto the couch where I had my turn, tasting the sinewy muscles I'd been admiring for so long. Just when the ecstasy was almost too much to bear, he decisively pushed me to the floor, threw on some protection, and, holding my arms back above my head, made me come so hard I forgot all about my future as a data entry, sandwich-board-wearing hotel maid.

Almost instantly, with a sudden, deep thrust, Irwin exploded too.

As we collapsed together rapturously, he stroked my hair and blew softly on my sweaty face.

After a few blissful minutes, he threw on his clingy black boxer-briefs and padded to the kitchen to blend some drinks. We brought the piña coladas out to the deck by his swimming pool in the fenced-in backyard. Wearing only a black velour thong, I dipped my feet in the water, and he started tossing rose petals at me. "I want to decorate you with flowers. You are so beautiful the way the sun is reflecting in your eyes, the natural highlights in your hair, and God, those luscious tits," he said, kicking water playfully in my direction.

I laughed and slipped into the heated water, diving under into its soft depths. When I came back up, he said, "This is what my pool's always been missing: a beautiful nymph."

"Try nympho," I said, pulling him into the water and

wrapping my legs around him. We started insatiably kissing all over again, and he carried me to the Jacuzzi. "I'm going to have to keep a box of condoms in every room now that you're around," he said with a grin.

"How come? Didn't you need them with Marisa?" I asked coyly.

"Change the subject, please," he said. Right answer!

Amidst the hot, tumbling waters, we realized how much more we still had to discover about each other.

Later, after we'd showered and finally come up for air, we sat together on his bed, and he suggested we just cuddle up and watch a movie. Although I knew he'd never subject me to a four-hour drama about the peasants of Turkmenistan, although I'd never tire of touching his carved physique, and although I was perfectly comfortable in his home, which was a near-replica of the one I'd grown up in—split-level colonial on a quarter acre, foyer leading into stairs with kitchen to the left, living room to the right, and half-bath in the middle—I somehow felt restless.

Suddenly, I knew why. This was all so new, so momentous, I had to talk to Trish!

"Oh, God, that sounds so great, but I have some plans I can't break."

Irwin was perfectly understanding and loaned me one of his soft, worn-in shirts, which he buttoned up, pausing to kiss me at intervals. It still felt like his arms were around me after he'd dropped me off at my parents' house.

"Oh. My. God. He is SO SEXY!" I whisper-screamed, checking over my shoulder at the crowded Pizza Hut. It wasn't exactly gourmet cuisine, but Trish and I had our own special table there where we'd been talking about boys since we were eleven.

"Can I just say this once? I told you so," she squealed with delight. "Yay! So is he as good as Lucien the Silver Lamborghini?"

"This guy doesn't even have wheels—he flies. And he takes

me to heaven."

Following her usual habit, Trish peeled the pepperoni off of her pizza and popped each slice in her mouth. "And how perfect is this? He's best friends with my husband, and we're best friends!"

I smiled giddily, unable to even eat for all my excitement. Trish went on. "We can all go bowling together!" My best bud wasn't the most sophisticated sportswoman in the world, but the idea of knocking back a few pins with both of our guys did sound fun, if a little retro. "Totally," I affirmed.

21

My thighs were sore in the most pleasurable way, with the memory of Irwin's body against mine resonating as a physical sensation and enveloping my mind in a dream-like state. I don't remember the ride over to Gallant or the walk up Broadway, and I only regained my bearings when I faced the receptionist.

"Hi, Sherill!" I said. "I have a quick meeting up at legal."

Instead of buzzing me in with a friendly smile as usual, she motioned for me to take a seat and punched a light on her console. "Ms. Linden is here; she says she has an appointment." After a pause, she added, "Okay then," and pressed the buzzer without another word.

I was looking over my shoulder as I walked through the hall, wondering if they'd sent out some kind of e-mail warning all staff to shun me, and my suspicions only grew when I saw the lawyers. Without so much as a greeting, they placed a stack of papers in front of me to sign and initial.

When I was through, I smiled weakly. "Well, guys, it's been great working with you."

"You call that work?" one gray-suit replied. "Sixteen thousand dollars, and you never published a word. Wish I could get a gig like that." The other lawyer snorted, and I slunk out of the room.

At the far end of the hall, I could see my three publicists

huddled around a copy machine. They'd always been so friendly, and I thought I owed them at least a thanks. But as soon as I approached, they glared in my direction and tightened their circle. I'd been in enough high school cliques to read the body language and translated it easily as: "Go away, loser—we don't want to catch your germs." I didn't hang around to hear them say it out loud.

I had almost made it out of reception when Sherill stopped me. *Are they going to frisk me before I leave?* I wondered. "Almost forgot," she said. "Here." She handed me a plain white envelope with my name handwritten across the front. I would recognize that red pen anywhere. Nona. Her last contact with me had been so friendly, I held out hope that this might be a decent goodbye and opened the envelope in the elevator. When I peeked inside, I saw her familiar red ink all over a page of my now-dead manuscript. *Not anymore, Nona,* I thought to myself, shoving it back in my bag. *I'm a free woman now.*

Free! Free to live off of my dwindling savings and have crazy fun with my boyfriend. Over the next few weeks, interspersed with efforts to secure even moderately respectable employment, Irwin and I fell in love during a whirlwind of dates. In Manhattan, we indulged in guilty pleasures Lucien would have scoffed at, like ice skating at Rockefeller Center, surrounded by the colorful autumn leaves, going to a Broadway matinee like a pair of tourists, and coasting on bikes through Central Park. We always ended the evening the same way: with uncontrollable, hot sex.

One afternoon, as we sped toward Brooklyn with the top down, I peppered him with questions about Coney Island. "Do they still run the Cyclone? Can we get hot dogs? Is there an actual boardwalk?" I sounded like I was seven years old and going to an amusement park for the first time in my life.

We parked by the New York Aquarium and joined the crowds of people from all over the world, breathing in the tangy sea air and heading toward the rides. With his boyish energy, Irwin grabbed my hand and made straight for the Caterpillar, a goofy ride favored by kids. I couldn't understand why he was so keen on it until the Caterpillar's canvas skin covered the seats and we were suddenly plunged into total darkness. Irwin took full advantage of our minute of privacy, kissing my breasts until the light started peeking through as the hood lifted back off.

On the carousel, we fed each other popcorn, and after dismounting our painted horses, we strolled hand-in-hand over to the original Nathan's. I don't know if it was the famous grill, the wise-cracking cooks, or just my mood, but that hot dog was the most delicious thing I ever tasted.

The highlight, though, had to be the Cyclone. We grabbed the first car, and as the classic ride began its steep climb, we threw our arms up like teenagers, leaving us tense with anticipation. As it curved over the summit and began its terrifying plunge, I clung tightly to my lover, and we screamed in rapture. Just like the wheels clicking in the track of this rollercoaster, I felt my life was in sync with Irwin's, like we'd always been together and always would be.

Despite the thrills and peaks of my new romance, my lack of paid employment was bringing me down. Before I could even look at the classified ads, I had to figure out how a person could make money with a degree in English Literature, the ability to look at any mutt and guess its mixture of breeds, and a propensity for daydreaming.

That's how I found myself paying two hundred and fifty dollars to attend a workshop at the Levittown Marriott called "What Song is Your Dance?" It looked professional enough when I entered the large conference room and was handed a clipboard by one of the well-groomed staff, but as I sat down, I suddenly felt like I was taking an SAT, since I was older than everybody else by at least ten years. I tried to convince myself that I was that much more mature and would get that much more for my money.

A burly but hyper man took the microphone and repeated the pitch that had brought me there in the first place. "Congratulations on taking the first step in your new life," he said, exhorting us to applaud ourselves as if we had already landed dream jobs. "By the time you leave here, you'll not only be stepping, you'll be dancing your way to success, power, money, and satisfaction—not to mention the big bucks."

Sounds good, I thought. We had an hour and a half to complete a comprehensive survey that would reveal all. I picked up my pencil. At first, the questions were fairly standard—name, age, work experience—but by the fourth page they started getting difficult:

23. *When you dance, do you:*
a) *Lead*
b) *Follow*
c) *Sometimes lead and sometimes follow*
d) *Neither; I only dance freestyle.*

24. *Where do you pick up your latest dance moves?*
a) *The hottest nightclubs*
b) *The street*
c) *Music videos*
d) *I invent them*

25. *When you square dance, do you prefer:*
a) *Promenade left*
b) *Promenade right*
c) *Acey Deucey*
d) *Do-Si-Do your partner*

26. *When you do the rumba, do you think with your:*
a) *Hips*
b) *Butt*
c) *Neither*
d) *Both*

It only got worse from there, and by the time I finished, my wrist was aching, my head was spinning, and I never wanted to dance again.

During the twenty-minute break while they fed my answers into a computer, I wandered out to the hotel lobby and retreated into the refuge of *Celebrity Style*. Flipping to the People Profile section, I noticed that journalist Salli Simmer was covering a story in the nearby Hamptons. She set the scene beautifully and ended her article on a rare personal note.

> *As we wandered through the Japanese gardens of Karismah's magnificent thirty-eight-room, neo-Tudor–style mansion, she pulled a few dead leaves off of the only tired-looking plant for miles around. "They told me to throw this one away, but I just can't give up on any living thing," she said with characteristic expansiveness. Her million-dollar fingers can stand a little dirt if that means one rhododendron bush will enjoy a longer life.*
>
> *Walking next to this lithe and ever-youthful doe, I felt like a giant cow with thirty-five extra pounds of pregnancy weight topping my already hefty figure. Gads! But before I left, Karismah reminded me of the true miracle of birth. "There's nothing more beautiful than a woman with child," she declared, probably thinking back on her own nine-month odyssey to produce precious little Beeno. "As soon as you set eyes on your wondrous baby, you'll understand," she added knowingly. I can't wait until December.*

I could have devoured the entire issue, but it was time to go back and meet my career specialist. Sitting face-to-face with one of the experts, I was eager to hear the big results.

"Well, Laurel," he said, adjusting his tie. "I have excellent news for you." I leaned forward in my seat expectantly.

"You," he declared, "are a bossa nova."

I was dumbfounded.

"With just a touch of merengue," he added, "and a little cha-cha-cha."

"I'm sorry," I asked tentatively, "this has what to do with my career?"

"It has everything to do with your career. You came here to find out how your song dances. And I'm telling you."

"Umm . . . bossa nova, merengue, and cha-cha-cha?"

"A little cha-cha-cha," he corrected.

"So, I'm pretty . . . Latin?" I guessed.

"That's not a job!" he laughed. "We're much more scientific than that. I'm pleased to inform you that you are ideally suited to be—and remember, there is a one point seven percent margin of error—a retail specialist in the biotech industry."

"What?"

"Either that, or quality control in a transportation warehouse."

He handed me a scroll of paper with a ribbon tied around it. "Here's your diploma," he said, patting me on the back. "Show it around on your job interviews. And don't forget—Do the Hustle!"

Thank God Irwin rescued me from that disaster in his little red Audi, but even after a night of getting drilled by the dentist, I was still depressed about my aptitude results the next morning when we went to the supermarket.

"Where am I going to find a transportation warehouse?" I moaned as Irwin pulled a box of pancake mix off a shelf and threw it into our shopping cart. "And how do I do quality control? Examine containers to make sure they're not going to fall apart on the railroad?"

Irwin was as perplexed as I. "Dunno. Hey, you want some blueberries?"

I shrugged. "Either that or selling biotech stuff. Like what, I have to go door-to-door hawking genetically modified crop seeds?"

Irwin looked into my eyes tenderly. "That seminar was ridiculous—a total waste of two hundred and fifty dollars—but forget about it. Just concentrate on what *you* really want to do."

"That's the problem," I said, as we joined the line to pay. "I have no idea."

"If you could have any job in the world, what would it be?"

"I always wanted to be a writer, but the only person I ever respected in that business basically told me to forget it 'cause I suck."

"Come on, I don't believe they said that." His eyes were filled with such love and admiration that I almost felt there could be hope for me.

I tried to recall Nona's actual words. "Well," I admitted, "she said I wasn't the *worst* writer she'd ever worked with."

"Of course you're not!" he said, starting to put our groceries on the conveyor belt. "Tell me the good things she said."

I took a deep breath. "Well, she did say my character depictions have some insight and flare, and she liked my short sentences. Apparently I can be engaging . . . when I'm not trying to be deep."

"I don't know; the deeper I get into you, the more engaging you are," he said, grabbing my ass.

"Stop!" I wriggled away. "The point is, she made it all too clear that my abilities are insufficient to meet my ambitions."

"Well, maybe you just need to readjust your ambitions."

"Yeah, like a gig at *Girdle and Support Hose Quarterly*," I sighed. Irwin meant well, but he knew nothing about the business. To soothe my mounting anxiety, I grabbed a handful of junky magazines and tossed them on the counter.

We'd been so busy making eyes at each other on the way in that we hadn't bothered to notice where we were parked, so when we got out, it took us a good ten minutes of wandering up and down the asphalt before we found his car. It was the thing I hated most about shopping in the suburbs—except, of course, the congested traffic, which we encountered next.

When we got back to his house, Irwin mentioned that he'd cleared out a whole dresser just for my stuff. I should have been thrilled by the intimate gesture, but instead I felt strangely disconcerted. "That's okay, honey," I said. "I'd rather just bring fresh clothes every time." It must have been insecurity about my work prospects. I trusted Irwin would understand.

22

Nona, Nona, Nona. I couldn't sleep that night imagining those big, wise owl eyes watching me. Irwin had made me realize that she'd never said I sucked as a writer, only that I'd failed as a novelist. Suddenly, I remembered that letter she'd left for me at Gallant, the one I'd shoved to the bottom of my bag without reading.

I climbed over Irwin's sculpted body, slipped out to the living room, and retrieved the envelope. As I'd initially suspected, there was no card inside, just a sheet from my novel marked up with a note at the bottom in her trademark red. This was her parting gift to me, but what did it mean? I unfolded the paper:

        Marie Antoinette languished
        in the Bastille, awaiting the
        guillotine. As a kindly
        gesture, Napoleon had sent his
        hairdresser to the doomed
        monarch for her last updo.
        Marguerite was immediately
        impressed by the gracious

cordiality with which she was invited into the dungeon. Despite the dirt and grime, the deposed queen exuded an air of grace and sensitivity. Yes, she had spent the last three years chained to a wall, but her hair still shone radiantly in the one beam of light coming through the bars.

Despite the circumstances, Marie Antoinette's regal air hadn't faded. With that aristocratic chin pointed high, she demanded that the guards unchain her for the beauty appointment, and they obliged, clearly in her thrall.

As Marguerite lathered the royal locks in a bucket of dirty water, the daughter of the rulers of the Holy Roman Empire, who had grown up always believing her destiny was to become Queen of France, complained about the ingratitude of her subjects. "The stories you read in the citizen's press about my excesses are vastly overstated," she said with her lilting Viennese accent. "Okay, maybe I was a teenaged party animal," she conceded, "and I did indulge in a shopping spree now and then. But that 'Let them eat cake' line is pure republican spin. Look at this waist!" She gestured to her perfect hourglass figure. "Do you think I eat cake?"

Marguerite acknowledged the low-carb bod. "No, Your Highness."

"And how they go on about my spending! Sure, I never wear the same designer hoop skirt twice; what royal does? But the year before the revolution, I reduced the household staff at Versailles from twelve thousand to eight thousand. Whether it was helping to carry a fifty-five-pound side of venison or dusting that blasted Hall of Mirrors, I shouldered my burden around the palace. And what will I have left to show for it? Nothing but my shoulders!" she lamented.

The poor, beautiful head. Marguerite did her best to make it pretty for when it landed in the basket the following day. Reflecting on the soon-to-be-cut-short life of this extraordinary woman, she realized that no amount of eye-catching looks, heartthrob boyfriends, swinging minuets on the hottest dance floors, or flaunting the finest fads and fashions could save a queen from the guillotine.

I braced myself and read Nona's comments. She had given

me a report card of sorts:

> **Verisimilitude: F (timeline is way off)**
> **Plot sequencing: D- (doesn't fit the novel's structure)**
> **Literary possibilities: Zero (need I say more?)**
> **BUT**

That one word held the promise of a better future. *But what?* I thought, and read on:

> **Character profile: A+! This is an amusing, insightful glance at one of history's great, misunderstood women. Unfortunately, you've totally mangled the facts (low-carb diet?), and your voice is thoroughly modern (party animal?)—get out of the eighteenth century—but there's a market for this sort of profile. Maybe you should try the Biography Channel, or better yet, something that doesn't require fact-checking. Anyway, you're a brave girl, and buried inside this hopeless novel there is evidence of talent. Get out there and use it.**
> **Best of luck, Nona.**

She was encouraging me, but the Biography Channel? Ugh. And anyway, that was fact-check city.

Then another idea struck, keeping me up for the rest of the night, this time not with anxiety but with an electric sense of possibility.

I didn't discuss my inspiration with anyone—not even Irwin, and least of all Vanessa, who surprised me out of the blue to invite me to lunch at her apartment. I dreaded going, but I had to give her the benefit of the doubt. Hoping she'd heard me and that we could start our relationship on a new footing, I showed up that week at the familiar lobby and was let up for the first time.

Standing before the apartment door, I was ready to be blown away. I had been inside the most fabulous New York apartments, but I'd always imagined Vanessa's would be extraordinary, just like her—expansive and bright and filled with interesting intimate objects, souvenirs of the deep relationships she'd cultivated over the course of her life. Like a temple of wisdom, I'd thought those allowed to enter would leave with some profound insight.

But when a bulky, middle-aged man opened the door, wearing a faded argyle sweater, I almost had to laugh at my delusion. The fantasy faded quickly as I took in the sterile surroundings. Her place was decorated like a suite in a chain hotel—everything standardized to fit a dull color palette of grays and pastels.

Vanessa came scurrying over. "Darling," she said to Mr. Pixley, "meet Laurel. I told you about her."

"The one who just got a divorce?" he guessed. She shook her head and tried to interrupt.

"No—"

"The one who started her own business?" he asked again.

"No—" she repeated.

"That's good," he said brightly, "'cause you always say she's such a whiner."

It was an awkward moment, but Vanessa covered it by quickly ushering me into the living room and pushing him off to the bedroom.

Seated on her cloud-colored couch, I could tell Vanessa was eager to bring me back into the fold. She took my hand in hers and locked eyes with mine. "Laurel, I thought about everything you said, and it's true; I haven't shared enough about myself. So today, I want you to learn all about me. Where shall I begin?"

She had me there. It wasn't exactly a normal friendship if someone had to hold a debriefing about their background all in one afternoon, but I gave it a go. "Where'd you grow up?"

"Mom and Dad met at our town church in Lofton,

Massachusetts," she began. "Dad's grandfather's father was a Scotsman, but Mom's side of the family was Irish-Dutch-German-Swedish."

"Is that so?" I asked, wishing she would let go of my hand so I could sit back comfortably. No such luck. As Vanessa droned on about her genealogy, birth, childhood, and the rest, I struggled to look interested. This was worse than one of Lucien's endless lectures about obscure art—at least he'd been sexy to look at. Vanessa just looked small and sad. The woman I'd always thought was larger than life—a force of nature, beautiful, uninhibited, and strong—was actually just another Vassar alum who'd made herself out to be more than she was.

And I'd been a willing participant in the charade. All too keen to find a magic solution to my problems, I'd embraced her in the role of fairy godmother, or more accurately, substitute sister.

"...I used to teach our dog, Chestnut, to fetch Dad's slippers. It was the cutest thing..." she was saying. For all the spa treatments and fancy meals, Vanessa had always shown signs of being mortal; I'd just conveniently ignored them so I could preserve the image of her as my savior. The way she always put Splenda in her coffee, just like my mother. The way she sometimes pretended to know all about matters, like the publishing industry, by dropping facts that she had culled from her news feed. I was working for Gallant at the time but suppressed my more informed opinions to not undermine her authority.

"...my dress was made of taffeta, and I wore the same necklace Mummy had worn to her prom..."

Yes, Vanessa was an ordinary American girl turned self-proclaimed saint, but I'd been fully responsible for joining her church.

I managed to escape before she got to her tenth wedding anniversary by making excuses about walking Bogey and Bacall. Vanessa let me go but not without signaling first, pinky to mouth, thumb to ear, that I should call her. Although I nodded, I knew I never would.

Walking to Mrs. Lilianthaller's apartment, I consoled myself that my infatuation with Vanessa hadn't all been a waste and that the grandiose parts of her I'd imagined were in fact a projection of my own inner qualities. I didn't need her to take me to the Duplex anymore, to coach me on making my dreams come true, or to tell me what they were. She'd been great in her own way, but I was unhappy with Lucien and Gallant, and if I'd followed her, I'd still be stuck with them both. It was time to harness my impulse to believe in a greater future for myself and combine it with good old common sense.

Nona hadn't realized it, but she'd pointed me right to my dream job. Of course, how could I not have seen before? I thought of all those hours I spent at the library sneaking peeks at *Celebrity Style* when I should have been at *Celebrity Style* getting paid to do what I love!

I knew the destination; I'd just have to figure out how to get there.

When I arrived at Mrs. Lilianthaller's, I learned that the poodles were out with another neighbor, but she invited me up. In truth, the sweet retiree needed just as much company as the dogs did, so I climbed the stairs to her floor.

"How nice of you to stop by," she said, leading me into the dusty, cramped apartment. It was the perfect antidote to Vanessa's place, crammed with personal touches: dozens of pictures of kids, grandkids, and even a great-grandbaby competing for space with postcards sent by friends from around the world.

"So how's your new place in Tribeca?" She was referring to my planned love nest with Lucien.

"Oh, it didn't work out," I said.

"Found a better one?" she asked, tottering to the kitchen in search of some sweets.

"Nah . . . I'm back with my parents."

Mrs. Lilianthaller returned with a plate of graham crackers.

"Don't they live on the Island? I thought you work here."

"That's the thing," I said, crunching on a stale cracker. "I lost my job. But as soon as I get a new one, I'm looking for a place."

"Well, if it's in the next few weeks, let me know." She leaned in and whispered conspiratorially. "Apartment 4-F downstairs is moving out. I may look like just an old lady, but the super has a huge crush on me," she added with a wink.

Hmm... I thought. A couple of weeks to get a new gig. And wouldn't Irwin be surprised when I told him about a Village apartment in a rent-controlled building.

Salli Simmer's maternity leave would be my foot in the door. Task number one: Find out the name of her replacement. Task number two: Replace her replacement with me.

"Hello?" I said in my best business-like tone, calling from my parents' den and hoping the sound of the lawnmower out back couldn't be heard through the phone. "I'm with Central Supply. We're updating our records, and we understand Salli Simmer's going on maternity leave in December?"

"That's right," chirped a bubbly-sounding receptionist.

"So whose name should we put on the account during her absence?" My cheeks burned at my own audacity. Surely this woman would realize there's no such thing as Central Supply.

"That would be Fatima Smith," she said obligingly.

"Great, thank you." I hung up quickly and began my search of Fatima Smith's articles.

A quick Google revealed that this woman had more entertainment journalism awards than just about everyone except Salli Simmer. How was a girl whose last published work was a poem in the Hoboken Herald going to compete with credentials like that?

"It's our first double-date!" Trish squealed as we arrived at the Island Bowl-A-Rama. "Just like we pictured when we were kids!"

"Only it's not Richie Menzel and Jump-Shot Jimmy," I

laughed.

"Thank God," we both said at once.

The noisy alley was full of happy couples, and as with seemingly all other sports, Irwin was a natural, hitting strike after strike. I bowled nothing but gutter balls, but it was worth it to have him put his arms around me to try to improve my form.

Ever the provider, Trish had brought snacks for us all, but not the ones Tom wanted.

"What about my mom's cookies? Kids ate them again?" he asked.

"Every single one," she replied. When Tom went up to take his turn, Trish leaned in and confessed the truth. "I threw out his mother's chocolate chip wonders."

"Were they that terrible?" I asked.

"The opposite—they're divine. That's why I never let Tom have any. If I do, he'll realize what he's missing when mine come out of the oven."

Oh, the sneaky ways of wives, I thought. But at the same time, I grasped the strategy, and it was brilliant: Never let your understudy get on stage.

By the end of the evening, I felt like I'd heard enough clattering pins to last a lifetime, but Trish had other ideas. "We should make this a standing date. Like girls' night out, only all of us together!"

"How about we check out a movie next time?" Irwin suggested, as though he'd read my thoughts.

"Yeah, we could check out what's playing at the Film Forum downtown," I said. Just because I was no longer with Lucien didn't mean I'd given up on culture.

"You mean in the city?" Tom asked doubtfully. "Too much traffic. We've got movie theaters here."

Trish backed him up. "Last time we drove around for an hour looking for a spot. We ended up spending sixty bucks on a garage."

I complained about their attitude to Irwin in the car on the way home. "I love Trish and Tom, but don't they realize there's a whole world on the other side of the Midtown Tunnel?"

"Hey, baby, I'll take you to a movie in Paris if you want, but I can see their point," he said, a little too sympathetically. "When you get used to life around here, you don't really want to bother going to the city. It can be such a hassle."

That night, he showed me a closet he'd cleared out, but I didn't feel any closer to wanting to move my stuff in.

23

I had no hesitation, however, about trying to my make big move into Salli Simmer's job at *Celebrity Style*. I had worked it all out in my head, but, lost in the crowds pouring through the lobby of the Condé Nast Building, I realized how far plans can be from reality.

I got off to a rocky start, accosting four pregnant women who were not my prey, including one who turned out to be a male undercover cop. Luckily he didn't give me a summons for harassment, but I nearly lost my nerve after that.

My fears only grew when I finally spotted a harried-looking woman clearly in her final trimester who was screaming at an old merchant behind his candy stand.

"Again? Still no Mentos? What is it with you people? I can't walk across the street in this condition, and I need my Mentos!"

I could see she was frazzled, but I reminded myself that even the hungriest dog loves to be stroked, so I reached into my bag, pulled out a copy of the magazine and a pen I had at the ready, and approached her. "Oh my gosh. Aren't you Salli Simmer, the star reporter for *Celebrity Style*?"

She turned toward me with a suspicious snarl on her lips. "What's it to you?"

So it was her. "I'm your biggest fan. I've read everything you've ever written. Your coverage of the Winter Olympics—I cried my heart out, it was so inspiring. Could I please have an autograph?"

Salli rolled her eyes but took my pen obligingly. As she started to sign her name with a flourish, I went in for the kill. "So I hear Fatima Smith is replacing you when you have the baby. She's awesome!"

Salli blanched and handed me the magazine, keeping my pen. "Do you happen to have any Mentos?" she asked impatiently. "'Cause if I don't have one in the next five minutes, I swear this baby will start going through withdrawal symptoms." She clutched her stomach.

"I might have a Lifesaver..." I stammered.

"What are you, deaf? I want a Mentos. Ach," she groaned, "this kid is elbowing my bladder."

Before I could say another word, she took off toward the lobby coffee shop.

I followed her inside and saw her make a beeline to the bathroom. Frozen in place, I pondered the ethics of the situation. Surely Salli deserved to pee in peace. Just then, a hostess stepped up and made it clear that if I wasn't going to take a table I'd have to take it outside. Noticing there were two exits in the restaurant that Salli might escape from, I knew there was only one option for me.

Darting past the hostess, I slipped into the bathroom and headed into the one empty stall. Salli was farting loudly, and I considered giving up the whole project, but I knew I had to hold my nose and proceed.

I sat on the closed toilet and leaned toward the partition. "I'll say one thing for that Fatima Smith," I said loudly, my voice echoing off the dingy tiles, "she really knows how to convey the lives of the rich and famous."

"Did you follow me in here?" Salli asked angrily. "What are you—some kind of pervert?"

This was not going according to plan. "I had to pee, too," I said weakly.

There was a loud flush, and I could hear Salli trying to quickly zipper up her maternity jumper, so I rushed out of my stall to catch her before she escaped.

While I washed my hands next to the famous columnist, I gave it another try. "Wow, you must be really confident to let Fatima step in your shoes."

"Why—what do you mean?" She shot me an irritated look in the mirror.

"Fatima stops at nothing to get what she wants. Just look at her exclusive last week," I said, hoping she'd take the bait before I lost her.

"What, that little hospital bed nonsense? I get those interviews on a bad day." Toweling off her hands, she turned to leave and said, with finality, "Well, have a nice life."

I ran out, following her to Broadway. Salli stopped in her tracks and confronted me in a huff. "Look, you got your autograph. Are you some kind of stalker?"

"No, I'm just an admirer. I want to congratulate you for having the guts to choose somebody as good and clever and incisive and ambitious as Fatima to replace you. I mean, temporarily of course."

"Yes, well, thank you. Thank you." Salli looked at me with disdain and stuck out her arm to hail a cab.

"Most people would be too insecure to do that; they'd be worried that Fatima might try to steal their job," I said, feeling my desperation mount.

A taxi pulled over, and Salli stepped into it. "She wouldn't try to steal my job; she loves me. In fact, she threw me a huge baby shower at her own expense."

Salli squeezed herself into the cab, and as I took a step toward her, she closed the door between us. "As a matter of fact," she added through the open window, "Fatima bought me a two-year pass to Mommy and Me classes at Curves." Turning to the driver, she commanded, "Park and Seventy-Fifth," and they were off.

As the car pulled away, I ran alongside and hurled my last frenzied pitch. "But what did she write on the card?" I screamed.

I was left standing in the dust, watching the yellow cab drive off when it screeched to a stop and began backing up slowly. The window came down, and Salli stared at me, looking white as a ghost. "I remember exactly what she wrote on that card," she said. "It seemed so innocent at the time: 'Take a nice long rest, and don't worry about anything. I'll handle the readers so they'll never notice you're gone.'"

"Oh, I bet that's exactly what she wants," I goaded.

Salli stepped out of the cab and put a hand on my shoulder to steady herself. "Do you think it's all a big setup?"

"Either that, or she's genuinely sweet."

"In this business? Impossible. How could I not have seen it?"

"Well, it's not too late to protect yourself," I nudged.

"But this is my last week," she said desperately. "What can I do?"

"Just make sure your replacement is someone who makes your readers miss you," I suggested.

"How can I find someone bad enough to make me look good at such short notice?"

"Hey, I'm a failed writer!" I said brightly.

By the time I'd told her about my poem in the *Hoboken Herald*, "Total Eclipse of the Canoe Trip," and the fact that Gallant Publishing had paid me to *not* write a book, she was sold.

"I've got an interview now, but can you be back here at four?" she asked.

"Of course," I said, praying her water wouldn't break before then.

That's how I found myself, two hours later, seated in front of the editor-in-chief of *Celebrity Style*, Weldon H. Sutton.

"Maybe it's those hormones," he began, crossing his arms skeptically, "but she's threatening to quit if I don't hire you outright."

Yay! The plan had worked.

"Of course, I can't do that."

You can't? I thought. *What about my plan?*

"You have no published work, unless you count winning some crappy contest over ten years ago," he said, looking at me with pity. "But I told Salli I'd give you a chance—one chance— to prove yourself."

So I still had a shot!

"If you can deliver me a crisp, eight-hundred-word profile of an A-list celebrity worthy of publication in our magazine, I'll sign you on as her replacement."

Goal! I thought, wondering who they'd assign me to interview and feeling ready to jump out of my shoes with excitement. "So who's the big star?" I asked eagerly.

"That's what you have to tell us," he said.

"You mean I have to find the celebrity?"

"Aren't you supposed to be the reporter?"

"Yes, sir, I'll find someone huge. I have tons of phone numbers," I promised, my heart sinking, knowing they all belonged to failed writers, suburban housewives, and dog owners.

I desperately relayed the news to Irwin over a Middle Eastern salad at Saint Marks Place, where he'd sweetly brought me, knowing I'd had enough of Long Island *kultcha*.

"I have to be six degrees away from someone huge, but who? Don't you have any patients whose mom or dad or uncle or cousin or somebody is an A-list celebrity?"

"Closest I come is that crown I did for a guy who drives a limo," he laughed.

"I'm serious!" I whimpered. "This is my big shot."

"So why don't you go back to your candy-ass ex-boyfriend? He's supposed to know everyone in town."

Of course I'd already thought of Lucien. Pride wasn't the issue—I would have been happy to throw myself at his mercy— but he was so snobby that his idea of A-list was the Icelandic experimental photographer who only worked in the midnight sun, not the Hollywood hottie Weldon H. Sutton was after.

"Nah . . . he's useless," I said, happy that Irwin was so secure he wouldn't have minded me contacting an ex.

"What about that princess whose dog you used to walk; you know, in that fancy building on West Street?"

The Meier tower—of course! The princess was long gone, but it couldn't get any more A-list than Ruxandra del Mar, the star I'd seen on my last visit there. Except she was notorious for banning all reporters for miles around.

When I explained this to Irwin, he smiled. "Perfect," he said. "You're not a reporter. Now, what does she need that only you have?"

I strained my mind trying to recall every word of the conversation I'd overheard. "Pulverized rhino meat . . . or something?" I guessed, trying to remember the name of the diet aid she'd been so desperate for.

I expected Irwin to look at me like I was crazy, but instead, he calmly corrected my mistake. "You mean desiccated hippo liver."

"You know about that stuff?"

"Marisa was practically an addict. Used to sprinkle it on potatoes."

I nearly gagged at the thought but pressed him for more information. "Where did she get it? I hear it's impossible to find."

"In Flushing, where else?"

Half an hour and a short cab ride later, we found ourselves in a crowded, narrow alleyway. Hidden among the bright neon signs, storefront tanks full of swimming fish, and sidewalk vendors selling tchotchkes was a small pharmacy. Instead of aspirin and cough syrup, though, the place was overflowing with baskets of gnarly, dried roots, herbal tinctures, and strange-looking apparitions. We scored the last three packets of desiccated hippo liver, and I felt like Jack and the Beanstalk hurrying out with potential magic in my pocket.

The next day I went straight to the Meier building, hoping to run into Ruxandra del Mar, but Natan told me she wouldn't be back until Thursday. "The best time to catch her is at about four when she comes from breakfast," he told me. It was bumping up on my deadline, but there was no choice. I had to wait and pray that she'd have a big meal and feel really bloated that day.

When it arrived, Irwin drove me to the train station and walked me to the platform. It was a clear, bright November afternoon. "Everything's coming together for you," he said.

"Yeah, I already got the great guy, and now I'm going for the dream job."

"I'm the great guy? I'm the lucky guy." He zipped my leather jacket up, held me close, and spoke softly. "I have never been so happy as I've been these last couple of weeks. You know I'm dead in love with you."

He'd said it before, but hearing it again made me glow inside. "I love you, too." I had planned on waiting until I got the job to tell him Mrs. Lilianthaller's insider tip, but in the moment, it slipped through my lips. "And . . . I have a lead on a rent-controlled apartment in the East Village. As soon as I get this gig, it's back to the city!"

I expected Irwin to cheer, but he looked crestfallen. "Back to the city? I was hoping you'd move in with me." He took a step away as we heard the rumble of the approaching train in the background.

"This is even better. We can move together to Manhattan. Isn't that what you always dreamed of?"

"Yeah, maybe when I was sixteen, but I'm thirty now, and hello? I own a house and run a business on Long Island."

As the train pulled in, my heart sank, but rather than dwell on our different domestic tastes, I leaned in and kissed him. "Okay, I understand," I said. "I don't even have the job yet, so let's not think about it."

Ricardo was on duty at the Meier building. He let me hang around the lobby and, being an old friend, even agreed to go along with my scheme. So when Ruxandra's long, white stretch Hummer drove up, we began our fake conversation.

"Really, so you used to weigh three hundred and forty pounds?" he asked as the glamour queen walked into earshot. I almost forgot my lines at the intimidating sight of this world-famous diva. It was nothing like seeing Yelena Yelenovich slumped in a beanbag chair. Ruxandra had an impenetrable air of grandeur, plus the usual entourage shielding her on all sides.

"Yep," I said as they moved through the lobby. When I noticed they weren't paying attention, I added, "I lost two hundred pounds without even dieting." That got the group to quiet down and start eavesdropping, but Ruxandra still seemed uninterested. "This stuff is a miracle." I desperately held up the packet of fine brown powder.

"What did you say it was called again?" Ricardo asked loudly.

"Desiccated hippo liver," I said as slowly and deliberately as possible. I felt like an idiot, but this was the only bait on my hook. And just then, Ruxandra bit.

"Halt!" she commanded the entourage. "Did anyone else hear what I just heard? Or was it one of the voices in my head?"

Lars of Lars of Beverly Hills stared at me like I was some kind of intruder, but Missouri Culpeper, Personal Trainer to the Stars, rushed to my side. "How much do you want for that?" she whispered from the corner of her mouth. I couldn't give it to the assistant. I had to hit my target, so I brushed her off. "Not selling," I said.

Ruxandra herself swaggered over. I almost went blind looking at the stunning actress I'd seen in so many great films, and I almost went dumb trying to speak to someone who was the object of millions of people's dreams and jealousies.

Almost, that is, until I looked into her eyes. There I saw it, that familiar gaze I knew so well from the pleading stares of Slobodan, Kingpin, Mini, Bogey, Bacall, and every other dog I'd ever been master to. Whether in canines or humans, the meaning was the same: What do I have to do to get that treat?

"Everybody has their price," she said, towering over me and grinding her spike heel into the floor. "Name yours."

I let a pause hang in the air while I fingered the envelope

teasingly. Suspense was every trainer's secret weapon. The longer I waited, the more ready she seemed to give me the six-thousand-dollar denim jacket off her back. But I wanted more.

"Oh, you can have this," I said, sniffing the little packet and then rolling my eyes with delight. "And I wouldn't ask for anything in return. But—I've always been a huge fan of your acting, and when I saw you in that revival of *A Chorus Line*, I realized you were one of the truly great artists of American musical theater." I was counting on her to react the way Cadbury did whenever I commanded him to roll over. He'd immediately dive into his tumble, loving the attention, and when he was through, his eyes gleamed with pride and satisfaction. Ruxandra looked similarly mesmerized. "I'd just love to hear you sing 'Tits and Ass,'" I suggested.

"That's outrageous," said Lars. "Ms. del Mar isn't some street performer."

"No," Ruxandra announced regally. "If she insists, I can perform. The actual name of the song you're referring to is 'Dance 10, Looks 3,'" she added with delight. "But I will need my cane and top hat."

"What a brilliant idea!" fawned Missouri.

It felt like I had stepped into one of Ruxandra's caper films. She took my hand and started guiding me to the elevator. "Did you not love the outfit I wore for that number?" she asked in the same intimate tone Trish and I might share.

"Loved it!" I affirmed.

"Well, you are in for a treat, because I have it upstairs!" she squealed. We were in the dusted bronze elevator. "Where do I live again?" she asked. Lars pressed eleven.

Ruxandra's three-thousand-square-foot apartment had more mirrors than the Hall at Versailles. No wonder she worried about her figure; you could see dozens of reflections of her everywhere you turned.

She sat me down in her personal home theater and ordered a black-and-white-clad maid to bring me whatever I wanted before disappearing into a back room.

As I waited, sipping a ginseng seltzer, I prayed that
Ruxandra would still be my best friend when she realized I was
after an interview. Before long, the lights went dark, and the
strains of what sounded like a live orchestra but could only have
been the most high-tech of speaker systems started playing the
Broadway tune. A spotlight from an upper balcony beamed onto
the stage area in front of me, and Ruxandra emerged,
transformed into Val, the auditioning dancer in *A Chorus Line.*

Her moves showcased grace, rhythm, pizzazz, and beauty. I
was transfixed from the moment she started singing until she
took a sweeping bow at the end.

"Bravo! You're a genius! Incredible! Thank you, Ruxandra!"
I stood and applauded, wishing I had a dozen roses to throw her
but realizing I had something she wanted even more. "Here," I
handed her my three packets of the diet aid. "You really don't
need it—your body is just perfect—but there's always more
where that came from."

Ruxandra ripped open one of the bags and poured half of its
contents down her throat, momentarily looking less than
glamorous. "So it's not true what the tabloids say," I cooed.
"You really do your own dance moves. And you're so much
nicer than they claim. How unfair is the press?"

Throwing herself dramatically across the couch, Ruxandra
launched into a long speech about the cruelty of exploitive
reporters. "Even when I had my first bit role they started lying
about my love life, and I was only eight for God's sake."

I listened sympathetically as she ranted, cried, whimpered,
and cursed about the media. She punched a pillow when she
described how she'd only heard about Roberto's affair with the
elderly baron when "Entertainment Tonight" stuck a camera in
her face to film her reaction.

"That is so awful—you poor thing!" Ruxandra rested her
head on my lap, and I stroked her hair gently. "If only you could
tell your side of the story to someone you could trust."

"Trust a reporter?" She looked at me as if I had just told her
to jump off a bridge. "Are you kidding? They're all sharks.
Every last one. They're only after my blood. They'll rip me limb

from limb."

"Oh, I agree completely," I said. "I went to school for writing, and the journalists were always looking for a salacious angle. But not all writers are journalists. What you need is somebody who can put into words the poetry of your existence."

Ruxandra looked intrigued. "I've always wanted to let the world know what a beautiful person I really am inside."

"They only focus on your outer beauty, but they don't know how much time you spend helping other people."

"Exactly!" she said. "Like, I'm really working on promoting literacy right now. After all, if people can't read, how can they appreciate the credits at the end of a film? Who's done my hair, my makeup, my wardrobe? I don't look this beautiful without the help of others."

"You obviously care about making sure everyone is appreciated. It's a story that needs to be told," I said solemnly.

"Did you say you were a writer?" she asked.

"I did go to Vassar, but I haven't published anything since I was seventeen, unless you count a poem in a local New Jersey newspaper. I'm afraid I've earned more money by not publishing my work than by publishing it." For the second time in as many weeks, I was flashing my loser credentials.

Ruxandra was even more intrigued than Salli by my total lack of professionalism. "You know what? Maybe it is time for the world to know the real Ruxandra," she said. "Are you game?"

Are you kidding?!

I had offered her treats, she did her trick, I rewarded her, and now she was a puppy in my arms.

And they said dog-walking is a useless skill.

24

While Irwin slept peacefully, I worked by the glow of my laptop at his desk, hour after hour, transcribing, organizing, writing, rewriting, polishing, and finalizing my draft. When it was done, I collapsed into my lover's arms.

The next morning, I asked Irwin to drive me to the train, but he wouldn't hear of it. "On such an important day? You're not relying on the LIRR. I'll be your chauffeur." He promptly canceled his first three appointments.

We battled traffic on the way in, and although Irwin was driving, I was the one who was a bundle of nerves. I kept checking to make sure I hadn't somehow lost the envelope with my printed-out story, which was way too hot to send electronically and risk a leak, along with exclusive photos Ruxandra had allowed me to shoot.

When we reached the Time-Life building, Irwin tried to calm me down. "Don't worry," he ran the back of his hand across my cheek. "They're going to love it!"

"What if they don't? This is my only shot."

"They will! But listen," he took me in his arms, "no matter what happens, you'll never be alone. It took me a lifetime to find you, and I'm not letting go. I don't care if you're a top columnist or a dog-walker, as long as you're mine."

My nervousness turned into joy. "Of course I'm yours," I

said, looking into his bright eyes and realizing that I was already as lucky as they get.

He kissed me tenderly. "As long as we're always together, everything's going to be great."

I murmured in agreement, kissing him back. "You mean that? You really love me?"

"Hey," he said, "a guy like me doesn't face a morning commute to Manhattan during rush hour if it's not love."

Celebrity Style's offices were located on the forty-fourth floor, and each time I thought I was headed up there, someone else would enter the elevator and stop it along the way. That ride felt like it took forever, but I knew it would be nothing compared to having to wait for Weldon H. Sutton to react to my article. I'd probably hear within a week, if I was lucky, and what would I do in the meantime?

I went straight to the editor-in-chief's receptionist, who regarded me impassively and stuck my article on top of an in-tray. "So will I be hearing from you soon?" She merely nodded in response, and I turned to leave, pausing to gaze at some of the framed covers on the wall. I had read each one of these chronicles of the vicissitudes of fame. It was like looking at a museum dedicated to my favorite pastime.

I was momentarily lost in the fantasy of rushing through these halls with my latest column when a voice behind me bellowed, "STOP! YOU!" I froze and then turned to see Weldon H. Sutton holding my article and pointing at me, his neck veins bulging. I was gripped by fear, thinking I'd have to beat another disgraceful retreat like I had at Gallant.

"You had the nerve to bring me a personal interview with Ruxandra del Mar?"

I gulped. I must have crossed some line. Maybe she was a persona non grata at *Celebrity Style*. Maybe they'd sworn her off years ago.

"This is unbelievable. We've sent every one of our reporters to get an exclusive with her, and she's turned us down for the past three years. And now you've done it. You're a genius." I didn't know whether to trust my hearing, until he added, in no uncertain terms, "Hey everybody, meet our new star columnist, Laurel Linden."

Streams of staffers started crowding into Weldon H. Sutton's office. Squeals of wonder traveled through the room as they competed to get a first glance at my exclusive photos.

"She looks fabulous!" cried one staffer.

"This is a miracle—how did you get to her?" wondered another.

"Eat your heart out, *People Magazine!*" guffawed Mr. Sutton. "This is the scoop of the year." I was feeling dizzy from all the excitement.

Suddenly, a face I recognized from my Google search moved up from within the crowd. "Yeah, but is it well-written?" asked Fatima Smith, plucking my exclusive from the editor's hands and looking at it with disdain.

"Don't you worry about that." Weldon grabbed it back. "This writing's spicier than four-alarm hot sauce." Setting his glasses on the tip of his nose, he began to read to a hushed crowd.

> We all know who she is . . . or do we?
> Her molten eyes and volcanic talent have
> sizzled movie screens and melted hearts
> for nearly a decade now, not to mention
> those off-screen eruptions! Yet Ruxandra
> del Mar may be the most misunderstood
> woman since Marie Antoinette (who,
> incidentally, never said "Let 'em eat
> cake." She was a low-carb Queen.)
> The six-foot, sultry stunner hasn't
> given an interview in three years, since
> she bid adios to Roberto in a live
> television breakup . . . until now. She
> bares all about her most intimate
> concerns, deepest fears, secret desires,

and, oh yeah, that bisexual bullfighter who bumped her for a Bavarian baron.

"It's been just awful having to hide all this time," she says, that honey-sweet voiced tinged with bitterness as she curls up with a mink pillow on a white leather couch in her fifteen-million-dollar penthouse overlooking New York Harbor. "God knows why anyone would care about my love life," she adds modestly, as if millions around the world weren't fantasizing about Ruxandra between the sheets at night.

"But if they're curious, I've always been happy to share with my fans, just don't stick a camera in my face before I've had a chance to wax my unibrow."

The perfect blonde crescents above her eyes—separate, thank you very much, courtesy of Mandolina of Malibu—furrow at the memory of that particular public humiliation. Roberto was never the issue, she insists. "His tepid temperament was no match for my blazing passion."

She'd long been planning to put out the flame of their love and only continued wearing that spectacular five-carat engagement ring because she hadn't found the right time to break it to him gently.

Too bad "Celebrities Uncensored" found Roberto first as he played freaky footsie with his geriatric German in a hot tub in Baden-Baden.

"Why anyone cared so much about a silly fetish when there are over six hundred million illiterate people on the planet is beyond me," she says, characteristically turning the subject away from herself and to the world at large — the world that rarely sees how much Ruxandra does for it, because she doesn't invite the cameras along when she's out in jeans and a sweatshirt giving her all to the cause she cares so passionately about.

"Children need to learn to read — after all, how else will they be able to tell the ingredients in their packaged foods or understand the care labels on their garments? Without reading, we risk a world of badly nourished people in shrunken clothes!" The fourteen-thousand-dollar, sapphire-studded suede pantsuit she sports was never in danger of shrinking. After all, between shooting her remake of *It Came from Uranus* and hawking her wildly successful line of sushi-flavored edible panties (she swears by the spicy eel), Ruxandra's too busy to do her own laundry, but her concern shows just how much she's able to relate to the average person.

"Woo-hoo!" Weldon whooped. "And there's plenty more — she actually got the ice queen to cry about her big dis at this year's Golden Globes. You," he turned to me, "really know how to mix up the celebrity dish, and we're gonna sell it like hotcakes."

They showed me my bright, airy office overlooking Radio City Music Hall, gave me all manner of applications for press ID, assigned me computer passwords, and introduced me to Salli's—or rather, my—personal secretary. My first assignment would be to attend the Oscar nominations and write about Hollywood's Hottest Hairdos.

I floated out of there like one of those giant balloons in the Thanksgiving Day Parade. I felt larger than life, and even the strangers I met on the street seemed to sense my excitement and regard me with wonder.

"Irwin, honey, they loved it—I got the job," I bubbled into my cell phone while I sat next to the gushing modern fountain in front of the Time-Life building.

"God, that's incredible!" he said. "I'm so happy for you, my love—hey!" he suddenly broke off. "You trying to kill someone?"

"What? Where are you?" I asked, sensing he was probably still in his car.

"Traffic's a bitch; I haven't even made it across the bridge. Hey, fuck it!" he said, struck by a new idea. "This is the biggest day of your life, and I'm headed back to work? I don't think so. I'm canceling the rest of my appointments and coming back to sweep you off your feet."

He was so spontaneous, and I was struck by an idea, too. "Meet me at Twelfth Street and Avenue A. There's a place I really want to show you."

I got there before Irwin, and, as expected, Mrs. Lilianthaller was home. In the second miracle of the day, apartment 4-F was still available, and she arranged for us to meet the super in half an hour.

While waiting outside for my love, I called my parents and relayed the news.

"Cookie, I am so proud of you!" squealed my mother. "This sounds right up your alley."

My father had picked up another extension. "So can you get

me a date with Ruxandra?"

We all laughed. "Listen, Laurel," my mother said when our giggles had subsided. "I want to throw a party for you."

Not again, I thought, picturing the nightmare at Leonard's.

"But this time, you tell me how you want to celebrate."

I would have said thanks but no thanks, but since my mother was actually willing to listen to me for a change, I took her up on the offer.

"How about a nice, quiet family dinner at your place; invite Jenna, Rob, and the kids, and I'll bring Irwin. It's about time you had a chance to get to know my boyfriend."

"Sounds like you two are getting serious," Mom observed, and I realized she was right. "So, tonight then?"

"Tonight's perfect," I confirmed.

Even though I had just kissed him goodbye that morning, when I saw Irwin again my heart leapt. Those dark eyes sparkled with so much happiness for me I could think of nothing more wonderful than us spending a lifetime together supporting each other in our dreams and making them come true.

He took me in his arms on that crumbling little stoop and kissed me deeply. "I love you," he breathed. "I knew you could do it. I always believed in you."

I was nearly moved to tears when I realized how true that was. His wasn't an egotistic, consuming kind of support that sought reward but rather a true partnership where we made each other strong.

"So why did you bring me here?" he asked with cheerful curiosity, looking up and down the battered block.

"Come with me." I took his hand and led him inside.

Apartment 4-F was bigger than Mrs. Lilianthaller's and faced the front, so the excitement from the street below could be felt inside its walls, with radios providing a backbeat to the sounds of children playing and cars rushing by. It was nicer than my old place—no exposed pipes, and the toilet flushed completely in one shot.

"Check out this water pressure!" I said, turning on the sink with enthusiasm. Irwin looked puzzled. "You're planning to live here?"

"Us, we, together." I kissed him.

"We are?" he stammered.

"Look," I demonstrated. "We can put our bed against the wall, and we can each have part of the closet. And there's even space for your mountain bike."

"Isn't it kind of small?" he asked hesitantly.

The super, a gray-haired man who had let us in and was arranging the deal, issued a warning. "You better make up your minds. I've got a dozen people in line for this place."

"How much do you want?" I asked.

"They pay thirteen hundred, but they want fifteen hundred from you. And I get two thousand key money."

A sublet. Even better, I decided. No landlords to hassle with. "We'll take it."

"You got the money now?" The super held out his hand.

"Well, uh, I don't have my checkbook with me," I said. "Can you give us 'til tomorrow?"

"If you weren't friends with Roselyn, I wouldn't hold it a minute, but I've seen you walking her dogs. So okay, three p.m. tomorrow. But no later."

The minute we were back out on the street, Irwin looked at me like I'd lost my mind. "Is this your surprise for me? What makes you think I'd want to live in a dump like that?"

"It's romantic," I said defensively.

"Romantic? It's dark as a dungeon, noisier than the LIE, you can't even turn around without hitting something, and it smells like cabbage soup. Not to mention, from here it's at least forty-five minutes to get to Penn Station before I even catch the train to Long Island. Imagine doing that every morning and night. Plus, I'd have to give up my swimming pool, my peace and quiet, and my tax deduction. No thanks."

I was devastated. Had I completely misread him? All the signs had seemed to indicate that Irwin wanted to live with me. "I thought you wanted to shack up," I said shyly.

Irwin pulled me close. "Are you kidding? I desperately want to live with you. Why do you think I keep clearing out drawers and closets for you? I want to wake up with Laurel, go to sleep with Laurel, breathe Laurel."

Thank God. I felt like I was floating on air again.

"But not in a one-bedroom dive in the East Village," he explained. "Come on, Laurel. I have a big, comfortable house. After the tax break, I pay less in mortgage for ten times the space than they want here. Sure, Massapequa's not the most exciting place on earth, but as long as we're together, we can make it fun."

I thought about it a moment, lacing my fingers in his strong hand. Irwin was right. Why push my luck? An incredible job, a devoted hunk, and a decent home. The suburbs would be a small price to pay for so much happiness.

25

Any doubts I might have entertained about my parents loving Irwin were put to rest the moment we arrived and he started marveling at my father's weedless lawn. "You can't tell me that's not sod," my boyfriend said. "It just looks too perfect."

"The real thing," my father replied proudly. "It's all in the timing of the watering. I've got a book—I'll lend it to you."

"Would you do that?" Irwin asked.

"Sure, it's called *Sprinkler Magic.* Explains the whole science of it."

Mom was charmed completely when Irwin went wild over her pot roast and mashed potatoes. "I hope you give Laurel your recipe," he said.

To me, the meat was totally tough and undercooked, and the potatoes were lumpy and bland. Why would I want that recipe?

After dinner, we moved to the living room. Emily and Bobby Jr. were delighted to have Dr. Turnov in Grandma's home and demanded that he play the same silly games that always entertained them at the dentist's office. As he sent them into fits of giggles with funny voices and gentle wrestling, Mom leaned over and offered her assessment. "You'd better grab this one and not let go. He'll make a great father."

I glowed inside, knowing it was true. Mom continued to sing Irwin's praises. "And to think, he has his own business right in Massapequa—and he owns a nice split-level colonial not ten minutes from here. You'll come over every week! You'll join the country club; Dad and Irwin will play golf; and you, Jenna, and I can hit the mall—it's every mother's dream come true."

For some reason, I felt a growing sense of suffocation as she spoke. I wanted to talk to Irwin, but by then he was engaged in a deep conversation with my father about pool chemicals, so I excused myself politely, threw on my coat, and stepped out into the cool November air.

My years in the city seemed like a mirage—the crackling excitement of close friends everywhere, the freedom of no need for cars, the twenty-four-hour everything right around the corner all fading into memory. And in its place, a predictable future, with its predictable rituals—one that looked startlingly like the life I'd tried so hard to escape.

I heard a rustle behind me and turned to see Jenna, just the person who would be thrilled that I was joining her in the march to suburban sanity. Over the past few months, our mutual understanding had grown, but I knew that on the subject of my lifestyle, she would never budge.

Until she spoke.

"You are so lucky. This guy is definitely totally sweet and crazy about you. And I've got to admit, even I couldn't have thought of a more perfect career for you than entertainment writer, much less secure the job the way you did. You've come a long way, Laurel."

From the tone of her voice, I knew there was a "but" hovering in the air.

"But are you really prepared to settle down in Massapequa, ten minutes from me and Mom? What happened to the off-beat city girl I used to admire?"

I felt my anger rise. What a hypocrite. "Admire?" I challenged. "You hated all that! You were the perfect suburban wife and mother I could never live up to with my messy, unconventional life that you were always trying to talk me out of."

"Perfect? What are you talking about? I'm the screwed-up sister, remember? The one with shrinks starting at the age of thirteen."

"Oh, sure, you had a troubled adolescence; wasn't that fun and dramatic," I said, feeling my Jenna headache approaching. "But then you got into the fitness business, married the perfect man, and became Mrs. Together."

"Come on, Laurel; you're not serious. Me, together?" Jenna sounded sincere, not angry. "I'm just as compulsive as I ever was, only now I obsess about my perfect lifestyle instead of my perfect body. But believe me, it's still a prison inside my head. I always thought you knew how nuts I am and that that's why you acted so distant."

I stared at Jenna. Who was the crazy one here, her or me? She had never once admitted that anything was wrong, and now she was saying she was still as conflicted as she had been all those years ago—and that she admired me! "I acted distant because I thought you hated everything I was."

"Well, yeah, I wasn't comfortable with the fact that you couldn't succeed at a career and you were living in a dump, but I was always jealous of your ability to be comfortable with being different."

Jealous? I couldn't believe my ears.

"You always had a creative streak; that's why I thought you were more interesting than me. You were always breaking the mold, and I was just filling it." Suddenly, I felt a rush of affection for Jenna. "Really?" I asked.

"Really," she confirmed. "That's why I'm so surprised to see you turn your back on all of that so easily. I mean, Irwin's perfect, he's great, but that was so much a part of you, I'm going to miss the old Laurel from Manhattan."

I am, too, I realized.

After we'd said our goodnights, Irwin and I went back to his car. "Is that all you're bringing?" he asked as we settled into the leather seats. "You might as well grab some more of your stuff so we can start moving you in."

Part of me was afraid to tell Irwin what I was thinking, but the part of me that was deathly allergic to suburbia knew I had to. "Look, Irwin, I love you. If there was anyone who could make me want to live on Long Island, it would be you. But I can't do it. I'm a city girl."

"So what are you saying? You want to break up?"

"No, no," I pulled him close and kissed his neck. "I just told you I love you. You're the only guy for me. But I can't see myself in a future of making pot roast, mixing pool chemicals, and trading gossip at the country club."

"Pot roast? I was just trying to flatter your mother. I don't care if you never cook."

"That isn't the point," I said. "A big part of my life is missing out here, and I feel like you just don't acknowledge that."

"Laurel, it's not like this is Siberia. You're going to be working in Manhattan. And what about me? A big part of me is out here. Haven't you ever heard of compromise?"

"Me? What about you? You act like you're more interested in your swimming pool than your girlfriend."

"Well, excuse me, but I like to swim every day," he said.

That hurt. He was supposed to say, "I love only you, darling," but here he was sticking up for a tub of chlorine instead.

"Well, I guess we'll just have to have a commuting relationship then," I snapped, laying it all on the line. "Apartments like the one we saw today don't come around very often, and I'm going to take it."

"That piece of shit?" he asked angrily.

"That piece of shit is going to be my new home. If you want to move in with me, you can come along at three o'clock tomorrow to cosign the sub-lease. Think about it." I slammed the car door on the way back to my parents' house, tears streaming down my face. I knew I was being stubborn, but as much as I wanted to join my life with Irwin's, I didn't want to lose my own self in the process.

I tossed and turned all night. When Irwin didn't call in the morning, I had to figure he'd chosen not to live with me. I knew he had his reasons, and it would be difficult, but there was no backing down. I went online, transferred money to my checking account, and hopped the train toward my new home.

I watched my phone all day, but it stayed dark, and whenever I called Irwin, I just got his voicemail and hung up. While I dawdled outside my future building fifteen minutes before our appointment, I thought I saw him coming around the corner more than once, but it turned out to be total strangers. Irwin was nowhere to be seen.

It should have been a triumphant moment, but when I met the super in 4-F and looked at the dark little space, I felt completely depressed. It was one thing to imagine moving in there with my honey, but to go it alone made me wonder if I was really making progress. Sure, this place probably had fewer mice than my last apartment, but that wasn't saying much. Still, knowing it was a steal considering New York prices and that I'd earned it through inconspicuous good deeds, I handed over the check. It would make a good story, and maybe some future dog-walker would be encouraged to help out a pooch or two in need.

The super handed me the keys and then showed me how to use them. "Turn this, and then give it a good push with your shoulder," he said. He might have saved his breath; I'd been here before.

When I walked out into the cold, gray afternoon, I was shocked as a pair of familiar hands wrapped me in a warm bear hug from behind. "Oh my God! You showed up! Let's go back in and get your name on the lease!" I was elated.

"I told you I'm not living in that dump," Irwin said.

"Then why are you here?" I asked, confused.

"To bring you home where you belong," he announced, pulling me inside a cab he had waiting. He started kissing me passionately, and I felt my resolve melt. *What the hell*, I thought. I could just keep the apartment in the city as a pied-à-terre and move most of my stuff into his place.

As we headed in the direction of Penn Station, my suspicions were confirmed. He was abducting me back to Massapequa, and with his sensuous scent filling my head, it seemed kind of cute.

But when the taxi stopped six blocks short of the LIRR hub, I started to wonder. Irwin paid the driver, grabbed my hand, and led me through a hidden courtyard with a two-story waterfall cascading along one side. We entered a revolving door and were welcomed by the sweet scent of lilies.

It was a lobby but nothing like the tiny vestibule on Twelfth Street. This was understated elegance—modern orange and red chairs surrounding a small, black table, and a concierge behind a large, brushed stainless steel counter who apparently knew Irwin. "So you brought the lady this time?" he asked before turning to me. "This guy doesn't waste time."

I was tingling with excitement, and once in the elevator, I showered Irwin with questions. "What are you up to? Why are we here?"

"I want to show you something," he said. The doors opened on the third floor, and I was stunned to see an Olympic-sized swimming pool. "This is a little better than the one at my house, don't you think?" he asked.

"I don't get it. Is this a health club, or—" Irwin put a finger over my lips. Back in the elevator, he said, "I told you I didn't want to live in a dump. I never said I didn't want to live in the city." He had pressed 28. When the doors opened, we walked down a wide hallway toward a corner apartment. "It's a five-minute walk to the train station, I get all the light and quiet I need, and someday, if I'm lucky, we can raise our kids in the city."

"You mean…" I didn't even dare say it.

"Yup. I put down the money this morning. You're going to have to chip in your share, but I think when you see the place you won't mind." He opened the door, and we were flooded with sunlight, thanks to the floor-to-ceiling windows that ran the length of the living room.

Looking out at the ocean of tall buildings and broad, crowded avenues spread before me, I realized Dorothy in *The Wizard of Oz* had it wrong: Home is okay, but there's no place like New York.

Irwin looked into my eyes, we burst out laughing, and before I knew it, he had swept me off my feet and carried me across the threshold.

ABOUT THE AUTHOR

Jessica Jiji, also the author of *Diamonds Take Forever* and *Sweet Dates in Basra*, lives in New York with her husband and three children. For more information, and to contact Jessica, visit www.jessicajiji.com.

Made in the USA
Middletown, DE
21 September 2021